BEYOND
THE SCARS

BEYOND THE SCARS

Jacqueline Grandey

atmosphere press

To the WHIP-ettes...thank you.

He is my rock
I am his spine
No one can come between us ever again
...I'll never let him go.

CHAPTER 1

DALLAS

"Thank you for supporting Tyler on this project," Trent whispers in my ear as he glances down at the black bird tattooed on my ring finger that was gently tapping on the sound console in the recording studio.

"I'm glad he accepted your apology, Trent. You know I'll always support any musical project that Tyler gets himself involved in. Plus, he gets to stay in Dallas while y'all record, which pleases me to no end." I smile as I glance up at Tyler, who is standing once again in the vocal booth with his headphones on in the middle of *Head Rush Studio*.

"I need my creative brother back. Even though we're involved in separate projects—me with my composing and Tyler still singing with the Black Rifle Coalition—I feel we could set aside our history and focus on our professional careers from this point forward," Trent says as I nod my head in agreement. Trent had come to terms with mine and Tyler's union. He knows how important Tyler has been to me ever since he joined the band WHIP. He made the decision to accept it and ask for forgiveness for the sake of the music. I finally let go of the betrayal I felt when he had the affair with Tonya. It feels so good to let it all go. I've really had no more time to fixate on it now that my life revolves around Tyler. He is my best friend, my husband, my songbird...he is everything to me.

"I'm so happy for y'all that Zack is fronting this project, Trent. You on piano, Tyler on vocals, and Edward on violin. Who knew you three could create such a beautiful piece of music," I compliment the trio.

Trent presses the button on the sound console to speak to Tyler. "You need to push it, Tyler. Come on, I know it's in you." He orders the engineer to go back and re-record the verse.

"I'm not using studio magic on this one," he huffs.

I smile at Tyler while he sticks out his tongue at me from behind the glass booth and sips his water, preparing for another take on the song.

"Okay, buddy, are you ready?" Trent asks and Tyler nods his head. He takes in a deep breath, closes his eyes, and begins to sing:

"*There were times I let it fall through. There were times I cursed you. I know I left you alone. I know I used the wrong tone.*" He releases a breath. "*I wish I could change and go back. I wish I could put it all on track.*" His voice goes up a few octaves as he belts out: "*I regret the tears. I regret dismissing your fears.*"

Trent smiles as he elbows my arm, knowing Tyler is nailing it.

"*It fell apart, it's all gone. It fell apart, it's said, it's done.*" He drags out the word "*done*" as I shake my head in approval.

This is going to sound so beautiful with a haunting piano line, a weeping violin, and Tyler's voice aching into the microphone, I think.

"Got it, dude!" the engineer says into the microphone as Tyler nods his head, takes another sip of water, then removes his headphones. "Hey Trent, I think that was the take!" The engineer smiles as he stretches his arms out.

Trent slides on a pair of headphones and listens in for himself just as Tyler walks up to the three of us.

"Whatcha think, baby girl?" Tyler asks, softly kissing my lips a few times.

"Wow, songbird! You sound incredible!" I giggle as Tyler keeps kissing my lips, my cheek, then my neck. I love how he is never shy about kissing me in front of anyone.

"I love you," he whispers in my ear, and I blush while Trent removes his headphones. "Sounds good, brother." Trent reaches out his ink-covered hand and shakes Tyler's hand. "Thanks, dude. When does Edward record?" he asks.

I place my hand in Tyler's while the two of them banter back and forth about the single. I can sense Trent is trying real hard not to let our PDA get under his skin; he remains professional, discussing the project at hand as he glances down at our intertwined fingers. I just don't care.

"Well, we need to play around with the mix a bit, but y'all can swing by later this week to listen in on Edward's recording if y'all want," Trent offers. It's pretty cool that they're pulling in Black Rifle Coalition's guitarist to play on the violin.

My, what amazing talent these guys possess, I think.

"Sounds good," Tyler says as he turns toward me. "Ready, lovebird?" he asks and I nod my head.

"I'm ready," I reply, batting my lashes up at him. We then turn and walk hand in hand out of the recording studio.

The summer evening is unseasonably warm as Tyler opens the balcony door.

"It's fixin' to storm, Alex," he calls back to me as I pour myself a glass of iced tea. "Hey Ty, do you want some tea?" I ask as I drop in an ice cube and take a swig of mine. "Sure," he answers as he walks out onto the balcony and lights up a joint.

I pour him a glass then go meet him outside. "Here, songbird." I press the cool glass against his tattooed arm, laughing.

"Ahh, that feels good," he says as he takes the glass from me and hands me his burning joint.

I sit down on the wicker chair and inhale while I watch Tyler lean over the railing. He still takes my breath away in his black ribbed tank top, his unbuttoned black jeans, black shoulder-length hair, and no shoes. I smile—I am never happier with anyone else the way I am with him.

"You sounded so beautiful in your recording session today," I compliment him. I always refer to the way he looks, the way he sings, the way he writes, the way he loves me as "beautiful."

"You think so? I need a break from all the metal screams I've belted out on tour!" He laughs as he reaches back to take the joint from me and inhales a second hit.

"Ooo, did you hear that?" I ask—the sky is talking. "I love storms!" I lean back in my wicker chair in my white tank and cropped denim jeans. "Every time it rains, I think back to when we were 'partners in rejection' and we kissed each other in the pouring rain," I giggle as Tyler takes a seat in the wicker chair next to me.

"I remember that." He smiles. "I also remember fuck-ing you twice that night," he says as I play-slap his arm. "Is your little monthly visitor gone?" he asks while flashing me a grin.

God, I melt every time he smiles at me. I nod, and his makeup-lined eyes light up as he readjusts himself in his jeans.

"Got a problem over there, Mr. Black?" I tease, knowing he has sex on his mind.

"No problem; it's just been a little while, that's all," he moans as he takes a swig of iced tea and runs his hand through his black feathered bangs. "I miss you," he whispers.

I smile at him.

Suddenly, lightning lights up the sky as the storms move in closer.

"We better head in," I suggest, standing and turning toward the balcony door.

Tyler stands up and blocks me. "Kiss me," he says as he leans down and pecks my lips. I smile then part my lips, allowing him to slowly insert his warm tongue. He swirls his pierced barbell around my tongue a few times as I step back on my heel, steadying myself.

"Oh, you taste so good Ty," I whisper as he lightly pushes me against the metal balcony railing and kisses me more deeply.

"I want to make you come twice tonight," he whispers as he unbuttons my jeans.

"Ty, we better go inside," I say, but he ignores me. He slides his hand down the front of my jeans and inside my satin panties. "Oh, Ty," I cry out as he owns me right then and there.

A few raindrops start to bounce off the railing as I let out a heaving breath. Tyler inserts a second finger and slowly moves them back and forth.

"I want you to fuck me," I quietly plead as I lick his neck. "You're not ready yet," he says as he slips in a third digit.

"Oh my God," I pant as my clit begins to swell with excitement.

"Come on, baby, come for me," he whispers once again with his lips against my ear as he rubs then pushes his fingers in deeper. I allow him to play with me.

"Okay, I..." I lose my breath. "I'm almost there." I bite on his neck as I am quickly aroused by the magic of his fingers.

"Come on my fingers." He pushes as I gyrate my hips slowly back and forth, inhaling his scent. He knows how to work my body. I rub my hand along his hardened dick over his jeans, which turns me on.

"Oh Tyler, I'm going to come for you." I squeeze his arm with one hand and hold the metal railing with my other hand as I start to quiver on his fingers.

"That's it, baby girl—I can feel that." He sucks on my earlobe as he keeps finger-fucking me, waiting for me to finish before pulling his hand out.

"Oh, I need to catch my breath!" I smile as he peppers my lips with kisses.

"That's orgasm number one. Let's go inside so I can get you off good this time," he says. I lick my lips, then grab his hand and follow him into our bedroom.

Walking into the darkened room, which is only lit up by flashes of lightning from time to time, I push Tyler against the wall, unzip his jeans, and slide my hand in.

"My turn," I say. He groans while I rub on his thick, velvety, hardened cock. His core tenses as I pull my hand out. I grip his tank top in my hands and pull it up and over his head, letting his "best" charm necklace with our platinum wedding band scrape across his chest.

He smiles, then grabs ahold of my jeans and my satin panties and pulls them all the way down to the floor. He sticks out his tongue and licks me from my ankle all the way to the line of my hip, then slides his finger in once again.

"I love how wet you get for me when I make you get off," he whispers as he pulls his finger out. He grabs my tank top and pulls it up and over my head as my "friend" and diamond ring necklace dangles between my breasts. He tugs on each peaked nipple one at a time then drags his heated tongue up toward my neck as I throw my head back in ecstasy. I close my eyes as I exhale. He licks my bottom lip, then flickers his tongue inside a few times as I moan.

"More!" I cry out.

"My, aren't we greedy tonight?" He laughs as his tongue darts inside my mouth once more. *I can't get past how good he tastes.*

He pulls his jeans down as I bite my lower lip, watching him.

"I want to taste you," I say as I reach my hand out and rub along his endowed cock. I run my fingertips over the pulsing veins as his length extends. He nods his head as I push him back against the wall and go down on him. I lick his head then insert him into my hungry mouth. I suck as Tyler threads his fingers into my hair, watching me.

"Oh, Alex," he moans as I stroke him. I lick his erection

once more then push him back inside my mouth. "Oh, I need to fuck you, baby," he cries out as I slow my rhythm.

The thunder continues as the rain starts to pelt the bedroom's floor-to-ceiling windows.

"Lay back, baby," he instructs. I move over to the bed and lay back on the unmade covers. I grab a fistful of the satin sheet as Tyler opens my legs. He slides himself in as I gasp.

"I'm so hard for you, Alex," he says as he slides in then out, slowly teasing me.

"Oh, Tyler," I pant, arching my back and squeezing my butt cheeks. He keeps sliding in and out, then gives a good thrust as he moves my whole body further up the sheet. "Oh!" I let slip out as he shocks me with his forceful thrust. "Again!" I say, and he obeys. He makes me mad—crazy with lust—as I scratch his back with my nails.

"Oh Alex, you know what that does to me!" He laughs as he nestles his nose against my ear, panting. He begins to slowly thrust deeper and steadier as I drip for him. My legs shake underneath him as he keeps fucking me. He rubs one hand along my curves, over my abdomen, then down to my clit. He flicks it and I cry out uncontrollably.

"That's it, baby. I want you to let loose." He kisses my neck as he works his finger and fucks me simultaneously. I continue to cry out as he hits all the right spots. He looks down at me with his endless dark eyes and whispers, "You're going to come." He knows my body so well as he picks up his pace and thrusts harder. "Come for me, Alex," he says as I feel him thicken while sweat drips down his back.

"Oh, Tyler!" I call out as I let myself release, feeling

my whole body tremble underneath him just as he starts to climax.

"Ahh," he cries. I tighten my grip on his hips as he releases inside of me just as I finish. As promised, I came twice tonight.

"I can't get enough of you," Tyler says as he pulls out and rolls over onto his back.

"Good!" I stretch my legs. "I don't think I'll be able to walk tomorrow, Ty!" I laugh as I roll my head in his direction. "Thank you," I whisper as he lights up a cigarette and smiles.

"I'm so happy I get a break from the tour." He inhales a hit as I push up on my side and run my fingers through his hair. "I missed my wife," he groans.

"You did so good—I can't believe how far you've come with your sobriety." I keep sifting my fingers through his hair.

"I promised you 'all in' and I think I'm holdin' up my end, right?" He looks over at me for confirmation.

"You are the *best* husband," I say as I flick his "best" chain with my nail.

Tyler laughs. "And you, Alex, you're an amazing wife. I still can't believe you're my wife sometimes."

I smile hearing those words that make my heart flutter. Sometimes I couldn't believe it myself.

<h1 style="text-align:center">CHAPTER 2</h1>

The next morning, I stumble out of bed, my legs almost giving way from the sex last night. I sit back down at the foot of the bed and pull on Tyler's black tank top, then glance back at him. He is sound asleep on his stomach, his black silky hair flopped over his face, and his pouty lips twitch as he dreams. I smile as I take him in for a minute, then head to the bathroom.

After brushing my teeth, I slip on Tyler's jogging pants that are hanging on the back of the door, pull my hair into a loose bun, then go into the kitchen to make some coffee. I stew on the projects that need to be addressed today. I have to scan and send Tyler's contract for the newly recorded single over to our attorney, William. Then I need to construct a follow-up email to the accountant to be sure Tyler is always making money from the single, to Black Rifle Coalition, to the interviews he partakes in on behalf of the band. When he was in WHIP, he didn't know where or how the money came in as he snorted a portion of it away. So, as his wife, I took on the responsibility to make damn sure that he is getting paid for everything. He is a performer—a famous one at that—and I made certain the right people from Zack to William are in his close circle of responsible business allies.

I walk over to the fridge, pull out the milk and sugar, and set them on the counter. Beatle and Beethoven greet me with meows as I set up their bowls and feed them their breakfast.

"I need coffee!" I hear Tyler groan.

I laugh and take out a second mug from the cabinet. "Are you hungry?" I call back. "Yes!" He laughs as he is always hungry.

"French toast?" I offer. I hear "Ooo" and pull out a skillet to get started with breakfast.

A few minutes later, Tyler meets me in the kitchen wearing last night's unbuttoned black jeans, smeared eyeliner, and bedhead.

"I swear you always look as if you just had sex," I say as he hops up on the kitchen counter to watch me prepare breakfast.

"I did just have sex—incredible sex, I might add." He laughs as he puts his leg up to stop me from getting into the refrigerator. "Morning, wife," he greets me as I lean in for a kiss.

"Good morning, husband." I smile as he licks his lips. "Here, eat your vitamin," I say as I grab the multivitamin off the counter and feed him one.

"You take such good care of me," he says as he picks up my coffee mug and takes a swig.

I dunk the bread into the batter and place it into the skillet. "I have a lot of work to do today." I rinse the blueberries in the sink.

"I'll give you space, baby girl. Anyway, I'm meeting up with Zack today," he says as he pops a blueberry into his mouth.

"Let's eat on the balcony," I suggest, collecting plates and silverware and setting them on the counter, then flipping the French toast.

Tyler takes another swig of my coffee and I smile and pour a second cup for me. "Zack?" I ask curiously as I fix our plates.

"Yeah. I wrote some tunes that he wants to review. If he likes them, then some of his artists on his label might use them—I'd be credited as the songwriter," he says proudly.

"Paid as the songwriter?" I laugh as I shut off the kitchen light.

Tyler hops off the counter and follows me out to the balcony. "Of course. It'll be my fallback gig for when I'm done touring with Black Rifle Coalition," he says and I smile. I am happy that he is thinking beyond the band and touring. His talent definitely lies in lyric-writing. "Trent kinda set himself up the same way; he composes music and sells it, so I figure I could write it and sell it as well." He shrugs his shoulders as he takes a bite of the French toast.

"Sounds good, baby," I say as I steal one of his blueberries off his plate.

"I caught Trent staring at you yesterday at the studio," he says, sipping his coffee. "Did it make you uncomfortable?" I ask. Our eyes meet.

"No. But you know he feels like shit for what he did to you." Tyler glances away.

"I let it all go, remember? I'm glad y'all are working together again. We've all moved on, Tyler," I say sternly as he leans back in his chair.

"Do you miss him? I mean, when you see him, do all those feelings surface?" His insecurity has joined us on the balcony.

"No. I do not." I sip my coffee, a little irritated that I have to address the Trent conversation for the millionth time. "I love you, Tyler. I've always loved you."

He looks away, a little embarrassed that he had to ask the question.

"Your touch erased Trent," I say as his eyes widen. "Do you remember how many times I held your hand during my relationship with him? Or how I kissed you? How I always bought things for you or how you were the first one I ran to when my heart was broken?" I pause. "It was because I've loved you all along. I'll always love you more." I blink my lashes as Tyler nods his head, knowing I am right. "I'll never leave you, Tyler," I say.

He smiles. "Promise?" he asks as I push his dish closer to him.

"Promise. Now eat, beautiful," I direct, and he picks up his fork and pierces a blueberry.

My cell phone buzzes on my drafting table just as I hit "save" and close my laptop. "Hi, bitch," I answer, leaning back in my chair.

"Hey, Mama," Nova says. "Am I disturbing you at work?" she asks. "No, I just wrapped. What's up?" I ask as I stand up and stretch my back.

"I know your bird's birthday is coming up soon. Are we still planning something?" she asks.

"Oh shit, that's right. I want to just have a little something for him at the cabin. Whatcha think? I mean, you're the event planner now." I laugh, smiling into the phone, proud of the business my gal-pal started.

"Girl, I'm always up for a party. How about a surprise one?" she asks as I blow out my breath.

"Humm. Do you think Tyler would like that?" I ask.

"If he's the center of attention, of course he'll like it," she says, and I laugh again, knowing she is right.

"Let's do it, girl. Small gathering, though—I mean, the cabin isn't very big," I suggest. "I'll email you a guest list. You can add or subtract whomever you like," she offers. "Oh, but should I invite Trent?" she asks.

I let out a deep breath. "Well—umm." I have to stew on that question for a moment. "Birthdays are kind of personal, and inviting Trent would be inviting him back into our lives. Maybe. I mean everyone else in our circle will attend, and if he's the only one left out, I mean..." I pause. "What do you think?" I toss the ball back into her court.

"I'd say...hum—that he's an asshole. But I'll ask Zack and get back to you," she promises. Nova always puts up with stupid drama from the leather twins.

"Okay, send me a list," I huff.

"I will. Talk to you later?" she asks.

"Yeah. Again, thank you, girl," I say as I click off the line. "Humm, what am I going to get Tyler for his birthday?" I ask Beethoven, tapping my foot as the black cat rubs against my leg.

Suddenly, the key turns in the front door and I feel the butterfly in my stomach flap its wings.

"Hi, baby girl!" Tyler greets me as he walks in, shuts the door behind him, then kicks off his Converse.

"Hi." I smile. "Hey, are we still on for a weekend at the cabin? What's your recording schedule look like?" I ask, fishing for a good day to plan the birthday party.

"Ooo, the cabin!" Tyler flashes me a perverted grin.

"Yes, our cabin," I say as I walk over and peck his lips. The cabin was a wedding gift from my parents and I intend to use it as much as I can.

"I want tongue," he teases. I open my mouth and give his barbell a good swirl. "That's better." He licks his lips. "I should be done recording my part by next weekend," he finally answers.

"How was it today?" I ask, turning to head toward the kitchen.

"Ahh, a little boring. Trent was mixing more than recording. His part sounds killer, though," he calls out to me as I go to the fridge to pour us something to drink.

"Trent's a very good piano player, Ty. Of course he sounds good, especially paired with your vocals," I compliment him as he smiles. "Here." I hand him a glass of sweet tea, then I pour myself one.

"I think that when the band plays live somewhere in Texas, we're going to have Trent join us for a show to try the song out on a live audience," he says.

I raise my eyebrows. "Man, you already had Vincent join Black Rifle Coalition, now the keyboardist?" I laugh as Tyler shrugs his shoulders. "The song would sound so beautiful live. Ooo, just imagine you at the microphone, Trent on the piano, and Edward playing his violin with candles flickering everywhere—it would be something." I try to get Tyler to imagine the vibe that the song portrays.

"I see it." He smiles as he sips his tea. "What are your plans for tonight?" he asks. I lean back against the fridge. "I want to paint. And your plans?" I ask.

"I'm going to watch you." He laughs, finishing off the tea and setting the glass in the sink.

I change into my painting clothes, which consist of a paint-covered Nirvana T-shirt and a pair of Tyler's old jogging pants. I then spread out a beige drop-cloth on the floor and toss a canvas down on top of it. I open the balcony door, then walk over to my CD player and put in Mazzy Star.

Tyler pops a squat on one of our large colored floor pillows and just watches me go about my routine.

"Can I sketch you?" I ask. I've only painted him once, going off a picture on the computer when I was in Miami and my ex, Gage Heston, fucking ruined it.

"Really?" Tyler perks up. "What do I have to do?" he asks as he taps his jeans with his fingers.

"Nothing. Just sit there. I'll sketch you in black first then I'll paint it afterwards." I smile while I sift through my galvanized metal art box, looking for my charcoal pencil.

Tyler leans against the wall, blows his feathered bangs out of the way of his mouth, and lights up a cigarette. I kneel on the floor, bend over my canvas, and begin sketching. I glance up at him and our eyes meet. He blushes while he blows out smoke.

"Don't be shy," I say. "You have thousands of fans watching you perform on stage and you blush when your wife watches you?" I laugh as I start drawing his thick black hair. "I love your hair, Ty," I say, blending my lines with my fingertips.

He smiles. I draw his almond-shaped dark eyes and long black eyelashes. He just blinks them back at me while he takes a hit off his cigarette. When I begin to draw his mouth, I lick my lips. Tyler sticks his tongue out at me. I laugh and home in on their fullness as he bites his lower lip, watching me.

"You sketch pretty fast," he says and I smile.

"I know your features so well, Mr. Black," I say as I hollow in his chiseled cheeks and defined jawline. I then sketch his neck and the chain that hangs from it with our platinum wedding band. I draw his shoulders and then his right arm, angled upward as he holds the cigarette in his hand, the other arm hanging by his side. He has on a black V-neck T-shirt, exposing his inked sleeves and unbuttoned black jeans.

"I'm only sketching you from the waist up because you're a tall drink of water, Ty. I'll need a larger canvas!" I laugh. He runs his hand through his hair, still watching me intensely. "You're so beautiful," I say as I shadow his ivory skin on my canvas. He shakes his head and blushes as he always does when I call him beautiful. "I just might leave this as a charcoal piece—it looks so good." I lean back on my heels and admire my work for a minute.

Man, he is utterly beautiful, I think to myself. I pick the canvas up and flip it around as Tyler puts out his cigarette.

"You're kidding me, right? Alex, that's fucking amazing," he says, leaning forward and crawling toward me. I drop the charcoal art piece as he grips my neck with his forceful hands and pulls me in for a kiss. "I love it," he whispers.

"Oh, how I love when you kiss me," I say as he retracts his tongue, bites my lower lip, then lightly pecks my chin, my throat, and begins sucking on my neck. "Oh, Ty." I lose my breath as he sucks harder, marking me.

He pulls my hair out of its bun and grabs my waistband. I unzip his black jeans and pull them down as he tugs at my jogging pants, leans me back on the floor, and pulls them off. He then crawls over me, spreads my trembling legs, and enters me.

"Tyler," I cry out as wind blows in from the balcony door, lightly blowing his hair. "God, you're beautiful," I whisper.

He leans down and slowly begins to rock back and forth. "You're the one who is beautiful," he whispers in my ear as he sucks on my earlobe. "You're so talented, Alex," he whispers again. "Can you feel how hard I am?"

I moan as I hold onto his hips as he slides in and out.

"I could tell you were getting excited as you sketched me." He lets out a subtle laugh as I reach up and push his hair behind his ears.

"I can't control it," I pant as he licks my neck. I rake my fingernails slowly down his back and over his buttocks as he tightens his abdomen from the sensation. I then slowly insert my middle finger inside his ass.

Tyler is taken aback and pauses.

"Don't stop, baby," I whisper as he exhales. "Just go slow," I encourage him, pushing my finger in a little deeper as Tyler lets out a breath and starts to thrust.

"Oh my God, Alex," he says as he paces himself, sliding in and out of me. I lick his neck as he pants in my ear. "Oh, Alex," he repeats. I can feel him lengthen as he hits the right spot.

"Oh, Tyler," I whisper back. "Baby, you're right there." I lose my breath as he rolls his head toward me, kisses my cheek, then slides his heated tongue back into my mouth. I accept it and massage his tongue with mine as he thrusts slowly.

I know my finger is exciting him. I love how he always

lets his vulnerability take us to new sexual heights. I move my finger back and forth as he slides in and out, keeping rhythm. I open my eyes and watch him as ecstasy flashes across his flushed face. *I am completely infatuated with him.* The feeling of his cock rubbing inside me makes me very slick.

"You're so wet," Tyler mutters as he looks down.

"Come for me," I say as I know he can't hold out much longer. He pushes a little harder, gripping the drop-cloth with his fist as he moans, letting himself go. "You always make me come so hard," I pant. I climax just as I feel him thicken inside of me. "Oh, Ty," I cry out, a wave of euphoria rushing through me as he releases inside of me. "That's it, baby. Come inside of me," I say as he moans once more, finishing off.

"God, I love you," he says, and I laugh. I pull my finger out as he brushes my damp hair out of my face and leans down and kisses me once more.

"No, I think I love you more," I say as he smiles, taking my breath away.

CHAPTER 3

The next morning, I stand at my computer, reviewing Nova's birthday party guest list.

Trent is on it. I shake my head and exhale as I continue to read. I see the guys from the REVENUE listed and I didn't really mind since Tyler and Roger are close friends—I just have to make sure that Tonya doesn't tag along. The Black Rifle Coalition, WHIP, and my brother Austin are also on the list.

"This looks about right," I say as I type in my approval.

"Hi, lovebird," Tyler says. He takes a sip of my coffee that is sitting on the counter. "Hi," I greet him as I hit "send."

"Whatcha working on?" he pries.

I smile. "I have to approve a project I have to take on," I say slyly as Tyler searches the kitchen drawer for his Jeep keys. "*Head Rush?*" I ask as I shut my laptop and walk over to him and run my fingers through his freshly showered hair.

"Yeah, Edward is recording today. Do you want to swing by?" he asks as I take back my mug and finish off my coffee.

"We will see. I don't need to hover," I say.

Tyler takes my mug from my hand, places it in the sink, then picks me up and sets me on the counter. "Thank you for last night," he says as he nuzzles his nose in my neck.

"Did you like that?" I ask, and he laughs deeply. "I take that as a yes," I say as I push his hair back and kiss him on the lips. "You better get going," I giggle as he grunts, kisses me once more, then goes over to the door and slides his shoes on.

"I love you," he says as he opens the door.

"I love you more," I say back as I jump off the counter, and he smiles and locks the door behind him.

A WEEK LATER

Nova has Tyler's birthday party all planned out. Everyone on the guest list has been confirmed, and I am thrilled that we pulled this all together so quickly without Tyler suspecting a thing.

"Hey, songbird, are you ready for our overnighter at the cabin?" I call out as I adjust my white satin top, which has delicate ties behind my neck and waist and exposes the black angel wing tattoo on my back. I pair the top with high-waisted black leggings and black heels.

"Wow, a little fancy for just the two of us," Tyler says as he stands in our bathroom doorway, watching me brush my platinum-blonde hair over my shoulder.

"I want to look good for you. I told you I am having a light dinner for two to celebrate your birthday tonight, remember?"

"I never celebrated my birthday," he says shyly.

I stop fussing with my hair and turn around to face him. "Never?" I'm in shock. "I mean, you and I never celebrated it since you always lied and told everyone your birthday was on Halloween. But, with your father as a kid?" I ask. He shakes his head no. "Hum," I say, feeling a little nervous about tonight's party. "Well, consider tonight a first, Ty. Your birthday is an important day and you and I will always celebrate it from here on out," I promise as Tyler reaches for my hand, pulls it to his mouth, and kisses my inked ring. "Let's go, songbird."

Tyler grabs our overnight bag and the Jeep keys as I lock the door behind us.

As we pull up to the cabin, the driveway is empty. Nova had all the guests park down the street at a local church so Tyler wouldn't suspect a thing. He puts the vehicle in park, shuts off the engine, and hops out. He walks around to my side, opens the door, and helps me down.

"Thanks, birthday boy," I tease as he shuts the door. "Leave the bag," I say. Tyler takes my hand and I lead him around the side of the cabin to the backyard. "Do you hear music?" he asks as we walk up to the party.

Amongst all the trees, Nova has set up a few blankets with a long table made out of wooden crates with mason jar candles lit on it. Everyone is seated upon floor pillows, inviting a cozy atmosphere. String lights are wrapped around several trees as the summer sun shifts west. Another wooden crate table with Tex-Mex food is set alongside Nova's watermelon rum refresher, lemonade with blueberries, and iced tea. Gifts are wrapped and piled next to a chocolate birthday cake.

What an amazing comfy-style party. I am completely

impressed, I think. Tyler and I stand there in awe as everyone shouts, "Surprise!"

Tyler's eyes dilate two sizes as he squeezes my hand in shock. Everyone begins singing "Happy Birthday" as he blushes and shakes his head.

"Happy birthday, songbird," I whisper in his ear.

He lifts his hands, pulls me by my neck toward him, and kisses me. Everyone begins clapping. Nova gets up off one of the floor pillows and runs over to us, wearing a cotton blue sundress.

"He looks surprised!" she shouts as she leans up and kisses Tyler's cheek. "Come, come, I have you two seated in the middle." She directs us over to the wooden crate table under the trees. We both sit down and look around in amazement.

"Hi, Austin!" I wave to both Austin and Lilith.

Tyler shakes Gunner's hand, still taken aback by the surprise. He waves to Zack, WHIP, the Coalition, and the REVENUE. He squeezes my hand tightly as Nova brings us each something to drink and sits down next to me.

"Whatcha think?" she asks as she toasts me.

"You're unbelievable! Thank you," I say as I look back over toward Tyler and my eyes begin to water. He is so happy at this very moment and I am grateful.

"Hey, y'all, the food is ready, so please plate up!" she calls out, and everyone stands up and starts to make their way over to the food table.

"I'll get us something, Ty," I say as I go to push myself up off a floor pillow just as Tyler grabs my hand and pulls me in toward him.

"I love you so much, wife," he says as he kisses me. I lick his tongue as Nova whistles. "Let's go!" She snaps her fingers.

Tyler pulls his tongue out and pecks my lips once more.

After dinner, I push my fajita aside and sip my drink while Austin cuts the chocolate birthday cake and Lilith serves it. Everyone is chatting, laughing, and feasting as we all enjoy ourselves.

"Here, try your cake," I say. Tyler wipes his mouth with his napkin, and I pick up a small piece of the cake and feed it to him.

"Umm," he says as he chews while I lean in and lick the chocolate icing off his lower lip. "Oh, you taste so good," I whisper as he laughs, swipes the top of my piece of cake with his finger, and smears the frosting on my lips. I laugh as he leans in and licks my lips, removing all the icing, then flickers his barbell inside my mouth as I moan.

"I love watching the two of y'all," Gunner's wife says, and I smile while Tyler peppers my lips with kisses.

"Still red-hot!" Gunner laughs as he sips his drink.

I brush Tyler's lip with my fingertips. I then reach for a napkin in the center of the table and notice Trent watching the two of us.

He showed up. I am surprised. I was so self-involved that I never saw him sit down across from me.

"All right, y'all," Nova says, trying to gain everyone's attention. "Zack, as usual, has something to say."

Everyone laughs as they direct their attention toward Zack at the head of the table. "Tyler...what can I say about Tyler?" He shakes his head as Austin whistles through his fingers. "We love you, man. You've come so far and we're all so very proud of you. From your voice, your talent, your loyalty, to your beautiful wife..." He pauses. "You have everything you deserve, you're a very blessed man, and, like I told the Black Rifle Coalition once before...don't fuck it up!" He laughs. "So, happy birthday, my friend, we love you!" He raises his drink and everyone clinks their glasses and drinks to Tyler.

"Hey, Ty, here's a few gifts from your pretty lil' lovebird." Nova smirks as she sets three black boxes down in front of Tyler. "You can open the rest later but I think your bandmates will appreciate the efforts your wife went through," she says.

I smile excitedly, waiting to see his reaction.

He glances over at me, surprised once again as he unwraps the first box. "Holy shit," he says. "It's a brand-new microphone."

"Is that a Shure SM58?" Vincent the drummer asks. "In black, nice." He smiles as Tyler hands over the box so Vincent can get a good look at it.

"Baby girl, really? How'd you know?" Tyler asks, scratching his head in disbelief. "Go on, open the second," I say.

"Holy fuck! An SA-MEGA9 professional megaphone bullhorn!" He laughs. "I soooo wanted this for the stage!" He leans over and thrusts his tongue in my mouth as Gunner swipes the black megaphone from Tyler's hands.

"Ty!" I laugh as he hugs me. "The third present is for later," I whisper, batting my lashes up at him.

He takes the third box that says *"birds of a feather"* on it and opens it, then quickly shuts it and laughs. "It's a black feather tickler," he whispers as he shakes his head.

"That's for later," I say as he kisses me once more. "I love you, songbird," I say gleefully. "I love you, lovebird," he says, smiling.

"Now, go fraternize with your guests," I order just as I squeeze his butt.

Tyler gets up, walks over to the guys from the REVE-NUE, and lights up a joint.

A few minutes later, Nova interrupts everyone once again as she taps her drink glass with a fork.

"All right, y'all, the party is moving inside the cabin for dancing and games!" she hollers.

Everyone begins making their way into the cabin just as additional guests begin to arrive to join in on the party. Nova has a DJ set up in the corner, and he plays Massive Attack just for Tyler. Candles burn on top of the fireplace, the kitchen counter, and on the windowsills as the sun finally sets.

I reach out and wrap my arms around Nova. "Thank you for all of this. Tyler is beside himself," I say happily.

"Man, what you don't do for that bird!" She laughs as she squeezes me tighter. "Now that my drink is refilled, let's dance!" she shouts, spinning around and starting to dance in front of the fireplace on the fur rug. I sway along with her as Gunner and his wife join in.

"Knock, knock!" we hear two girls holler in through the screened door.

I stop dancing as I recognize them right away and huff. "Woman, are those two girls from *Vanity*?" I ask, tapping my foot and flashing Nova a dirty look.

"Ooo, yes, they are! Hey girls, come in!" She motions for them to join us. "Where is our birthday boy?" she asks as she scans the room, looking for Tyler.

I shake my head in disapproval and pout. *Ew, strippers.*

"Hey, Tyler, I have a surprise for you!" Nova grabs

Tyler's hand and introduces him to the two young exotic dancers wearing matching black bikinis and clear heels. "Sit, my girls want to entertain you," she says as she pushes Tyler onto the couch.

The two girls step in between his legs and start dancing with one another. He leans back, lights up a cigarette, and watches their little assembled routine. One tries to lean in a little too close, but Tyler shakes his head no. I just laugh as I continue to watch. The girls then play-fondle one another, removing their bikini tops and swaying their hips to the music while guests whistle. Tyler finishes his cigarette, stomps on it, then taps one of the girls' asses.

"That's enough for me," he says as he stands up and looks around the room.

The girls move on to Austin and Lilith and begin entertaining the two of them. Austin gets a real kick out of it as Lilith plays along. I laugh as I love seeing my brother have a good time.

"You rocked the black bikini so much better than those bitches," Tyler whispers in my ear.

I smile, remembering myself in a black leather bikini, striking Tyler with a flogger the last time we were here at the cabin.

"Do you remember what I did to you that night?" I ask.

He licks the side of my neck, assuring me that he remembers. "Alex, you have sucker- bites on your neck!" He laughs and licks my neck once more.

"You sure like to mark your territory," I say as he nuzzles my neck and purrs.

"Hey girl, I don't want to play strip poker with those guys," Nova interrupts as she points to the table set up in the kitchen. "So, we're going to play Spin the Bottle!" she says excitedly, shaking two bottles of Jack Daniels.

"How old are we?" I roll my eyes as I turn around and look up at Tyler.

"Hey, I got to see some tits, so I'm good. That's all you, baby girl," he says. "I'm going to shoot the bull with Roger—have fun."

I play-pout as he kisses my lips and walks away. Nova hands me one of the bottles, clutches my hand, and bee-lines for the stairs.

Walking into the loft area, I see a few girls and a couple of guys scattered on the floor.

Nova places one of the bottles onto the floor and slides it over with her foot.

"Who's in?" she asks, and everyone shrugs their shoulders and agrees to play. "Now, if the person the bottle lands on is someone you don't want to kiss, then you have to take a sip of the liquor in place of the kiss," she says, making up her own rules. "I love voyeurism!" she squeals, excited to watch the guests kiss. I sit down on the floor as people scoot in closer, feeling silly, like I'm in seventh grade all over again.

"I'll start," Nova says. She spins the bottle and it stops, pointing to a guy from the REVENUE. "Ooo." She licks her lips and leans in to kiss the drummer with the shaved head. She pecks his lips then tongues him hard as he moans while kissing her back intensely.

"Easy, guys!" I laugh as I smack Nova's butt.

The drummer wipes his mouth, then grabs the bottle and spins it. It lands directly on Trent and he laughs out loud. "Now, I know you're pretty and all, but I'm fucking taking a drink instead!" he howls as he opens the bottle of Jack and takes a large swig.

"Okay, you're the spinner," Nova says to Trent.

He shrugs his shoulders and spins the bottle. I bite my lower lip as I watch the two exotic dancer girls sit down and join us.

"Alexandria!" the circle shouts.

I turn back around and the liquor bottle is pointed straight at me. "What?" I ask as Nova smacks my leg.

Trent nods and crawls toward me. "Not like I haven't kissed you before," he says as he leans in to kiss me. He softly presses his lips to mine then slides his warm tongue in as I circle my tongue around his a few times. I then gasp and pull my head away.

What am I doing? His kiss could be very dangerous. He tastes all too familiar but very different from Tyler. *Maybe this wasn't such a good idea after all,* I think as my eyes widen.

Trent leans back in for a second kiss.

"No, I can't, Trent," I whisper, but he ignores me and grips the back of my neck, pushing his heated tongue inside my mouth for a second time, swirling his tongue with mine. I lose my breath as the circle hoots and hollers. "No," I say once again, putting my hand on his chest to try and stop him as he kisses my lips, my cheek, and my neck.

"She said fucking no, Trent!" Tyler hollers out as he walks through the small crowd of people and pushes Trent off of me.

"Easy, dude, it's just a game," Trent says sarcastically as he leans back on his heels and licks his lip.

"Not when it pertains to my wife—you may pull that shit with Roger's wife, but stay the fuck off of mine!" Tyler grabs my hand and pulls me to my feet.

"What about Tonya?" Roger asks as he walks up and

stands behind Tyler. "Oh, shit," Nova mutters.

"What about Trent and Tonya? Vegas? You talking Vegas, dude?" he asks once more. "Trent and Tonya? You knew about their affair?" Tyler curiously asks as Roger registers surprise.

Trent gets to his feet as Roger pulls his fist back and clocks Trent right in the mouth. "Oh my God!" Nova hollers as everyone backs up. "Take it outside, assholes!" she yells. Tyler pushes Trent and Roger punches him once more. "You fucked my wife?" he asks.

"And you call yourself a friend? I thought Alex was just upset about one night swinging in Vegas; I had no idea y'all carried on with one another." Roger shakes his head, trying to digest everything. "Wow, Alex, I'm embarrassed by Tonya's behavior," he says apologetically as he looks at me with disgust. He then turns around, snags the bottle of Jack Daniels from Nova's hands, and walks down the stairs and out the screen door.

Tyler grabs my hand once again, pulls me into the bathroom off the loft area, and slams the door shut.

"Rinse your mouth out," he demands, trembling.

I open the mirror cabinet, take out the mouthwash, and rinse, then look over at him. He steps up into my personal space and roughly wipes across my mouth with his hand. I know at that very moment that just a kiss from Trent would tear open the wound on both of our hearts.

"I'm sorry—it happened so fast," I cry out as I reach for his hand.

Tyler pulls away. "That fucking asshole," he mutters. He punches the back of the door and I jump. "I had to tell my best friend that his wife cheated on him with Trent right after my wife kissed that asshole!" he says angrily.

He steps toward me and gives me a slight push. I push him back as he flashes me a dirty look. "I want to go the fuck home," he mumbles.

I fold my arms and huff. Tyler swings open the bathroom door and heads straight downstairs. I follow him, passing the circle of Spin the Bottle players, who keep on playing with the second bottle of Jack Daniels.

Nova quickly gets to her feet. "Alex!" she cries, following me down the stairs and out the screen door.

Roger is drinking the bottle of liquor while Tyler stands beside him, lighting up a cigarette in frustration.

"I'm sorry—I really thought you knew, dude," Tyler tries to apologize to Roger as he shakes his head. "I mean, y'all are swingers. I thought the marriage was open, I guess."

I stand behind him, just watching Roger's reaction.

"Yeah, we are, but we never keep secrets from one another. I wanted Alex as much as Tonya wanted Trent in Las Vegas, dude," he confesses as he takes another swig of Jack. "I never went behind my wife's back," he huffs. "An affair? Trent? I'm shocked," he says.

I swallow, not saying a word.

"Well, I'm sure it's over by now," Tyler says.

Roger rolls his eyes. "She always had a thing for musicians—that fucking slut."

I glance over at Nova next to me. Tonya did love fucking musicians. She kept calling Trent "rockstar" in Las Vegas.

"Let me drive you home," Tyler offers, stamping on his cigarette to put it out. "I got him!" a voice calls out.

Tyler turns around and sees the REVENUE drummer standing next to me and Nova. "Fucking bitch is probably out banging a musician right now," the drummer says as

Roger tosses the Jack Daniels bottle aside and flashes him an evil look.

"Easy, bro—she's still my wife," he says as the drummer takes hold of Roger's arm and walks him to his truck.

Tyler glares over at me, then Nova. "Stupid fucking party games," he mutters. Nova looks down to the ground with embarrassment. "I just want to get the fuck out of here," he says, shuffling through his pockets for the Jeep keys. If he was still using, he would have had his ass parked right next to mine during any party game. However, this time was different—he was no longer that person on drugs.

"Let me get our things and we'll go, just hold on," I say, though disappointment flushes through me. I want to stay. "Give me a minute." I go back into the cabin to collect our things.

As Zack packs up our Jeep with all of Tyler's gifts, Nova steps up and hugs me. "The damn leather twins," she whispers in my ear. "I got this, girl. Zack and I are crashing here tonight. The cleaning company comes out first thing tomorrow and will take care of everything—no worries," she says as I nod my head.

Zack kisses my cheek and helps me into the vehicle as Tyler starts the engine. I wave, but Tyler says nothing as he peels out of the cabin's driveway and heads for home.

CHAPTER 4

As we hit the interstate, soft top down, I release a breath. I need to address this—and tonight. Tyler shifts gears, in deep thought. I can feel his anxiety over Trent smothering him.

When we pull into our parking garage, I hop out and help Tyler collect everything. He still doesn't say one word to me. We walk into our darkened place, setting all the gifts and our overnight bag down in the entry. Tyler goes over to the refrigerator and takes out a bottle of water, sipping it as I just stand there, watching him. He continues to ignore me.

"I need my husband to talk to me," I say as Tyler turns around and flashes me a dirty look. "I need you to talk to me," I repeat as I walk up to him and take his hand.

He says nothing; I know he is playing out every bad scenario in his head. I know him—I can feel it.

"I want you," I say. Tyler glances away. "I said, I want *only* you." My eyes tear up as Tyler squeezes his water bottle, trying to release tension. "Baby, it was a stupid party game— don't make this about us," I say, taking his hand and holding it over my heart. "You have the power to hurt, you know," I say, frustrated with his silence.

"I love you more than him." He finally speaks, giving me a slight push into the kitchen counter as I shake my head, annoyed with his attitude. "You said you'd never hurt me!" Tyler raises his voice.

"I won't. I need my husband," I say. He releases a breath. "I love you, Tyler—nothing can or will ever change how I feel about you," I plead. "Listen, if you love me more than him, you'll let this whole thing go. There is nothing to prove. I kissed Trent and I'm sorry. I..." I pause as I look at the floor, ashamed. "I want you, Tyler," I mumble.

Tyler just stands there and burns a hole right through me with his glare. "I want you," I say repeatedly.

"I want to hurt you just so I can hear you screaming my name," he says, aggravated, tossing his water bottle across the room.

I let out an exaggerated breath as he shakes his head. He then steps into me, grips my neck, and thrusts his tongue into my mouth, knocking me off balance as I grab onto the counter to steady myself.

"Oh, Tyler!" I cry out as he keeps kissing me heavily.

He feverishly rips at the satin tie around my neck and my top falls right off of me. I gasp as my breasts are suddenly exposed. He tosses the top onto the floor, then spins me around and bends me over the kitchen counter. He fists a hand in my hair and bites my shoulder.

"Ow, Ty!" I cry out.

He then scrapes his black-painted nails down my back and roughly pulls my stretchy pants down over my buttocks and slaps my ass.

"Tyler!" I gasp with surprise.

"You still want me?" he asks as he slaps my ass once more.

"Yes, I always want you," I say as he leans in and licks my neck. I start to pant. "I'll give you all of me, then," he says as he unbuttons his jeans and pulls out his hardened cock. He spreads my legs, opens my folds, and pushes himself in forcefully, filling me entirely.

"Ahh, Tyler!" I yell, biting my lip while he thrusts inside of me.

"Take it, Alex, take all of it," he says as he holds my hips and pushes his raging hard-on in deeper. My sex begins to swell as he roughly squeezes my buttocks.

"I'll take it, you asshole—go ahead show me how mad you are!" I taunt as I look over my shoulder, watching his feathered bangs dangle across his face as he focuses on fucking me. He leans forward and lashes his tongue inside my mouth. "Is that all you got?!" I call out, egging him on.

"Ahh!" he moans as he slides in and out, making me take in his entire length over and over. "Alex!" he cries out again as my nipples harden and my body begins to pulsate on his throbbing cock. He is pissed. He is taking it out on me sexually and I am enjoying every fucking minute of it. I rock my hips, stroking him fast and dirty as he moans for more.

"Alexandria," he pants heavily as our mouths slide over each other's once more. He grabs my breasts and tugs on each nipple.

I moan while sweat beads on my upper lip. I keep my grip on his cock as he tugs my nipples harder. My core tightens as I continue to push back on his shaft while he aches for more.

"Oh, Alex—take it out on me," he says as he pulls my hair. I keep pushing back toward him, feeling his legs slap against mine.

"I want you," I say as I know he longs to hear those words again. I close my eyes and rock him a little harder, knowing I am getting him off good. "Oh, Tyler!" I toss my head back and my long platinum hair whips across his face.

"I'm going to come so fucking hard, Alex!" he cries out. "I'm not holding out!" He loses his breath as I become dizzy with desire. "Come now," he demands, and his authoritative voice pushes me over. I open my eyes and let myself go as I begin to rapidly release all over him. "I feel it—oh, I feel you coming," he moans as he leans his head on my back. "Let yourself go, let it all fucking go," he says.

I bite my bottom lip as I keep coming for him. I suddenly feel his heat as he starts to come inside of me. I slow my pace, easing back and forth to finish him off.

"Oh, Alex," he exhales, releasing a breath of relief directly into my ear. "Oh, baby girl," he whispers.

"I love only you," I whisper back as I lay my head down on the cool counter, exhausted as I come down from the high.

"You called me an asshole," he says, and I giggle. He then leans down and hugs me tightly. His damp chest sticks to my back and I know at that very moment that we are going to be okay.

The next morning, I try to roll over to get out of bed as Tyler grabs ahold of me, pulls me closer to him, and just buries his face in my hair. I pause. He throws his long leg over mine and groans.

"Baby girl, you mean everything to me," he whispers.

I smile, knowing he is no longer cross with me after makeup sex. He is no longer addicted to drugs. His relationship with his father is finally getting back on track. His stage persona is in full force... *BUT* his insecurity regarding me can really be heavy at times. He's always loved me, but he has such a fear of losing me that it saddens me sometimes.

"I love you, birthday boy," I whisper.

He laughs into my tousled bedhead hair. "Thank you for the surprise party," he whispers and I just smile. I then roll out of bed and go out to the kitchen and feed the two cats.

"Are you hungry, baby?" I call back as I stand there, tapping my nails on the counter, looking at all the gifts scattered on the floor. *Tyler finally surrounded himself with good people that truly love him,* I thought.

"Yeah," he replies from the bedroom.

"I'm on it," I say. I take out the eggs and start breakfast. I hear Tyler's cell phone ring and his voice as he answers it shyly.

"Good morning, Mrs. Rae," he says, then pauses. "Sorry, Mama," he corrects himself.

I giggle. My mother is calling him to wish him a happy birthday. *Kinda sweet.* I smile to myself as he chats for a minute. I then hear "I love you too" as Tyler turns off his cell phone.

"Your mother called me," he hollers toward the kitchen.

I laugh. "She's your mother-in-law," I call back. "Come eat, Ty," I say as I set down a plate of eggs, toast, and fruit on our breakfast counter.

Tyler emerges in his jogging pants, with no shirt and messy hair, and slides onto the counter stool. "I got a text from Gunner," he says. "Zack wants to discuss some gig down in Austin. There's a summer music festival going on for three days and I guess he wants us to play next Saturday." He pokes his eggs with his toast. "Black Rifle Coalition will be the headliner."

"You can rock your new megaphone!" I squeal with excitement as Tyler laughs. "I'm going to meet up with him in a bit, if you don't mind, baby girl," he adds as he chews his toast.

I just run my hand through his hair and kiss his cheek. "Whatever you need to do. I'm just hibernating today." The surprise party wiped me out.

"Will you drive down to Austin to come to my show?" he asks as I continue to run my hands through his hair, tucking his bangs behind his ear.

"Of course I will." I smile as he exhales and sips his orange juice.

After Tyler left to meet up with Gunner, I went over to my laptop and sent Nova a bouquet of flowers to thank her for all her hard work with Tyler's surprise birthday party. I then cleaned up our place, showered, and called Austin.

"Yo, soldier, how ya holdin' up?" I ask.

He growls. "I have a fucking hangover," he says, then laughs. "Man, y'all can really throw a party."

I laugh back at him. "I think I've had my fair share of parties. I've been partying ever since I lived down the hall from WHIP," I huff.

"Yeah, well, I heard about the lil' spat with Trent and Tyler once again," he says as he lets out a throaty cough.

"Those rockstars are nothing but chaos." I exhale, not wanting to rehash last night's trouble with the leather twins. "Speaking of rockstars, do you want to ride down with me to Austin next weekend to check out Black Rifle Coalition?" I ask.

"Yeah, Lilith told me about that gig this morning. She is at band practice right now," he answers.

"So, you'll pick me up, say two o'clock?"

"Sounds good," he confirms. "Look, I'll talk with ya later, sis, I need to go throw up," he says, and I hang up and laugh.

CHAPTER 5

AUSTIN

The morning of the summer concert arrives quicker than anticipated.

I fuss with Tyler's garment bag. "I love that lil' boutique Mick and I found in Deep Ellum," I say as I tuck away his black cropped jacket with silver chains that attach from the right side of the jacket to the left, draping over the chest. I shake my head as I close the garment bag. *Ooo, he's going to look so sexy on stage tonight,* I imagine as I look back at him collecting his toothbrush, eyeliner, and hair gel.

"I gotta split, baby girl," he says hurriedly. "I need to be on the tour bus in twenty minutes or Zack will have my head."

I laugh. "I have your outfit." I hand him the garment bag while he searches the kitchen drawer for his keys and sunglasses.

"Austin's taking care of you, right?" he asks, pausing in front of me. I nod my head as he leans down and kisses me. "I'm off like a dirty shirt!" he howls.

"I love you." I smile.

"I love you. I'll see ya tonight," he says as I follow him to the door and lock it.

Now that Tyler is out of the place, I begin my routine of getting ready for the concert. I put on my Breaking Benjamin CD, turn it up, and head for the bedroom. I am going to wear my black cropped tank top that has "BRC" in silver across the chest and my black high-waisted leggings. I turn my curling iron on as I apply my long butterfly-like black eyelashes. I only roll on ChapStick because I know Tyler will smother me with his tongue tonight—there is no use in applying lipstick. I laugh to myself just thinking about him.

By the time I am finished spraying myself with perfume and packing my clutch, Austin is already anxiously tapping at my front door.

"I'm coming! Hold on to your britches!" I holler as I dash over to the door and open it. "Wow, sis, you look cool!" he says. He is wearing a Black Rifle Coalition T-shirt with the sleeves cut off, and he flexes his muscles at me, showing off his swag. "That works for Lilith, huh?" I tease.

He laughs and shuts the door behind him. "I reckon it does," he says as he removes his sunglasses and looks around our place.

"I just need to grab my keys and we can hit the road," I say. I search the kitchen drawer for my lovebird key chain Tyler gave to me when I first moved into the nest with him. I shut off the music, lock the door, and head down to Austin's truck.

Arriving at the amphitheater, we pull into the parking lot. Austin flashes a pass and the security guard waves him over to the VIP parking area. He shuts off the truck, reaches behind his seat, and pulls out a bouquet of a dozen red roses.

"Please don't say those roses are for me!" I tease with a laugh.

"If they were, I better fucking dunk, 'cause you'll bash every one of them all over my truck!" He laughs as we both recall the time I bashed the roses my ex-boyfriend gave me all over his condo in Miami the moment before I left him.

"Really, what a sweet gesture! Lilith will love them!" I praise him.

He smiles, then opens the door and we make our way in.

After the security checkpoint, fans brush past Austin and I, heading for their seats. The band Chevelle is slated to play first tonight.

"Wow, look at this place! Even the lawn is packed!" Austin looks around in awe as I take in the covered stage with Chevelle's logo hanging off the lighting rig. The rows of seats in front of the stage stretch clear back to the lawn, which is littered with fans and beer. Vendors are all lined up, selling swag. We pass one that is selling Black Rifle Coalition T-shirts and I smile.

"There's the VIP entrance," I say, pointing to the right side of the main stage. We make our way over to the guard wearing a tight yellow T-shirt that boasts the word "Security" in black. Austin and I flash him our all-access lanyards.

He nods his head, turns on his flashlight, and points it to the floor. "Just follow this red line to the first room on the right. Black Rifle Coalition is in there," he directs. Austin shakes his hand and we make our way backstage.

Roadies roll past us, pushing cases of equipment with the logo for Shinedown—they are second in line to perform. I smile and hold onto Austin's arm. Zack is standing backstage, talking on his cell phone, but he waves us over. He clicks the phone off and hugs me.

"Hi, Alex," he says, then shakes Austin's hand. "Roses for me?" he teases. "You shouldn't have!" I laugh as he then points to the room behind him. "Gang's all in there," he says.

We nod our heads. Austin opens the door and Lilith gasps.

"Awe, told ya she'd love them!" I smile as Austin rushes over to the bass player and kisses her while handing her the flowers. I just love how close they've become.

"Hey girl!" Mick—Edward's blond, slender boyfriend—calls out.

I turn around and hug him. "I missed you at the birthday party!" I say.

"Girl, family drama," he says. "But I heard Roger found out about that slut banging Trent!" He wags his fingers as I nudge him. "Serves him right—he needs a good ass-kicking!"

I laugh. I glance around the room, which is filled with the band and their significant others, searching for Tyler.

"Oh, girl, he's in a 'meet and greet' with Edward," Mick says, reading my mind.

I release a breath, then notice Trent sitting on one of the road cases, bullshitting with Vincent.

"Um, dude, why is Trent here?" I ask Mick as I look at Trent in his black sleeveless T- shirt, with his tattooed arms, multiple chains hanging around his neck, and rockin' the man-bun and split-lip.

"Oh, they're performing that 'It's Done' song they've

just recorded at *Head Rush*." Mick rolls his eyes. "Why is he trying to squirm into the Coalition? Not cool." He pouts then waves over to Edward. "See ya in the VIP, girl, my man is here!" he squeals as he sashays away.

"Hum..." I mutter. I reach into my clutch for a mint, unwrap it, pop it in my mouth, and roll it around my tongue as I stew on Trent's presence.

"There's my lovebird!" I hear Tyler's voice and a butterfly barrel-rolls in my belly. He struts over to me in his cropped black jacket with the chains flapping against his bare chest, tight black jeans, feathered hair, and eyeliner. He takes my breath away.

"Hey there, songbird," I greet him as he stops in front of me, leans down, and pushes his tongue inside my mouth. He swirls his barbell around my tongue then steals my mint. "Hey!" I laugh as I lick his lips, trying to steal it back.

"Yum—I'd rather suck on you than this mint," he whispers in my ear as I pull on his chains.

"I think I'd like that too much, Ty," I whisper back.

He licks my bottom lip and pushes the mint back into my mouth. "Do you know how horny I am for you?" he flirts while I suck on the mint and kiss his lips once more.

"I'm glad y'all made it down here all safe and sound," Nova says as she walks up and stands beside Tyler and I necking with one another.

"Ooo, safe?" he questions as he licks my ear. "We need a safe word," he flirts once more.

I know he is wound up.

"Baby, what's gotten into you?" I laugh.

Nova taps Tyler's butt. "Shinedown is up, so y'all have to get your act together pretty soon," she snarls, then walks away.

I rake my fingers through his hair and lick his ear. "You think of the safe word. You'll be playing master, after all," I purr, handing the control back over to him. "I want to be your faithful servant. I live to please you, Mr. Black," I say as he thrusts his tongue back into my mouth. I love how our sex life hasn't cooled off one bit since we've gotten married. I feel it's even hotter and heavier now that he is all mine.

"Hey, everyone! I need a quick meeting with the guys, so please head out to VIP and suck face later!" Zack hollers, glancing pointedly over at me and Tyler as everyone laughs.

"Code black," Tyler whispers in my ear.

I blush. "Okay, Mr. Black—code black it is." I smile. "Good luck up there, songbird. I'll see you afterwards," I say as he kisses my lips and squeezes my hand, then lets go.

Standing in VIP between Nova and Mick, I smile as I point to all the fans with Coalition signs. I then take in a breath as I appreciate the banner with my logo on it draped behind Vincent's drum kit. The stagehands are finishing setting up, plugging in the amplifiers and adjusting Tyler's microphone stand before scurrying off the stage. Excitement just radiates through me. I love Tyler's live shows.

"Can you believe they are the headliner?" Mick squeals. Nova and I laugh and Austin gives us a thumbs-up.

Suddenly, Vincent walks out on stage and sits behind the drum kit. Gunner, Edward, and Lilith all walk out next as Vincent beats down on the drumheads. The crowd erupts. Gunner starts his guitar riff as Edward and Lilith join in on the introduction. Nova screams as Mick whistles. Then finally Tyler walks out, grabs the microphone stand, and spins around as the drummer plays harder. All of a sudden, the band stops and Tyler slams his microphone stand down and belts out a long metal scream, then the band kicks back in.

"Holy shit!" Austin says, easily impressed.

Tyler picks up the stand and thrusts it toward and then away from his chest, sets it upright, and sings: *"I won't lay in your shadow. I'm always pushed aside. I'm sick of controlling my anger."* He pauses, then goes up an octave. *"Just go away and leave me behind!"*

The crowd goes nuts; people on the lawn start a mosh pit as the fans in the seats all jump up and down.

"This is heavy shit!" Nova screams as I laugh.

Tyler pushes his microphone stand outward, then kicks it up with his boot, grabs it, and sings the second verse: *"I don't want to be the second choice in your pathetic mind."* He pushes his feathered bangs out of his eyes. *"All I need is to do what I want and not fall for her kind."* He runs over to Gunner and shares the microphone with him as they sing together:

"I can't take this anymore, you're not what I'm looking for."

Tyler then put his foot up on the amplifier and sings, *"I need to break and be on my way, I'm walking out the door!"*

The heavy guitar riff wails on.

"You!" he screams, and the crowd hollers back: *"YOU!"*

"You can have the light, I won't take it from you!" Tyler takes a deep breath. *"You can play with someone else and I*

hope they TAKE IT FROM YOU!"

The fans all sing along as I stand there, speechless. *Wow*—the energy he has on stage, and the fans know every fucking word! I can't believe it.

Tyler then thrusts his hips along with the beat of the drums as his chains slap his bare chest. As he sings the last verse, the mosh pit goes a little bit wilder.

"I won't lay in your shadow. I'm always pushed aside. This time I'm feeling free now cause within my head you DIED!"

The fans all shout, *"DIED!"* in unison as Gunner and Edward wail on their guitars. Lilith cranks the bass as Vincent beats *boom, boom, boom,* then hits the cymbals as the crowd cheers their approval.

"Holy cow! What an opener!" Nova hollers.

I nod my head in agreement, never taking my eyes off of Tyler. As the song ends, he flashes his beautiful grin and grabs his megaphone, putting it up to his mouth, and calls out, "Are y'all with me, Austin?!" The crowd screams as he repeats, "Y'all with me?! We're Black Rifle Coalition, motherfuckers!" he hollers.

Gunner then starts the second song; their latest heavy cover version of Faster Pussycat's "House of Pain."

"Lord, I need a drink after all that!" Nova says as she shakes out her damp Coalition T- shirt to try and cool herself off.

After a few songs, Vincent plays a drum solo while Tyler goes to the side of the stage and sips his water. When the solo finishes, Tyler calls out with his cordless microphone: "Let's hear it for Vincent!"

The crowd cheers as Vincent stands up, tosses his drumsticks into the crowd, then exits the stage. The fans fall silent as the lights dim. Trent, who is set up stage right, begins to play on the piano as lighters and cell phones start to flicker.

Tyler walks up to the centered microphone stand and begins to sing. *"Here you are, right by my side. I'm here trying to swallow all my pride. My mouth opens and I want to shout...but the words just won't come out."*

It is only Trent and Tyler performing my song. I can't believe it. Nova nudges me, sensing my surprise. Trent continues to play as the spotlights softly light up him and Tyler on stage. Tyler continues to sing:

"I want to tell you just how I feel. This fear rushes over me and I stand still. I could love you, I have no doubt...but the words just won't come out."

The tears begin to surface as I watch the two of them play beautifully together once again after all the bullshit they've endured.

"It does sound better with a piano," Mick whispers as I just stand there in awe.

After my song ends—the song that Tyler wrote for me and *not* for Trent—they go into their new song, "It's Done." I look around at the fans all swaying and just smile. Edward joins in on stage left with the violin as Mick gasps.

Tyler's range is tested as he begins to sing: *"It fell apart, it's all gone. It fell apart, it's said, it's done."*

I just stare at the stage as Edward's weeping violin and Trent's haunting piano melody compliment Tyler's beautiful voice. The three of them perform so well together. What a medley of heartfelt ballads—a nice, comforting surprise after the mosh pit settled down. When their new single comes to an end, the crowd claps and whistles. I feel relieved that they love it. I knew Tyler could make it a hit with just his fame and voice alone. Trent's "creative brother," so to speak, has just pulled it off live and the fans really did love it.

"Trent Van Zant, everyone!" Tyler points over to Trent, who stands up and takes a bow as former *WHIP-ettes* cream in their panties, screaming for the former keyboardist.

"That was amazing," I confess to Nova, but she rolls her eyes.

We listen to the entire set up until the point where the band walks to the edge of the stage, takes a bow, then heads backstage. Mick, Nova, Austin, and I all huddle in a group as stagehands rush past us, collecting BRC gear. Tyler walks backstage, spots our group, and runs up to me in his usual manner. He picks me up and swings me around, making me feel dizzy.

"Whatcha think, wife?" He smiles as he smothers my lips with damp kisses.

"I can't believe I'm saying this about an 'award-winning' band, but Black Rifle Coalition blows away WHIP!" I smile.

He laughs. "We're pretty solid, eh?" he asks, and I nod. "I sang your song." He grins as he wipes his forehead with a towel.

"I know, songbird—it was beautiful," I say. He lights up. "Even with the damn piano." I stick my tongue out at him and he laughs.

"You, my brother!" Austin walks up. "You never cease to amaze me—what a performance!" He pulls his brother-in-law in for a hug. "I'm so proud of you!" he says happily as he releases Tyler.

"Thanks, dude." Tyler smiles. "What are y'all doing now?" I ask.

Tyler stretches his arms, exposing his V tattoo as he looks around. I just lick my lips, admiring him.

"Amphitheater has a curfew so I was told by Zack in the meeting that after the show we're doing a quick panel with the reporters. Then I guess we're loading up and heading back to Dallas."

I smile with relief, as I was hoping no after-party was planned. *Tyler had his fill of after- parties for quite some time*, I think.

"Hey, Tyler! The band's all heading over to the panel discussion in Green Room 2. You better get your butt over there!" Zack hollers.

Tyler grunts, then leans down and kisses me. "Wait for me?" he asks.

I nod my head, straighten out the chains on his jacket, then run my hands through his damp hair. He smiles, turns around, and struts down the hall toward the green room. I release a breath as I look over at Austin. "Should we do a drive-by?" I ask.

Austin laughs and nods his head. I grab my brother's arm as he walks us over to the green room of reporters, and we stand in the doorway, eavesdropping.

Glancing inside the room, I see a long rectangular table set up with microphones on it.

Each band member selects their seat and looks over at Zack for direction.

"Okay, guys, fifteen minutes, that's it. I need to get my band back to Dallas," he says, and the reporters all nod their heads in agreement.

"Vincent!" one reporter hollers. "How does it feel to

join Black Rifle Coalition after the loss of Christian?" he asks.

Vincent leans forward to speak into the microphone. "Um, Christian was an incredible drummer; I had big shoes to fill. But I believe I'm kicking ass and the Coalition seems pretty fucking cool with me," he answers, then leans back.

"Tyler!" another reporter calls out. Tyler runs his hand through his feathered bangs and looks over at the reporter. "How does it feel to have Trent Van Zant join the Coalition after everything that happened between the two of you causing the breakup of your former band WHIP?" he asks, then starts typing on his cell phone.

Tyler shakes his head, smiles smugly, then answers, "Look, I'm not going to talk about the bullshit that happened between us again." He lets out a huff as I nudge Austin's arm, hoping Tyler isn't going to get himself all worked up about the gun incident. "Trent is just a guest musician on a few ballads—he's not a part of the Coalition," he sneers, leaning back and lighting up a cigarette.

"Burn," Austin whispers. We both know Tyler loves to stick it to Trent whenever he can. "Tyler, you're saying he's not a part of the band?" another reporter asks, and everyone glances over at Tyler, awaiting his response.

"Trent is a musician for hire, that's all. Coalition is hard-core. I don't think Trent can handle our music." He laughs as he takes another drag of his cigarette. I just roll my eyes as Austin nudges me.

"Gunner! What do you think?" the reporter asks.

"I have no comment. Coalition is rocking and rolling just the way it is. I enjoy writing music and performing. As long as I'm doing just that, I don't give a shit about the petty drama," he exhales, flipping his hair off his face and looking over at Lilith.

"Why is this conversation all about Trent?" I whisper to Austin. He shrugs his shoulders. "Lilith," says the reporter, "are you happy with the way things are with the band? I mean, Tyler and Edward are recording outside of the Coalition. Are you afraid that'll interfere with the band's success?"

Lilith smiles, then leans forward to speak into the microphone. "Hey, I'm just here for the music. If the other guys want to write songs with other members, then that's their bag—I'm cool with it. It's obviously bringing us some recognition." She pauses as she releases a breath. "I also have to agree with Tyler. Trent is a hired gun and only that. We have no intention of having him join the band permanently," she states.

Austin's face lights up. "She doesn't want Trent in the band either!" He laughs and blows her an air-kiss.

"Edward!" the reporter hollers over the band talking amongst themselves. "The 'It's Done' single is quickly becoming a hit; are you interested in Trent Van Zant joining the band?"

Edward speaks openly. "Trent Van Zant is a gifted composer. I enjoy working alongside him. However, he has his own projects. I'm not sure if he even wants to join the band—it never crossed my mind."

Mick taps my shoulder. "I told you Trent was trying to push his way into the band, girl," he grunts. "You tell them, baby, you focus on you," he urges Edward and I smile up at him.

"Tyler! Tyler!" the reporters start to shout in unison.

"Are you sober tonight? Have you finally kicked your

cocaine addiction?" one demands.

Tyler flips him off, scoots his chair backward, and stands up. "I'm outta here," he says and walks right out of the room.

"Okay, guys, that's a wrap!" Zack hollers as the rest of the band gets to their feet while photographers snap a few more photos.

Tyler walks over to me, leans down, and play-bites my neck. "Are you okay, songbird?" I ask.

He nods. "Fucking assholes," he groans, stomping out his cigarette. "If I knew that having Trent performing with us would ruffle my fucking feathers, I wouldn't have agreed to it," he says in a pissy manner.

"Well, the band seems to think he's just a 'musician for hire,' so..." I pause as Tyler reaches for my hand and squeezes it. "They're not stressing it," I say. "Look, let's just get you changed, baby, then I'll drive back with Austin and meet you at the nest?" I ask.

He leans down and kisses me. "Come strip me outta these sweaty clothes," he whispers as he nuzzles my neck and tries to play-bite me once more.

"Let's go, you hormone." I laugh as I pull him into the dressing room, away from the press, to help him change.

CHAPTER 6

DALLAS

It is one o'clock in the morning when Austin drops me off back at home. I kick off my shoes, then head straight for the shower. Afterward, I slip on my tank top and Tyler's jogging pants. Tyler will be home in a bit, so I set out something for him to sleep in, then crawl into our bed.

"Ugh," I moan as I stretch out on the bed. The cats jump up and lay down with me as I begin to nod off.

At two-thirty in the morning, Tyler walks in and goes through the same routine I did, showering and then falling into bed.

"Baby girl, I'm fucking beat," he groans.

I roll over and run my fingers through his wet hair while he lays on his stomach. "You did real good tonight, songbird," I whisper. "Get some rest." I kiss his cheek and close my eyes.

At four o'clock in the morning, my cell phone starts to buzz. I reach out and grab it off my bedside table, trying to focus on the name flashing across the screen.

"Nova?" I answer.

"Hey, Alex. Listen, Zack just called me. When he was

dropping Trent off at his place, I guess it got vandalized pretty fucking bad." She lets out a throaty cough.

"What?" I ask.

"Yeah. Then I guess Trent got a call from the chief of police and the fucking studio is on fire," she huffs.

"Fucking *Head Rush*? Oh my God, Nova!" Shocked, I roll my head, glancing at Tyler, who is sound asleep.

"Yeah, Trent has been burning a lot of fucking bridges lately and Zack thinks it's probably Roger and the REVENUE who are behind this," she says, and I gasp. "Serves him right, fucking cheater!" Nova laughs.

"Don't say that! I don't want his shit burned! I mean, maybe when I first found out about the affair, but girl, I kinda feel bad," I say as she lets out a breath.

"Well, you better go check on him—y'all live the closest. I'm going back to bed," she moans.

I hang up on her, then roll over to face Tyler.

"Tyler, baby, wake up." I shake his arm. "We gotta go get Trent," I say.

Tyler opens his eyes and looks at me. "Why?" He rolls onto his back and wipes his eyes. "What time is it?" he asks.

I get up out of bed and pull my hair back into a bun. "His place was vandalized and *Head Rush* is on fire!" I cry out as I go searching for my bag.

"Good, fuck him," Tyler groans as he rolls back over. "Zack thinks it was the REVENUE," I say.

"Karma." Tyler laughs.

"You need to get up, Ty. Do I need to remind you that he was there for both of us in Louisiana? He helped us when we were going through heartache, abuse, and detox—remember?" I say sternly.

Tyler finally sits up in bed. "What? So we have to save him now?" He flashes me a dirty look as he stands up. "I need to sleep," he groans once more.

I walk over and stand in front of him. "Not everything is about you and your needs, Tyler!" I say.

He slaps my face and I am surprised by the burning sting. I slap his face right back. He grabs ahold of his cheek.

"Get your fucking shoes," I say.

Tyler's eyes widen with shock. "Oh my God, Alex," he says as he tries to hug me.

I pull away. "You're exhausted Tyler," I say, fishing for the Jeep keys in the kitchen drawer. "Let's go." I exhale as Tyler follows me to the parking garage, humiliated.

Pulling up in front of *Head Rush*, the scent of smoke makes me want to choke. Multiple fire trucks are pulled alongside the curb as firefighters feverishly sway their rubber hoses back and forth, putting out the remaining flames. The building is completely gutted and blackened, ash littering the street. Metal cans are lined up along the curb to collect arson evidence.

I just put my hand over my mouth in shock. Tyler hops out of the vehicle as a police officer walks over to him, warning him to stay on the sidewalk as the firemen work. I notice Trent talking with an ATF investigator and a police officer while they fill out incident reports.

Zack calls over to us as he runs across the street. "Holy shit, guys! It's all gone!" he shouts as I jump out of the Jeep and walk over to him and Tyler.

"Anarchy!" Tyler laughs. I flash him a look of disgust.

"Nova called me. Do you think the REVENUE did this?" I ask.

Zack nods his head. "They vandalized his apartment pretty badly, so can you guys keep an eye on him tonight?" he asks, to which Tyler lets out a huff.

"Of course we can," I say as I glance back over at Trent, who is shaking his head as the police officer pats his shoulder with sympathy.

"Tyler, go get him," I say.

"Roger knew he was playing the gig with Tyler tonight, so Trent's apartment and the studio were both vacant. I just can't believe this." Zack shakes his head once again.

I watch Tyler cross the street. "I'll take him back with us, and we'll check out his apartment tomorrow," I say.

"Man, this fucking affair cost him everything." Zack looks over at me. "I mean everything."

I know he is referring to mostly me, but Trent's home and studio are now destroyed.

Hope she was worth it, I think as I tap my foot in disbelief.

Tyler and Trent walk over to the Jeep.

I step up to Trent and hug him. "Come home with us—there is nothing here for you to do tonight," I say, and Trent quietly nods his head.

Zack taps on Trent's shoulder, then says, "Call me, let me know how I can help."

Trent huffs then crawls into the back seat of the Jeep. I jump in as Tyler shakes Zack's hand, then starts the engine.

Walking into our place, I head over to the drafting table and switch on the desk lamp. I open the balcony door as Trent and Tyler both stand there in silence.

"Ty, baby, why don't you go get the blow-up mattress out of the hall closet and set it up?" I ask as I go to the refrigerator and pour Trent a glass of iced tea and hand it to him.

"Got anything stronger?" he asks.

I shake my head, a little pissed—he should know better. I no longer keep alcohol stocked in our home since Tyler is still in AA. I go and collect some sheets and a blanket as Tyler moves some of the floor pillows and sets up the mattress.

"Thank you," I say to Tyler. "Go get back in bed, baby, you're exhausted."

Tyler turns, walks into our bedroom, and closes the door. Trent just stands there, drinking his iced tea, staring at the canvas with my sketch of Tyler leaning against the wall.

"Hey, you need to get some rest. Do you want a valium?" I offer, but he shakes his head no.

"Thank you," he whispers.

I reach out and squeeze his hand. "Here is a blanket and a pillow. The bathroom is that way." I point down the hall. "Feel free to leave the balcony door open," I offer, and he nods his head as he uncomfortably looks around our flat. "Good night," I whisper as I turn and slip into the bedroom, closing the door behind me and releasing a breath. I crawl back into bed as Tyler pulls me closer to him.

"Baby girl, I'm so sorry," he whispers in my ear.

My eyes begin to water. I roll over and face him. "We do this together, Ty. It's just you and me, remember?" I remind him as a tear of frustration slips down his cheek.

"I'll never do that again. I'm..." He pauses as I wipe his

tear, kiss his lips, then roll over so he can hold me as we try to get some sleep.

The next morning, I open my eyes and immediately recall that Trent is sleeping in my living room. I throw the comforter off of me and head to the bathroom. After putting myself together, I tiptoe past Tyler, quietly open the bedroom door, and slip out.

"Morning," Trent greets me, seated upright on the mattress, leaning against the wall. I jump, startled. "Hi," I whisper. "Did you get any rest?" I ask.

He shakes his head as he sits there petting Beethoven. "I missed these guys," he says, smiling slightly as the cat purrs on his lap.

"Hey, are you up for some coffee?" I ask as I begin to fuss around in the kitchen, starting our morning coffee.

"Yeah, but then I need to head over to my apartment," he groans.

I stop and look at him. "We'll take you over," I say as I pull out three mugs from the dishwasher and set them on the counter.

Tyler opens the bedroom door and joins us in his ripped-up tank top, jeans, and bedhead. "Hey," he says.

Trent nods his head and keeps petting the cat.

"Hi, songbird," I greet him as he smiles at me, leans down, and kisses me. "I have coffee brewing—y'all want some breakfast?"

Trent again shakes his head. "I'm good with coffee," he says as he sets the cat aside and gets to his feet.

"I need to feed you. How about an English muffin

and some fruit?" I ask Tyler as he smiles and slips onto a counter stool. I hand Trent a mug of coffee and then prepare breakfast.

Trent pours milk into his mug, then takes a sip and sits down at the counter next to Tyler.

I can't believe the two of them are once again sitting in my kitchen. I smile to myself. "Here." I push Tyler's English muffin toward him after pouring honey on it.

Trent just watches me. "I need to repaint my entire place," he says. "They fucking destroyed my pad, those fucking assholes," he growls as he taps his fingers on the counter, digesting everything. "I sure fucked shit up," he mumbles as I swallow my sip of coffee and look back at Tyler.

Trent *did* fuck everything up. The affair, the gun incident, the DUI, the breakup of the band...man, he is downward-spiraling. He brought this all on himself, but out of this whole damn mess, Tyler and I got each other—and Trent knows it.

"Well." Tyler breaks the silence. "We'll drive you over, dude," he says as I collect the dishes and place them into the sink.

CHAPTER 7

Tyler and I follow Trent inside his place, gasping as we look around. Furniture is ripped to shreds, vinyl records are broken, glass is busted everywhere, and the walls are graffitied with red spray paint.

"'I'll never forget the pain you brought,'" Tyler reads the words on the wall out loud. "Are those our lyrics from 'Betrayal'?" He registers surprise. "Fucking irony, eh?" he mutters as I elbow him and walk away.

"It says 'final sign of betrayal' down the hallway here in red too—kinda creepy," I shout back as the two of them step across the glass to come check it out.

We then walk into Trent's bedroom, where the bed is slashed and red paint is thrown across it like blood splattered everywhere. Words such as "traitor," "liar," and "long-haired faggot" are spayed painted above the bed.

"Assholes." Trent shakes his head while Tyler stands there, pulling out a cigarette and lighting it.

"You have to throw everything out, get a new mattress, then paint," I suggest as I read the word "traitor" once again. *Fucking Tonya.* I shake my head then glance back at Tyler.

Trent's cell phone rings as he steps out of the bedroom

to take the call. "Where do we start?" I ask Tyler.

He blows out smoke. "We?" he asks with a groan.

"Yes, we," I say as I walk into the kitchen and grab the Hefty trash bags under the sink. I walk back into the bedroom and start stuffing the ripped-up linens into the bags.

Tyler steps on his cigarette to put it out then begins to help me.

Trent walks back into the room. "That was the police station. They filed a report, all the photos were taken, so I can call the insurance company and clean my place." He groans as he kicks a hanger across the floor.

"All this shit is replaceable," I say. Trent releases a breath as he agrees.

Over the next few hours, we clear the entire apartment out and sweep up. Then the three of us stand in the living room, staring at the graffitied wall.

"Why don't we paint tomorrow?" I suggest. "Let's go back to our place, grill, get some rest, and we can start again tomorrow," I say.

Trent looks over at me and Tyler. "Thank you, guys, I really mean it. I did this and I'm so sorry." He bows his head in shame.

"It's over," I say as Tyler takes my hand in his and squeezes it.

"How about burgers?" I call out to Trent and Tyler, who are shooting the bull on the balcony.

"I'll fire up the grill," Tyler calls back, and I begin pulling out everything for our dinner.

Tyler then walks inside, goes over to the record player, and puts on the *Peter Frampton Live* album. I smile, knowing he is trying to make the place as comfortable as possible.

Trent walks into the kitchen and stands there, watching me. "Can I help with something?" he asks, and I smile.

"Here, mix this salad with the olive oil," I say, handing over a bowl. Trent mixes while I pull plates down from the cabinet and whistle for Tyler. "Hey, baby, put these on the grill," I say. He takes the burgers and heads toward the grill. "I've got avocado, tomato, lettuce, and buns," I say happily as I tap on the burger bun package.

"Looks good. I'm actually pretty hungry," Trent confesses.

I smile again. "Well, I'll feed ya, then you can shower and turn in since today kicked all of our asses." I laugh as Tyler walks back into the kitchen and tosses the burger package in the trash bin.

"'Ooh, baby, I love your way...'" He sings along with the album, grabs my hands, and starts dancing with me. I laugh when he pulls me closer and kisses my lips.

"Gotta flip the burgers," I say as he sways with me.

"I got it," Trent says, walking out to handle the grill as Tyler leans in and kisses me once more.

"You're in a good mood," I tell him as he puts his lips to my ear. "I love you," he whispers. I kiss him once more.

The three of us sit on the balcony, enjoying the summer evening, eating and just chatting about the concert, the success of their new song—anything to keep Trent's mind off of his personal life.

"Oh, the mastered tape to 'It's Done' is with Zack, along with WHIP's music," Trent says as Tyler blows out a sigh of relief. "I don't keep any of that shit in the studio just in case shit like this happens…" He pauses. "A fire, I mean." He sips his drink as Tyler lights up a joint. "Can I have a hit, dude?" he asks.

Tyler raises his eyebrows and hands over the burning joint. Trent inhales then hands it to me. I accept it with two fingers and take a hit.

"This will definitely help us sleep," I say as I hand it back to Tyler. I then stand up and collect the plates. As I walk inside, I hear Trent talking once more and I pause to eavesdrop.

"She could never love me because she never stopped loving you," he says. "I promise to respect that, Tyler."

"Dude, I thought I loved her back then—it's so much more," Tyler says. I smile, exhale, then head to the kitchen and load the dishwasher.

After our showers, Trent stays out on the balcony as Tyler and I turn in. I shut the door as Tyler lights a candle next to the bed, then taps the mattress.

"Come here, baby girl," he says.

I toss my damp hair towel back toward the bathroom, crawl into bed, and lay on my back.

I'm wearing a summer silk nightgown, while Tyler lays under the sheet naked. "Ooo, this feels nice," he teases as he runs his hand along my nightgown.

"What a day," I whisper as he leans on his elbow and continues to stroke my silk-covered thigh. "Are you tired?" I ask. He pulls up my nightgown to my hip as I giggle. "Trent is out there," I whisper, but he just smiles, leans in, and begins softly kissing me. I exhale as he very slowly slides his tongue around mine. I gasp.

"I can be very quiet if you can, Alex," he whispers as I lick his bottom lip and nod my head.

What are we doing?

He traces his hand up my nightgown and slides his finger inside me as I open my legs wider. "You're so soft and relaxed," he says as he pets me then slides in two fingers.

My breathing becomes ragged as our eyes meet. He blinks his long black lashes at me as pleasure radiates through me. He slides in between my thighs, gently parts my folds, and starts to lightly suck as his tongue piercing flickers inside of me. I twirl his hair around my finger as I watch him. He slips his hands underneath me, cups my bare butt, and sucks a little harder as my abdomen tightens. He then pushes his finger in again as he sucks my clit. I bite my lip, trying not to moan. He slides in a second finger as I tug on his hair.

"You're ready," he whispers as he reads my body's signals—he knows it so well. He pushes up my gown a little further and lightly blows on my stomach as I lick my lips. He then pulls himself up and easily slides his cock inside of me. I try not to speak as he leans down and bites my trembling lip, flashing a beautiful smile at me.

"Ty," I whisper as he pushes his tongue in my mouth and rocks back and forth. My limbs shake as he thrusts deeper.

"I love being inside you," he whispers in my ear as I grip his taut back. I push my head into the pillow as I feel his cock steadily rubbing inside of me. "Are you okay?" he asks quietly. He is so hard that it takes everything within me not to scream. I roll my head toward his lips and slide my tongue in, heavily kissing him. "You're going to come," he whispers as I release a breath, trying to slow my orgasm down. "It's okay, baby, come for me," he says quietly.

I rock my hips with his slow rhythm. "You feel so good," I softly pant. "I can't help it." I try to control myself as Tyler thrusts deeper. "Oh, that's it," I whisper as I bite his neck, feeling sudden waves rush over me. I am coming and I am coming hard.

Tyler keeps his pace, then joins me as he sucks my neck, claiming me. "Uhhh." He bites my ear. "Oh my God," he says softly as he comes inside of me.

"Oh, I needed that," I whisper as he licks my neck then my lips.

"I couldn't hold out, baby girl. I needed to fuck you tonight." He laughs in my ear as I tug on his hair, knowing I always give in to him.

"Now I'm going to sleep well—thank you." I smile as he kisses my lips.

The next morning, I stand in front of the mirror and rub the bites on my neck as I recall Tyler fucking me slow and good last night. I wiggle my hips in my nightgown, then slip it off and pull on Tyler's clothes that are hanging off the back of the door. I walk over to the bed and stare at Tyler laying there sound asleep on his stomach with his hair over his eyes and his inked arms wrapped around the pillow. *I can't seem to get enough of him.* I smile as I quietly turn and walk out of the bedroom.

Trent is sound asleep as well on the blow-up mattress with Beatle under his tattooed arm. I catch a glimpse of his bare olive-skinned chest as he sleeps on his back. *He is sexy and Tyler is pretty.* I exhale as I look away.

"Hey," Trent whispers, opening his eyes and trying to focus on me.

"Hey," I say, hoping he doesn't notice me staring at him. "Did you sleep better last night?"

He nods his head and stretches his arms as he reaches for his T-shirt and slips it on. "That's good—me too. We've got more work to do today." I smile.

He groans as he stands up, adjusting his athletic shorts. "I know I've already said this, but thank you again for all the help," he says and I smile once more.

"I'll start the coffee so we can head out to pick up paint and purchase a mattress." I laugh as I tap the deflating blow-up mattress on the floor with my foot.

"Sounds like a plan," he agrees.

It is nice that our lil' trio is back together once again, I think.

"Hey, man," Trent greets Tyler, then turns and walks out onto the balcony.

Behind me, I feel Tyler slide my hair to my opposite shoulder and kiss my neck softly. "You marked me again," I tease as I turn around and he leans in and kisses me on the lips. "Just letting everyone know that you're mine." He laughs.

I tap his butt. "You're so bad. I got the coffee if you go and get dressed," I say. We have a lot of work ahead of us.

CHAPTER
8

"Wow! This paint conceals pretty well!" I shout as Trent and Tyler drop the new mattress in the bedroom and I roll my paint roller up and down on the wall.

"You're right," Trent says, standing beside me, staring at the blank wall. "You're even an artist at painting over graffiti," he compliments me.

I laugh and continue to roll. "Hey, pizza will be here shortly," I call out over my shoulder. Tyler huffs. "Thank you, Jesus! I'm fucking starved!" he says as I shake my head.

"What are you going to do about *Head Rush*?" I ask Trent as he bends down, picks up a roller, and starts painting.

"I'm not sure. I have projects I'm working on, but the insurance money will probably take some time to come in," he moans, and I flash him a sympathetic look. "I want to open another recording studio, but I'm back at square one. The REVENUE really fucked me on this one," he says.

I stop to take a sip of my water. "Are you looking for partners?" I ask as I hand my water bottle over to Tyler so he can have a sip as well.

"I'd love one, but I've burned a few bridges lately so I'm unsure how that will all play out," Trent answers just

70

as Tyler's cell phone rings.

"It's Zack," Tyler says, and he walks into the other room to take the call. "Why don't Tyler and I go in on a studio with you?" I ask suddenly.

Trent stops painting and looks over at me, surprised. "You two could afford that?"

"I'd be a silent partner, though. I'm not intervening on too much band business!" I laugh, recalling how I got myself tangled up in WHIP's affairs once before with the film soundtrack contract and I promised myself that I would never do it again.

"Let me hunt for a space and I'll let y'all know." Trent grins, pleased.

"I set Tyler up with a real good attorney, too. So if we do this, let's do this right," I say. "You really take care of him, don't you?" he asks.

I glance over at Tyler talking on the phone and I smile. "I do," I say proudly.

"Oh, pizza is here!" Trent calls out. He goes to answer the door, fishing in his jean pockets for cash.

"Hey Ty, pizza's here," I holler toward the bedroom door, and Tyler lets out a "Yeehaw!" "What did Zack want?" I ask as he dives into the pizza box, takes a slice out, and bites into it.

"He wants Black Rifle Coalition to perform a few more dates with Chevelle and Shinedown to finish out the summer fest," he says through a mouthful of pizza.

I raise my eyebrows and wipe cheese off of his lip.

"That's killer, dude," Trent says as he pops a squat on the floor and eats his slice. "Yeah, it's the New Mexico–Arizona leg of the tour after we finish out west Texas," Tyler says.

"Is Trent going with y'all?" I ask.

Trent's eyes widen and Tyler just shrugs his shoulders.

"'It's Done' and 'But the Words Just Won't Come Out' sound so beautiful live with the piano," I add to compliment Trent, and he smiles and gives me a nod.

"Not sure, lovebird, it's not up to me, but I can bring it up to Zack." Tyler flashes me a look, urging me to drop it.

"Oh, Trent. Are you going to stay one more night with us? I mean, the paint fumes are pretty strong in here," I offer.

He wipes his mouth with a napkin. "Nah, I've smelled worse in WHIP's rehearsal space," he says as we all laugh, remembering how disgusting their first rehearsal space was when they played together down the hall from my very first loft.

"Okay, well, we'll help you clean up, then I believe we're done," I say happily, looking around at the freshly painted apartment.

"Thank you again. I mean it—I owe y'all one," he says as Tyler glances over at me.

I collect the paper plates and begin to clean up. When I'm finished, I ask, "See you soon?" as I pick up my keys and reach for Tyler's hand.

"I'll be in touch," Trent promises. He stands up and walks us out.

"So, you have to go back out on the road?" I ask as we sit at a traffic light with the windows down.

"It's only a handful of shows—I'm going to be *fiiiine*," Tyler groans.

I play-slap his leg. "I'm not worried about that," I say, knowing he is referring to his history of drug and alcohol abuse. "No—I'm proud of you, boo. I just always get a little sad when you have to leave me, that's all," I confess.

He reaches for my hand, pulls it up to his mouth, and kisses it as I continue to drive. "Actually, Roger also texted me back at Trent's place," he says. I flash him a concerned look.

"Tonya left him—the bitch just took off." He shakes his head, glancing out the window. "They have a kid, you know. I've only seen him a few times." Tyler glances back over at me as my eyes widen.

"I'm sorry for Roger," I mutter. "I know y'all are good friends and he's been nothing but nice to me. But their swinging relationship is just something I don't respect. I couldn't do it. I'm too protective of you—I just wouldn't share you." I look over at Tyler as he smiles then changes the subject.

"So, what's all that studio shit y'all were talking about back there?" Tyler asks. "Well." I pause. "I offered—I mean, I offered for you and I—to go in as partners for a new recording studio, that's all," I say.

"Oh, that's *all*," he says, rolling his eyes as he leans over and starts to tickle me.

"Don't!" I squeal as I try to steer. "Code black!" I holler—our safe word—and Tyler pulls his hands away and laughs. "Anyway, I'm setting us up with other projects. I have my design work and you have your vocal career, but now we'll have your songwriting and a partnership in a recording studio." I release a breath and look over at him. "You can't tour forever, Ty," I say. I stick out my tongue and he returns the gesture.

"You're the business-savvy one—whatever you think, baby girl." He smiles. "Now, business is boring; let's talk about the safe word!" Tyler flirts. He pinches my side as I pull into our parking garage and park. "I want to dominate you before I leave on tour," he says matter-of- factly.

"Is that right?" I lick my lips and lean over to kiss him. "Mr. Black, you can start by ordering me to go into the house and take a shower!" I laugh.

He play-bites my bottom lip. "Chop, chop Mrs. Black!" He taps my butt as I groan and slide off my truck seat.

The next day, I receive a text from Tyler:

Lovebird, I'm going to be a little later than I thought. I have a band meeting first then rehearsal.

I reply:

No worries. Love you songbird.

Then I hit "send" and exhale. I boot my laptop back up and begin searching for listings for potential recording studio spaces.

"Ooo, this one is close to *Head Rush*!" I say excited-ly, scrolling through the pictures. It is smaller than *Head Rush* with no rehearsal space, but Trent really didn't need a rehearsal space since WHIP was broken up and the Black Rifle Coalition has their own space. It looks perfect. It is close to Dragon Street, which is an artist's dream and very affordable. I decide to email the listing to Trent to get his opinion on it.

I text him:

Hey there. I just found an intimate studio over off Dragon, interested? Check your email.

I hit "send," close my laptop, and go over to the refrigerator to pour myself an iced tea. It's not long before Trent replies:

I'll check it out, Alex. I would love to stay in that same neighborhood. Thanks for the research.

I smile, excited for the new business venture. I walk over to my vinyl record player and put on a David Bowie album, then go out onto the balcony. I find the remainder of Tyler's joint in the ashtray and laugh, pick it up, light it, and inhale. Everything is good—I am happy.

Just then, Tyler walks in the front door, kicks off his Converse, and hollers teasingly, "Are you listening to your boyfriend again?"

"You have some big shoes to fill!" I tease back as I sing along with Bowie. Tyler joins me on the balcony and takes a seat in the wicker chair beside me. "Baby, I thought you were going to be late?" I ask him as he takes a swig of my iced tea.

"Are you smoking my joint?" He laughs and I push the ashtray toward him so he can finish it off. "Zack just had the meeting. Rehearsal is tomorrow. I'm leaving Friday," he says as he inhales.

"Boo," I pout. "I picked up your dry cleaning today so all your stage gear is clean and ready to go," I say. Tyler smiles while watching me lean forward and pull dead leaves out of a flowerpot. "Is Trent going out with y'all?" I ask.

"Zack wants him there in Arizona, but he has to draft up a contract and all that bullshit," Tyler huffs.

I glance over at him. "Not 'til Arizona?" I ask.

"I think the song we wrote will be released as a single since Black Rifle Coalition's album is already out." He runs his hand through his hair.

"You know he's a good musician," I say.

Tyler nods his head. "You're right, baby girl," he mumbles.

"He's *good,* but not great like you, Tyler." I stick out my tongue as Tyler releases a breath. I swiftly change the subject. "Do I get a date with my husband before y'all leave?"

His face lights up with a smile. "Of course you do. I have one rehearsal, then I need to rest my voice 'til Friday," he says.

"Good. I look forward to it," I flirt.

He leans over and kisses me. "I love when you call me your husband," he says, and I laugh.

"Not on our date, though. I'll refer to you as Mr. Black." I smile as he licks his lips.

CHAPTER 9

It's the middle of the week and I am getting dressed for my date with my husband. We are going to a little trendy restaurant down in Deep Ellum. I pull the hot rollers out of my hair, slip on my black sheer thigh-highs with the lace around the top, then step into my black cocktail dress.

"Baby girl, I made reservations, so we need to boot, scoot, and boogie!" Tyler calls out from the bedroom.

"I'm almost ready!" I call back as I slip on my black high heels, fluff my lashes, then grab my clutch.

Opening the door, Tyler's mouth drops open as he gives me a once-over in my evening attire. "You look gorgeous," he compliments me, biting his lower lip, appreciating his wife.

"You!" I gasp. I love to see him all dressed up. He has on his black button-down shirt with his black dress scarf wrapped around his neck and his black slim-fit dress pants. "Mr. Black, all in black," I tease as he leans down and kisses me. "Are we ready?" I ask, and he nods.

Walking into the quaint, dimly lit restaurant, I feel a butterfly somersault in my belly as my wide eyes pan around the romantic scenery. I just love dinner by candlelight and elegant music. I squeeze Tyler's hand as he checks on our reservation.

"Of course, Mr. and Mrs. Black, follow me," the hostess instructs as she leads us to a secluded booth. I slide in and Tyler slides in next to me. The hostess smiles. "Y'all are a stunning couple," she says bashfully, setting a menu between us.

A waiter immediately walks up to the table and offers us a drink.

"My wife will have a glass of red," Tyler says. "And you, sir?"

"I'm not drinking. I have a performance coming up, so bring me a Perrier," he says.

I flash the waiter a smile, then reach for the menu. I am so proud of Tyler that he's keeping his word and maintaining his sobriety.

Tyler places his hand on my leg. "Ooo, Mrs. Black, I love these thigh-highs," he whispers in my ear as he traces his fingers up my stocking. I blush as he kisses my ear.

"Here are your drinks, sir," the waiter says, setting down our drinks in front of us. "Ooo, *sir*," I whisper back into Tyler's ear as he squeezes my thigh.

"What can I get you for dinner?" the waiter asks.

Tyler orders for the two of us as I sit there quietly, relishing the moment of Tyler taking control. He made the reservation, he ordered the drinks, he ordered dinner—*he is turning me on!* I think excitedly to myself as the waiter takes back the menu and walks away.

"To you, Mrs. Black." Tyler holds up his glass and toasts me.

"And you, Mr. Black." I return the gesture, lick my lips, then sip my wine.

"I want you to eat and build up an energy reserve, Alex,

because I'm going to fuck you hard tonight," he whispers.

I gasp. "Yes, Mr. Black." He leans down and inserts his tongue into my mouth. "Oh," I say, never one to mind the PDA Tyler always shows me. He swirls his barbell piercing twice around my tongue, then pulls out and kisses my lips.

"Maybe we should skip dinner?" He laughs as he shifts his weight. I hesitate. "Can I ask a question, sir?"

Tyler plays along. "One." He smiles as he sips his drink and glances around the restaurant.

"What will you be using tonight?" I ask in a husky voice.

He flashes a grin. "My birthday present from my beautiful wife and..." He takes my hand and slides it over his waist along his leather belt as I blink my lashes up at him. "I want to pleasure you, Alexandria. The combination of the two is very freeing," he whispers.

I sip my wine once more, feeling a warmth flush through me.

"Are you shaved down there?" he asks nonchalantly, and I nod my head. He then trails his fingers up my stocking, under my dress, and feels for himself. "Good girl," he says, and I smile, knowing just what he likes when we play rough.

The waiter walks up to our table with a tray and places our dinner in front of us, then asks, "Can I get you anything else?"

"No," Tyler responds, squeezing my thigh once more as the waiter nods and walks away. "Okay, Mrs. Black, I want you to eat," he orders me.

I pick up my fork and taste the food. Tyler picks at his plate as he remains calm and in control.

When we finish dinner, Tyler pushes our plates forward,

then pulls my hand up to his mouth and kisses it. "Are you ready to play?" he asks.

I melt as I look back into his dark, make-up lined eyes and he blinks his long lashes at me. I nod my head as he flashes his intoxicating grin.

"Check, please," he says to the waiter.

Tyler and I walk hand in hand up to our place. I allow him to open the door and pull me inside. He shuts the door behind us, then leans down and whispers in my ear, "Go into the bedroom and sit in my chair by the mirror. I'm going to put on some music," he orders.

I nod and walk into our darkened room, rubbing my hands over my backside to smooth out my dress as I sit down in the black velvet chair in front of the floor-to-ceiling windows and full-length mirror. I hear the sultry song "Love is a Bitch" by Two Feet start to ooze out of our bedroom speakers as I clench my legs with excitement.

Tyler stands in the doorframe, long and lean, as he unties his dress scarf and smiles at me.

He tosses the scarf onto the floor, then walks over to the bedside table and lights a few candles.

I bat my lashes as I take in the sight of him and the flames flicker. *I am mad about him and I am not going to control it tonight.* I exhale.

Tyler then opens the drawer and takes out the black feather tickler I bought him as a birthday gift. It is made out of ostrich feathers that are vivid and exquisitely soft and is equipped with a sleek 24K gold-plated metal stick.

He smiles as he closes the drawer and walks over to stand in front of me.

"Do you remember our safe word?" he asks as he runs his fingers through the black feathers.

"Yes, Mr. Black," I reply as he grins.

"Good girl, now open your legs," he says. He stands there, watching me slowly spread my legs open on the chair. "Wider," he commands, and I do as I am told. He stares for a moment, licks his lips, then takes the tickler by the handle and runs the feathers over my pussy.

"Oh," I mutter as he steps up into my personal space, gently takes ahold of the straps on my dress, and slides them off my shoulders. He lightly passes the feather along my collarbone, then across my cleavage as goosebumps surface.

"Do you like that?" he asks. "Yes," I answer excitedly.

He grabs the fabric of my dress and pulls it down, then completely off of me. I stay seated, left only in my black stockings and high heels.

"You love to not wear any panties around me. Oh, how you torture me, you little slut," he says as I bite my lower lip. He then glides the feather up my thigh-high, over my hip, and across my waist. The thrill tenses my core. He leans down, licks each one of my erect nipples, then swipes my breasts with the feather a few times as I moan. He pauses for a moment, then walks around to the back of the chair, moves my hair over my shoulder, and runs the feather down my neck while intermittently giving me light kisses. Then he continues over my exposed shoulder.

"Ahh," I moan as he traces his fingernails down my chest to my nipples once again and squeezes them both. I push my head back against the chair in ecstasy. He leans down over me and licks my lips. His tongue is so warm as he licks again.

"Do you want more?" he asks.

I nod my head and stick out my tongue. He lets out a subtle laugh, then walks back around to the front of the chair and begins to unbutton his dress shirt, tossing it to the floor. He then squats down in front of my spread-open legs.

"Touch yourself for me," he says.

I blink my lashes and slide my hand over my bare hood to lightly rub myself.

His dark almond-shaped eyes watch me with pure intensity. "Insert your finger," he says. I place my heel on his hip as he kneels, and I insert my finger.

He leans in and runs his barbell up my fold and over my hood. "Keep finger-fucking yourself; get wet for me," he orders. "I know you want me—you fucking slut," he says.

I do as I am told while he licks me once more. I am breathless; he is getting me so worked up.

"That's it," he whispers as he runs the feather over my pussy once more, sending a thousand sensations rippling through me. "Now, pull it out. I want to taste you," he says, and I hold up my finger. He licks it, then leans forward and slides his tongue in my mouth. His heated kiss sends me into overdrive.

I would do anything Tyler would ask—I am so hot for him.

"Take off my belt," he whispers as he withdraws his tongue and stands up in front of me.

I reach out, unfasten his belt, and pull it off from around his waist. I watch his cock harden underneath the fabric of his pants as I hand him the belt.

"Good girl," he says, taking my hands and pulling me to my feet. The candlelight flickers across his porcelain skin as I reach out to touch his chest. "Turn around," he says.

I drop my hands and obey him.

"Put your knee on the chair, bend over, and hold on to the back," he instructs, and I take position. Tyler then snaps his belt together with both hands, the sound making me flinch. He lightly runs his fingers down the tattoo on my back to soothe my nerves, then swings the leather belt across my buttock, making a jarring *slap* sound as I gasp. He then immediately runs the feather over my butt cheek as I feel heat escape through my skin.

I stay firmly planted as he runs both his hands up my stockings and sighs.

"Oh, Alex, I want to fuck you hard," he says as he grips my hair and pulls my head back, licking my neck while he thrusts his finger inside of me. "You're so wet for me," he whispers.

He pulls out his finger, then steps back and slaps me harder with the belt, then drops it to the floor. "Go get on the bed on all fours, you fucking slut," he says.

Aroused, I put my leg down, turn around, walk over to the bed, and do as I was told. He unzips his pants and steps out of them as I sway my hips, ready for him.

"Tell me you want me," he orders.

I swallow hard. "I want you, Tyler," I call back as he opens me up and pushes himself into me. His cock is hard and he is forceful as he stretches me while he thrusts once more.

Next to being fucked on cocaine in Vegas, this must have been the rawest encounter of my life, I revel, panting.

He leans over me and growls in my ear, "I can feel how bad your pussy wants to come on my hard cock."

I rock my hips back and forth along with his thrusts. "Don't stop, Tyler," I call out as sweat starts to drip down my back.

He pushes me onto my stomach and lays on top of me as I grip the sheet with my dampened palm. I tighten myself around his hard cock as he moans in my ear.

"That's it, Alex, I own you," he says. I feel him drag his thick black hair across my shoulder as he turns his head to suck on my neck. He sucks so hard that I lose my breath. "Come on, you feel close," he urges while he bites my neck. "Open wider," he demands, and I spread my hips wider. He starts to fuck me a little faster and a little harder.

Holy shit, this hurts, I think to myself as Tyler is getting himself all worked up. The pain from him pounding inside of me escalates as I cry out, trying to not let our safe word slip as I am anxious to see what Tyler will do next.

He backs up, pulls me up onto my knees once more, and leans me against his chest, letting his fingertips scrape down across my breasts, then slides them over my bare hood and flickers his finger on my swollen clit as he fucks me from behind.

"Come for me," he says breathlessly as I push back against him. "That's it," he says, roughly sliding back and forth inside of me, getting himself off.

"I'm going to come," I pant as he thickens with anticipation.

"Good girl," he says. He holds me close against his chest while I rock my hips and drip all over him. "Oh Alex, I can feel that, keep coming," he orders. "Oh, I'm going to come so hard for you," he moans. He climaxes while scratching his nails up my waist as he rocks back and forth, ejaculating inside of me.

"Oh my God," I pant, turning my head and biting his wrist where it rests on my shoulder as he pulls his cock out of me.

"Oh my God is right, Alex! Holy fuck, girl, we've never took it that far," he says. I blush. "Oh, what I wouldn't do for you!" I laugh.

He kisses my hair, wraps his arms around me, and squeezes me tightly. "I get so turned on by you," he admits, then backs off the bed. I glance back to look at him. He leans in and slides his tongue in my mouth, rolling it a few times.

"Good," I say, "it'll give you something to think about when you're out there on the road." I laugh as I push his sweat-soaked bangs out of the way, and he leans in for one last kiss.

The next morning, I open my eyes and roll my head toward Tyler. He is on his stomach, hair curled from the sweat of last night's sex, sound asleep. I smile, then slowly sit up. *Oh lord*, I think as my entire body aches. *My neck hurts from Tyler's bites, my ass hurts from his belt, and my vagina hurts from his dick.*

I shake my head in disbelief as I slide off the bed and go into the closet. I pull on Tyler's Nine Inch Nails T-shirt and tiptoe into the bathroom to pee. I sit down on the toilet, then jolt upward as the welts on my ass make me shudder. I ease back onto the seat and pee. *Are you kidding me?* I shake my head, wipe, then go over to the sink to wash my hands.

Looking into the mirror, I turn myself around and glare in shock at the marks the leather belt left on my cheek and lower back. Man, when he dominates, he dominates with fucking authority. *I wonder if all the pent-up Trent bullshit got him all wound up?* I think as I brush my teeth and pull my hair into a bun. Back in the bedroom, I stand there, staring at him as I laugh to myself.

"Hey, baby girl," Tyler says, rolling onto his back and brushing the hair off his face. "When you said you like to mark me, well, Ty—I'm fucking branded!" I laugh as I go into the kitchen to make coffee.

"What?" Tyler calls out as he sits up and scratches his head then heads into the bathroom.

I pull out the milk and sugar as I wait for the coffee to brew.

"Good morning, my lil' slut," Tyler teases as he walks into the kitchen and hops up on the counter in just a pair of jeans. I smile and turn to grab coffee mugs.

When I reach for two mugs on the shelf, my T-shirt lifts and exposes my bruised buttock. "Holy fuck, girl! Did I do that?" he asks as he pulls my arm toward him and turns me around to look at the welts on my backside.

"Yes, Mr. Black, you did—along with these bite marks," I groan, showing him the side of my chewed-up neck.

"Baby girl, we have a safe word! I was so worked up, I'm..." He pauses as he puts his hand over his mouth in shock.

"It's okay. I like rough sex with you," I say. I pull his hand away from his mouth and kiss it.

"Oh my, I'm sooo making this up to you tonight," he promises.

"I'm not sure my vagina could handle another go-round with you." I laugh as he blows out a breath.

"I need a cigarette," he says, fishing through the drawer in between his legs for his pack of smokes and the lighter. He places the cigarette in his mouth and lights it as his hand trembles. He quickly inhales, then glances back over at me.

"It's okay," I say once again. "I enjoyed every fucking minute with you," I reassure him as I brush his hair away from his face.

He blows out a puff of smoke. "You're not lying to me, are you?" he asks softly, flashing me a shameful smile.

I melt once again. "No, I'm not lying. I love having sex with you, Tyler. I love everything we do during sex." I kiss his pouty lips as he flicks ash into the sink and releases a breath. "Everything. We always told each other that we trust one another," I state, kissing him once more. "Now, I'll just need a donut pillow to ease the pain and we're all good!" I laugh, and Tyler shakes his head, laughing with me.

CHAPTER
10

The next evening, Tyler comes home from rehearsal in a good mood, singing while he removes his Converse at the doorway.

"Whatcha singing, songbird?" I ask as I close my day planner and look up at him. "Definitely not this shit!" he says, mocking the country music station that I have on in the background.

I just laugh and roll my eyes. "I have a covered dish of leftovers for you on the counter there," I say.

Tyler goes into the kitchen, tosses the aluminum foil aside, and grabs a fork. "I hate you having to eat alone when I'm out on the road," he pouts, leaning against the counter as he chews.

"Aw, me too." I smile as I organize my drafting table. "How'd practice go?"

He groans. "Oh, it was fine. I didn't sing. But we have our set down. We'll just make adjustments when they fly Trent out for the Arizona show." He rolls his eyes.

These two, I swear—they are always on each other's nerves. I nod my head as I listen. "I'm going to miss you, baby," Tyler whines softly as he wipes his mouth with a napkin. "Yeah..." I pause. "Me too. I guess Austin is still running security for y'all?" I ask, and he nods. "You'll at least have some family around with you."

Tyler ignores me while he sips his water. "Hey, baby girl, isn't this our song?" He pauses as he turns his ear to listen to Garth Brooks's "To Make You Feel My Love" playing in the background.

"Well look at that, you remembered," I tease.

Tyler sets down his dish, walks toward me, takes my hand, and pulls me away from the drafting table. "Come on, wife, dance with me," he says as he pulls me into his chest and wraps his inked arms around me.

I smile as I sway with him, gripping him tighter just as the tears start to surface. I danced with him when my heart was broken at the country dance hall. I danced with him after he lost his friend in our living room, in my parents' snow-covered driveway, and I danced with him to this very song at our wedding reception. An emotional storm cuts right through me as he holds me closer.

He leans down, lifts my chin up, and kisses me softly. He then wipes my watery eyes with his fingertips as he flashes an endearing smile. "It's okay, baby girl," he says.

I reach up and pull him in for a heavier kiss, circling his tongue with mine as tears slide down my cheek. He lets out a slight moan as he keeps kissing me. He then kisses my cheek, my ear, and softly kisses my bruised neck.

"Oh," I gasp as he begins to lick down my neck, toward my cleavage, and my nipples harden under my tank top.

"Alex, I know we were fucking around rough last night. But tonight I want to make love to you so bad," he pants in my ear.

I lean up and kiss him heavily once more as I push him in the direction of our bedroom. He steps backward until we reach the bed. I pull his T-shirt up and over his head as he unbuttons my jeans. He pulls his jeans off just as I shimmy out of mine. He grabs my tank top, pulls it up, and tosses it onto the floor. He takes ahold of my lace panties and slowly pulls them down and over my butt cheeks, trying not to hurt me as I still feel the sting of last night's leather belt. He pushes my hair off my shoulders and softly kisses my neck bruises once more. His lips give me the same sensation the feather tickler gave me, and I ache for more. He guides me to the bed and I lay back on our satin sheets as he crawls over me. I brush his bangs out of the way as he leans back down and pushes his tongue inside my mouth. The warmth of his tongue heats my desire—just like that.

"I want you inside of me," I plead, having I had my extra dose of foreplay last night.

Tonight I just want to *feel* him inside of me.

He blinks his lashes back at me as he opens my folds up with his fingers and gingerly slides in.

"Ahh," I moan, squeezing my red-welted buttocks while lifting upward.

"Baby, I don't want to hurt you," he whispers as I open my legs a bit wider. He grabs my hand, puts it above my head, and holds it there as he slowly thrusts forward.

"I'm okay," I whisper back breathlessly as I feel him thicken. "Just go slow," I say. My bruised vagina wall needs more than twenty-four hours to heal.

He slides softly, rocking me as he nestles his face in my hair. Turning his head, he whispers, "I've never loved anyone the way I love you." I feel tears begin to well up as I long for his soothing, sensitive side tonight.

I roll my head towards him and lick his lips. "I love

everything that comes out of these lips," I whisper back as I lick again.

He smiles, then continues to thrust as I become slick. "Oh, Alex," he moans as his cock lengthens, hitting the right spot. "You're so wet for me." His face flushes as he squeezes my hand and pushes deeper.

"That's it, Tyler," I pant, biting his ear. "That's it," I repeat as his cock slowly slides back and forth. I close my eyes and just relish the intensity. "I feel you're about to come," I say, sensing the change in his rhythm.

"I want to feel you come with me," he says, and I open my eyes and watch ecstasy flash across his beautiful face. He pushes lightly but deeper, heightening the sensations in my body as I bite my lip and begin to release. "Ahhh," he moans, starting his release with me. "Oh, Alex, I'm going to miss you so much out there," he whispers as we climax together.

I kiss his neck as we come down from our orgasm. "I love you, Tyler," I say as he leans back and looks into my watery eyes.

"I love you more," he says.

The next day, I collect Tyler's garment bags as he zips up his suitcase.

"Hey, two of these garment bags are for Lilith. I'm giving her some of my clothes," I say, glancing over at him.

"That's nice of you," he says. He sets the suitcase upright and rolls it over to the front door. He then picks up his sunglasses off the counter and pushes them up on his head as he rummages through the kitchen drawer.

"I packed tea and honey in a bag for you," I call out as I go into the bedroom to get his backpack.

"Just toss them in my backpack, baby girl. Are you ready?" he calls back.

I walk into the kitchen. "I'm ready. Grab the Jeep keys—your stuff can fit in the back," I say.

He hands the keys to me. "Okay, let's rock and roll!"

I laugh as I tap Tyler on the butt. We lock up the place and head out to meet the band on the tour bus.

I pull up next to Zack's vehicle and shut off the ignition.

"Hey girl!" Nova hollers, walking up to the Jeep as Tyler jumps out and begins collecting his things.

I step out and give her a hug. "What are you doing here?" I ask, reaching for the garment bags from the back seat.

"I thought I'd go back to your place with you and hang out after your bird left." Nova laughs as I turn my head to stick my tongue out at her. "Holy shit, Tyler! Does she have any blood left in her body?" Nova hollers as she smacks Tyler's ass. "Look at those bite marks! You damn vampire! Control yourself!" she says, moving my hair off my neck and shaking her head.

Tyler laughs and heads toward the tour bus as I adjust the garment bags on my arm. "Girl, you think *those* bruises are bad—you should see my ass cheek and my vagina wall," I whisper as she cracks up.

"Holy shit, you two!" She shakes her head once more as she hoists Tyler's backpack onto her shoulder and walks with me over to the tour bus.

"Here, Lilith, these are yours," I say, and she squeals and kisses my cheek. Austin gives me a nod as he puts her bag onto the bus. Gunner is hugging his wife goodbye as Edward kisses Mick. Vincent seems to be alone this time around as I scan the parking lot, looking for his new bride.

"Everyone about ready?" Zack calls out.

Tyler steps back off the bus. "No. I need to say goodbye to my wife," he says as he walks over, lifts me up, and spins me around. "I love you, lovebird," he whispers as he leans in and thrusts his tongue into my mouth.

I step back and return the kiss with the same intensity. "I love you, songbird," I say, and I peck his lips while he groans.

"Okay, let's go!" Austin calls out as everyone begins stepping back onto the bus.

Tyler hugs me one last time then steps onto the bus himself. Nova wraps her arm around my waist as we wave to everyone, then turn to head back over to the Jeep.

"You need a drink, girl, and I brought wine," she says as she pulls a bottle out of her bag and shows it to me.

"My girl!" I laugh as I start the vehicle up and take off back toward home.

"Here's the wine opener." I slide it toward her as I retrieve two glasses from the top shelf in my kitchen and set them on the counter. "You pour. I'll put on some tunes and open up the balcony door," I call back as I walk over to the CD player and push "play."

"Y'all's place is so bohemian—I love it. Still rockin' the floor pillows, eh?" She laughs as she hands me a glass, looking around while I take a much-needed sip. "How amazing is that piece!" Nova hollers. She points to my sketch of Tyler leaning against the window behind me.

I turn around and smile as I stare at the painting. "You know, I never sketched Tyler in person until then. I've always sketched Trent, but I destroyed all of them." I laugh as she toasts me.

"Have you heard from your ex-beau?" she asks as she sips more wine. "I mean, since the fire at *Head Rush*?"

I nod my head. "We took him in for a few days, then we cleaned and repainted his place for him," I say. Nova's eyes widen. "The REVENUE did a real number on his apartment and his recording studio," I say as I walk outside onto the balcony.

Nova follows me. "Karma," she mutters.

I shake my head and sit down in the wicker chair. "You sound just like Tyler." I laugh. "I've just moved on. We were constantly hurting one another. It wasn't as toxic as mine and Gage's relationship—nevertheless, it was toxic," I huff, sipping my wine. "I'm glad Tyler and him have made up and the music they're producing is something else."

Nova rolls her eyes. "Those damn leather twins will never fully get along as long as you're in the middle."

I shrug my shoulders. "We might go in on a new studio together—me, Tyler, and Trent," I say as my cheeks flush.

"Be careful there," she warns. "I'm so proud of Tyler, though. Zack told me he's keeping up with his AA and NA meetings, he's still with the vocal coach, he's healthy, he's happy..."

I interrupt, "Yeah, his only addiction is sex!" I laugh as she slaps my leg. "It's so much better now. I mean, it's so fucking intense sometimes." I blush at the confession. "Soft, hard, fast, slow, dom or sub." I blush deeper. "I don't care, I love it all!"

Nova gasps as she rapidly fans herself with her hand. "Good for you, mama. I do love y'all together," she says.

I bite my lower lip, missing Tyler already. "What about you and Zack?" I put the heat under her, seeking a confession.

"Oh, the days of *Vanity* come in handy," she rhymes, and I giggle. "He loves a good striptease."

I throw my head back, laughing. "Ugh, no more *Vanity* for either of us!" I salute her as she lifts her glass to celebrate us moving on.

CHAPTER 11

A few days later, I am sitting and watching videos of the Black Rifle Coalition on the internet. I miss Tyler. I sulk as I scroll through the band's list of songs.

Bing! A text message pops up on my cell phone from Trent:

Hey Alex. I called about the studio you sent me—interested in touring it with me?

I close my laptop, lean back in my chair, and reply:

Sure, when?

I hit "send." I get an immediate response:

In an hour. The realtor gave me the combo to the lock.

I huff then, type my reply.

Meet you in one hour.

I slide off the chair and drag my feet to the closet to change.

Driving down Dragon Street, my stomach barrel-rolls as I push the brakes and stop to look at the remnants of *Head Rush*. I shake my head as I stare at the black, hollowed-out building with no roof that was deemed condemned by the city of Dallas. *All those WHIP memories are now turning to soot,* I think, suddenly saddened.

"Another chapter burned in my memory," I say out loud as I shift gears and turn down the next block.

Pulling up in front of the listed studio, I see Trent leaning against the brick wall in his black T-shirt, black jeans, and man-bun, holding a motorcycle helmet. I put the Jeep in park and hop out.

"Hi Alex," Trent greets me.

I shield my eyes from the late afternoon sun and smile. "I like it already," I say as Trent laughs and turns to open the door. I follow him inside and stand there with my hands on my hips.

"It's not as big as *Head Rush,*" he complains.

I flash him a dirty look. "Yeah, but think of the possibilities! Make it an intimate studio— just the engineer and the band. No *WHIP-ettes* taking up space!"

Trent laughs. "Intimate, huh?" he asks as he begins to walk around.

"Look, this area could be the 'chill' couch." I blush as I recall having sex with Trent on *Head Rush's* "chill" couch. "You could hang your records and a few pictures of the bands that record here." I smile as I point to a plain white wall.

"Everything is a blank canvas to you, huh?" He laughs.

I keep envisioning the studio. "Look, the old recording studio was in there, the vocal booth is over there, and down the hall is a small bathroom." I smile. "What else do y'all really need?" I ask.

Trent pans the room with his handsome dark eyes. "Everything is soundproofed and wired. I mean, it's pretty much set up." He smiles. "All we need is equipment."

"Yeah, that'll help. What would we name it?" I poke at his waist and he smacks my hand away.

"Hum," he says, thinking.

"*Brimstone*," I suggest. "I mean, 'fire and brimstone,' right?" I make light of the fire set to the studio.

Trent nods his head. "I like it," he says.

"Well, it's affordable, Trent, and you need to get back to work," I say.

Trent puts his hand over his chin and pauses. "I say fuck it, let's make an offer," he says.

I clap my hands. "Yes! Call the realtor! I'll call my attorney and financial advisor and let's touch base soon," I say, trying to sound professional. "One question." I pause as Trent looks over at me with concern. "Can you *really* handle going into business with Tyler?" I ask, and Trent lets out a deep breath. "I mean, I'll be the silent partner if you want me to be," I suggest as he smiles.

"Can I make Tyler the silent partner and have you go into business with me? You have a much better head for this sort of thing. I mean, how impressed am I of the roster you built yourself of design clients alone?" I feel my cheeks flush at the compliment. "And Tyler, I mean, he's getting paid for everything because of you. The contract I had to sign and honor when we recorded recently, that alone was fucking impressive," he says, and I smile, taking pride in my relentlessness in having Tyler get paid for being the star that he is.

"Well, I can talk to Tyler, but he has to be in on it or there's no deal," I say.

Trent nods his head in understanding. "Let me make an offer and I'll call you," he says. I reach my hand out and shake his hand. "To *Brimstone*," I say as he laughs.

"To *Brimstone*," he says.

That evening after my shower, I lay in bed with my drawing pad and sketch out a few ideas I have for the studio. I am actually pretty excited about the new business venture I am about to embark on.

Suddenly, my cell phone rings, and I smile, answering it. "Hi, my beautiful songbird," I greet Tyler.

"Oh, lovebird, I miss you so much it hurts," he whines. I hate hearing the sadness in his voice. "We've moved hotels," he says as he starts laughing.

"What? What's that supposed to mean?" I ask, setting my drawing pad aside to listen. "You're never going to believe this!" Tyler laughs again. "Umm, Vincent's new wife left him already for the drummer of the REVENUE," he says.

"What?!" I shout. "You're kidding, right?" My mouth hangs open at the abrupt news. "Nope, I'm serious!" Tyler laughs once more.

"Man, those REVENUE guys are fucking trouble," I say in utter disbelief.

"Well, we had to switch hotels because Vincent destroyed the room and the band got kicked out." He couldn't stop laughing. "He smashed the lamps, the television, the mirrors—I mean, he went nuts! Rock and roll!" he howls.

"Are you okay, baby? You didn't get involved, did you?" I ask.

"Nope, I heard all the banging and just started to pack my suitcase," he huffs. "I knew our asses would be thrown out," he says. "Anyway, how are you, baby girl?" he asks. I hear him take a sip of something.

"Are you drinking hot tea?" I smile as Tyler laughs. "Well, I went to check out a potential recording studio and..." I pause as my stomach flutters with excitement.

"Wait, did you see Trent?" Tyler interrupts me.

"Yes, but it was only to check out a potential listing. I drove past *Head Rush* and it's condemned and..." I pause again. "Tyler?"

"I'm here." He sounds irritated. "Go on, you checked out the listing," he says. "Yes. It's small, it's perfect, and we're going to make an offer!" I squeal. "Who? You and Trent?" he asks with a sharp tone.

Why does he always give me pushback?

"Yes, me, Trent, and you, Ty," I say. "I told him I wouldn't go in on the recording studio unless it was both me and you. Trust me?" I ask.

"Yes," he whispers.

"If you want me to back out, I will—nothing is set in stone. Oh, speaking of stone, I want to call it '*Brimstone*.'" I giggle as Tyler lets out a slight laugh.

"Okay, I trust you, baby girl. We're in this together," he says, and I smile.

"Yes, I'm doing nothing without you, Tyler. When I said I was 'all in' with you—I mean all in," I say.

"I miss you, baby," he whines once more.

"You have no idea how bad I miss you." I blow him a kiss over the line and I can hear him smile through the phone.

"Hey, can I call you tomorrow?" He yawns and I know the road is taking a toll on him. "I love you, songbird," I say.

"Love you more." He hangs up and I toss the cell on the bed.

I sit there for a moment, wondering if it is a good idea to go into business with Trent. I then text Zack my dilemma and he replies immediately.

Trent is business and Tyler is personal. I think it's a good idea. I'll kick some business your way.

I feel relieved as I shut off the light and roll over, tucking Tyler's pillow into my chest, and fall asleep.

The next morning, I open my eyes and look around, still holding Tyler's pillow. I release a long breath, then pull myself upright. I check my cell and notice a text from Trent.

The offer is in, fingers crossed!

I smile, then pull my hair back into a braid and crawl out of bed. I go into the kitchen to feed the cats, then start to make coffee for one. I am a little saddened as I cut the serving in half. Little things make me miss Tyler. I pour water into the coffee pot and wipe my hand on my T- shirt. I pout as I note that it's Tyler's shredded Alice In Chains tee.

"Man, I need to get it together," I say to the cats. They both meow and go on eating.

Why am I so emotional? I think. Tyler is working, just like I should be.

I go over to my laptop and boot it up to review my calendar for the day. I have a few projects to invoice and then I have a little time to dedicate to the studio if all goes well. I feel my stomach turn as I release a breath and get to work.

A few hours later, my cell phone rings. I shut the laptop down and answer it. "Please tell me you have good news!"

Trent whistles. "Our offer is accepted!" he hollers.

I shake my head. "No shit? Yeehaw!" I holler back.

"I'm sending over the paperwork for you and Tyler to sign!" "Do you feel better?" I ask.

"I do, Alex. Thank you. You and Tyler have really come through for me," he says gratefully.

"Well, looking back, you've done a lot of shit for us too—so it's all good," I say. "I already talked to Zack and he's going to throw some business our way."

Trent laughs. "Wow, you don't stop, do you? That's great," he says. "I'll send the docs over now."

I feel elated, ready to take on another project.

"Sounds good, I'll text you when I'm through," I say. I hang up and wait for the email. I then dial Tyler.

"Morning, baby girl," he greets me with a froggy throat. "Did I wake you?" I ask.

"No, I'm about to shower then head over to the venue," he says. "What's up?"

"Well, aside from missing you, I made coffee for one and almost fell apart this morning." Tyler laughs.

"The offer on the recording studio was accepted!" I holler. "All right, baby girl!" Tyler perks up.

"I'm sending you some documents to sign, so after your shower please check your email," I direct.

"I'll do that. Hey, good job, baby girl," he says happily as he comes around to the idea of owning a recording studio.

"Okay, I gotta review the docs. I love you," I say.

"Love you more." He clicks off the line and I open the

laptop to scan the email from Trent.

After signing everything, I stand up and feel a little dizzy. I quickly sit back down and release a breath. My stomach turns once more as I bend down and vomit in the trash can next to my drafting table. *What is the matter with me?*

I sit back on the floor and wipe my mouth. I pull the trash bag, set it outside the door, and go into the bathroom to rinse out my mouth. I stand there, staring at my reflection, and gasp

I'm pregnant.

The next morning, I tap my pen on my lap as I fill out paperwork with my new insurance plan information at my gynecologist's office.

"Mrs. Black, the doctor will see you now," the nurse says.

I stand up and hand her my paperwork, then follow her into an exam room. She weighs me and takes my vitals.

"How are you, Mrs. Black?" the doctor asks as she walks in and takes my medical chart from the nurse. "So, you're here for a pregnancy test? It says here that you're on birth control?" she asks with concern, to which I nod my head. "Well, have you been consistent with your birth control?"

I shrug my shoulders. "I might have missed a day or two."

"Okay, hon, let's take a test. Everything else is up to date, so it'll be a quick visit, I promise." The doctor flashes me a warm smile as she hands me a cup for urine collection.

"Okay." I whine as I slide off the exam table and go into the restroom to pee in a cup.

Afterward, the nurse tells me to wait in the exam room, and I nervously sit back down on the paper-covered examination table. I feel like I'm five years old again as my legs dangle off the edge.

A baby? I ponder. I really want a family, but is Tyler ready? He is still so childlike himself—could we handle one? I begin to panic as I rub my sweaty palms together.

"Okay, Mrs. Black," the doctor greets me, closing the door behind her. "Looks like you're pregnant!" She leans forward to hug me.

I feel a little dizzy and grab onto her white coat. "Whoa," she says with a giggle.

"I am?" I ask again. *Wow. I am pregnant.* I smile as I bite down on my nail and just stare straight ahead, processing everything.

She laughs and squeezes my hand. "Everyone looks shocked at first. Now, here's a prescription for some vitamins and we'll schedule you for some lab work," she says enthusiastically.

I wipe my palms on my jeans to dry them. I snag the paper out of her hand, jump off the table, and collect my bag. "Thank you," I squeal.

She laughs once more as she shakes her head while she fills out my chart.

When I get home, I kick off my shoes, go straight over to our bed, and collapse on it. "I'm pregnant!" I cheer as I make snow angels on the sheet. "I'm having the famous Tyler Black's baby!" I holler as Beatle meows back at me. "Take that, Olivia!" I smirk as I lay there, relishing the thought of having a child with Tyler.

The next morning, I wake and immediately read a text from Trent:

Inspection and appraisal are complete. Docs are signed. I've got the keys!

I reply:

I'm on my way!

I hit "send" and roll out of bed. I throw on my HEART T-shirt and tapered jeans, braid my hair, and grab my bag. I jump into Axl and drive straight over to the new studio. I am in a good mood.

"I say we paint the building black," Trent suggests as I lock my truck door.

I turn around and nod my head. "Yeah, I agree," I say. "And just a small, subtle sign in white that says '*Brimstone*' right there." I point to the brick building.

"*Brimstone* it is," he says as he unlocks the door. "Here's a key for you." He hands me a set and I tuck it away in my bag and follow him inside.

"Let's paint it a better shade of white. Let's just keep everything black and white," I suggest as Trent raises his eyebrows. "I don't want it creepy in here; let's keep it clean and rustic," I say. "Well, musicians will be in here, so I'm not promising cleanliness." I elbow Trent as he rolls his eyes.

"Why don't we paint out in this area, then I'm heading to Arizona this week to play alongside Black Rifle Coalition, so feel free to decorate the sitting area as you wish," he says and I smile.

"I'm in an old concert tee, so I'm ready—are you up for painting today?" I ask, amped to get started.

"We're on!" he calls out. We lock the studio back up and hop into the truck to go and purchase paint.

❧

A few hours later, pizza shows up. Trent and I sit on the floor and dive into the box. "Didn't we just do this?" I tease as I bite into my slice.

"Maybe we're getting into the wrong business. Maybe we should start a painting business," he says, and I laugh, trying not to choke on the cheese as I look around, admiring our work.

"Are you ready for the Arizona show?" I ask, wiping my mouth and sipping my bottled water.

"I'm ready, but honestly I'm a little bit nervous. I feel a little out of my element with the new band." He glances over at me as I flash him a sympathetic look. "As you know, I'm just a 'gun for hire.'"

I laugh, knowing he heard about what went down at the Austin show with the panel of reporters. Tyler couldn't hold out; he had to stick it to Trent that Black Rifle Coalition was *his* band and not Trent's.

"Look, Black Rifle Coalition are professional all the way—the whole band is great. I mean, y'all played the show in Austin and it went well." I stick out my tongue and he smiles.

"I know, it did go well, thanks. I'm just nervous playing live again," he says openly.

"I remember your first show with WHIP at the *Steel Door* and you weren't this nervous." I laugh, recalling the very night I met him.

"That was a much smaller venue. Everyone was on drugs back then and everything was just a party." He laughs as I nod my head in agreement. "Tyler really made something of himself, hasn't he?"

I feel my cheeks flush. "Yeah, he has." I reflect for a moment on my husband.

"Hey, I'm sorry about the Fall Rock Festival a while back when you first told me about you and Tyler. My comment about him and drugs was just cruel. There is so much I wish I did differently," he says. "I never meant to hurt you. The whole Tonya thing after St. Louis was a total mistake. I was an arrogant son of a bitch. I just couldn't face the insecurity I felt about Gage and Tyler that I..." He shakes his head.

I feel a lump rise in my throat. "No need to relive it," I whisper as my stomach churns, feeling a bit nauseous from the greasy pizza.

"I just apologized to Tyler, but never to you personally. I'm just really ashamed of my behavior. I'm truly sorry, Alexandria," he says as I reach out my hand and squeeze his hand. "My mother ran off with another man whom I do not approve of, then I thought you ran off with Tyler, so I got all fucked up in the head and acted out stupidly with the piece and all," he confesses.

I swallow hard. "You did try to shoot Tyler." I shake my head as he bites his lower lip in disgust. "But you've always taken care of your mama," I say sweetly.

"Yes, that's why I took it so personally when she dismissed my opinion about this jackass," he huffs.

"I'm sorry you had all that on your shoulders. Look, us..." I pause. "It wasn't all bad— you were always good to me before all the acting out. I really do forgive you," I say, releasing a breath as all those feelings try to resurface. He was always the strong one and it hurt me to watch him in pain.

Suddenly, I hop to my feet and cover my mouth. "I'll be right back!" I mumble into my palm as I run down the hallway toward the bathroom. I kneel on the floor and vomit into the toilet, unsure if the nausea was induced by old feelings for Trent resurfacing or if it's my body alerting me that I am pregnant. I wipe my mouth with the back of my hand and flush the toilet.

"Alex, are you all right?" Trent asks, standing in the hallway.

"Yes, um, can you help me up?" I ask. My legs feel like noodles after barfing my lunch.

He opens the bathroom door and bends down. "Give me your hands," he instructs, and I place my sweaty palms into his warm hands and let him pull me to my feet. He holds on to my hands for a moment then pulls me into his chest and wraps his arms around me.

I inhale the familiar scent of him as I squeeze my eyes shut and let him hold me for just a minute longer.

"Trent." I pull back and glance to the floor. "I'm pregnant," I say.

"Oh, Alex," he sighs. *I bet he never thought mine and Tyler's marriage would last, and now this.* "Are you happy? Do you want this?" he asks timidly.

A smile stretches across my face as I nod my head. "I do," I say. "It's just that we weren't planning it, so I'm still kinda in a state of shock. I have to see where Tyler's head is in all of this." I wipe my mouth once more with the back of my hand. "We both know we can't overwhelm Ty with too much or he'll break down. He's been so good with everything, Trent."

I swallow hard as I walk over to the sink and rinse my mouth out. I then look into the mirror and Trent bows his head in the reflection. I second-guess my excitement for just a moment.

"I don't know," I mumble.

Trent turns me around, reaches for my hand, and squeezes it. "I'm here if you need me." I bite my lip and hit the bathroom light.

Holding my hand, he walks me out of the bathroom.

"Well, let's let the paint dry. You go pack for Arizona and I'll see you when you get back."

He nods his head as he pulls my hand up to his mouth and kisses it. "Congrats," he whispers.

I let go, turn and grab my bag, and head for the door, not wanting him to see my eyes watering.

The next day, I open my balcony door for some fresh air, then go into my closet and drag out a plastic storage bin full of pictures. I sit on a floor pillow and begin organizing them. I want to set aside all the photographs I could find of WHIP and the Black Rifle Coalition so I can frame them for the studio. I pick up the photo of the three of us in front of WHIP's tour bus and smile. I then set aside pictures from their live shows, their music video, pictures of Tyler sing-ing, and even the ones from the Billboard Music Awards. I make a pile of my favorite ones, then close up the bin. I am going to get these made into black and white prints, then frame them in black.

I decide to text Mick:

I need you! I need to decorate a recording studio. Are you free this weekend?

I hit "send," then lean back and try to relax as exhaus-tion overcomes my body. Mick replies:

Girl, free tomorrow then I'm cleaning house for Ed-ward's return home.

I laugh as I glance around my own place. I probably should clean for Tyler's return home too—but I long to sleep, so I shut the balcony door, pick up the bin, and go into the bedroom to pass out.

The next day, Mick and I wander around thrift stores, selecting all the cool pieces we can find for the studio. We frame all the band's photographs and swap stories about each one as we hang them up. We angle the couch, set candles on display, hang a metal sign and a new galvanized mirror in the restroom, and just giggle like two schoolgirls the whole time we decorate. *I love spending time with him.*

"Can I tell you something?" I ask Mick.

He wipes his hands clean on his pant legs. "Of course, girl, what's up?" he asks.

I motion for him to sit down next to me on the couch as I feel like I'm going to explode. "I'm pregnant," I say happily.

Mick's eyes widen as he begins to laugh. "Oh, girl, that's wonderful news!" He reaches his long arms out to hug me. "Does Tyler know?" he asks.

I bite my lower lip and shake my head no. "I only told Trent," I confess. "Girrrl, he's not your husband!" He waves his finger at me.

"I know. But it kind of slipped out with the vomit," I chuckle as Mick laughs.

"Ew, well, you better tell Tyler soon, hon—gossip spreads like wildfire." He looks me directly in the eyes. "We don't need anyone thinking this baby is Trent's since you told him first." I immediately slap his arm and he laughs.

"No, seriously," he says. "The tour bus is due back soon, so make your preparations," he advises.

We begin to collect the trash bags and toolboxes and set them by the door. Mick hugs me goodbye, then takes off so he can prepare for Edward's return. I stay back and just glance around one last time, admiring our hard work. Metal stars line the entryway corridor. The walls are freshly painted white with picture frames that hang above the black leather couch perched on a black and white cow-print rug. I glance at each picture; my heart flutters when I look at the ones of Tyler. There is a black trunk that is used as a coffee table with black and white candles on top of it. I even have a fully stocked drink station set up for the guest bands. I feel proud of the work that we've accomplished today. I place extra tape over the plastic that is blocking the studio area off so Trent and Tyler can handle ordering the equipment for that room as my part is now complete. I release a breath, hit the lights, grab the trash, and lock up.

CHAPTER 13

ARIZONA

Tonight is the big show in Arizona. Trent is joining the band to play piano on a few of the ballads and to test out their new single "It's Done."

I stand in my kitchen, eating crackers as I look around our place and appreciate how well I cleaned it. I am ready for Tyler to come home. I just have to brace myself for a temper tantrum of some sort when I tell him I'm knocked up.

I shake my head in disbelief. It's only been a few weeks, but I already don't feel like myself. I shouldn't have shared the news with anyone until my husband heard the news first; now I feel ill-prepared.

Come evening, I slip into my silk summer nightgown—the one Tyler loves—and stretch out on the bed. I light a candle and just lay there, thinking about him, when I am interrupted by my cell phone ringing.

"Hello?" I answer. "Alex, hey." It's Austin.

"Hey, soldier, what are you doing calling me?" I ask.

He laughs. "I've been distracted with the band and looking out for Lilith—I miss you," he says, and I smile.

"So, listen, the band's on stage now. Tyler asked me to get you on the phone so I could place it on the amplifier," he says.

My eyes widen with surprise. "Okay," I say, and Austin sets his phone down. I hear Trent begin to play his piano for the live audience. I release a breath when I hear Tyler join in singing as the audience applauds. My heart flutters—he sounds so beautiful. I am surprised when I recognize the song "But the Words Just Won't Come Out," and tears stream down my face. The two of them sound so perfect.

I am so proud as I lay back on the pillow and let the tears flow. *God, I miss Tyler.* I listen to his strong voice hit every note and I can't stop crying. I wish I was there, but I guess this is the next best thing. I then hear Tyler introduce Trent:

"Trent Van Zant, everybody!" The crowd roars with appreciation. I wait for a moment and hear, "That was for you, lovebird—I reeeally miss you," as Tyler speaks directly into the phone, then hands it back to Austin. I gasp.

"Hey, Alex, they sound pretty good, eh?" Austin asks.

Even though he can't see me, I nod my head, crying. "They sound amazing, thank you, Austin. You have no idea how much I needed that," I say as I wipe my teary eyes.

"They're finishing their set, then we're taking off early tomorrow. I'll see you in a few days," he says.

"Okay, soldier, thank you again." I click off the line and smile over at the cats lying next to me. "Oh, I needed that, you guys," I say, replaying that beautiful moment over and over in my head.

Then, guilt strikes me in the head. Trent and Mick know about the pregnancy and Tyler's oblivious to it all.

Shame on me; I should have held out, but my excitement got the best of me.

The day finally arrives—I have to go pick up Tyler from the tour bus. I blow my hair out, I have my nails done, my lashes are glued on, and I slip into a form-fitting tank dress. I want to look pretty for his return.

I glance around our place one last time. Everything seems to be in order, as I have dinner marinating to grill, and I just want a quiet evening alone with my husband. I open the kitchen drawer, pick up my lovebird key chain, and head down to the parking garage.

Butterflies slam-dance in my stomach as I drive over to the band's rehearsal space. I turn off the ignition and just smile as I watch everyone hug their significant other, relieved to be back in their arms once again. I then step out, shut the door, and walk over to Austin.

"Hi, soldier!" I greet him as he wraps his arms around me and squeezes me tightly. I shudder from the boob tenderness and step back.

"It's good to be on home turf," he says as he releases a breath, and I smile. My eyes then light up as Austin starts laughing, watching me stare at Tyler stepping off the bus. "He really missed you, Alex," he says.

I bite my lower lip and walk toward Tyler. He opens his arms and pulls me to his chest as I release a sigh of relief. *He is home.*

"I've missed you like crazy, baby girl," Tyler says. He steps back, leans down, and kisses my lips.

I grab his neck, pull him in, and slip my tongue into his

mouth as he moans. "I've missed you more," I whisper as I kiss his lips, his cheek, his ear, then his neck.

Tyler starts laughing. "Take me home," he says.

I nod my head and pull him in for one last hug before he releases me and walks over to collect his bags.

Trent steps off the bus and flashes me a grin. I bat my lashes at him then glance over at Mick, who shakes his head. I exhale and pick up Tyler's backpack, heading over to the Jeep to load it.

"Get in, baby girl. I've got this," Tyler says as he opens the door and helps me jump into the driver's side. He loads everything, closes the hatch, then hops in. "I'm tired of being in a constant crowd—I'm so ready to be alone with you," he says, placing his hand on my leg as I start driving home.

"Just leave the bags there," I say. "You go hop in the shower. I'll fire up the grill."

Tyler flashes me a smile of relief and nods his head, then goes straight for the shower. I select the *Cigarettes After Sex* CD and push "play." I then turn on the grill and pull out all the fixins for dinner.

As I am mixing the salad, Tyler walks into the kitchen and hops up on the counter.

"I missed you sitting there watching me prep." I lean into him and lightly kiss his pouty lips.

"I'm hungry," he says, and I laugh.

"I figured you would be," I say. I chop cucumbers and feed him a slice. I then take out the marinated steaks from the refrigerator.

Tyler takes the plate from me, jumps to his feet, and puts them on the grill. I roll the potatoes in aluminum foil, then toss them over to Tyler. He laughs, turns back around, and places them on the grill as well.

"Oh, you don't realize how much you miss home 'til you've been away," he says as I smile and dish our salad.

"Here," I say as I hand him his dish and fork. I grab mine and head outside to the balcony. "What can I get you to drink?" I ask while he flips the steaks.

"Ooo, I'm dying for your sweet tea," he says.

I smile. "Coming right up!" I go back inside, pour two glasses, then sit down on the wicker chair, a bit winded.

"You okay, baby girl?" Tyler asks as he sits down next to me and sips his iced tea. "So much has happened since you've left for tour." I bat my lashes as he pierces his tomato with his fork and pops it into his mouth.

"It seems like it. I want to hear all about it," he says excitedly, standing up and rotating the potatoes once more.

I'm not sure where to begin. I think I'll ease into the pregnancy conversation once we've eaten.

"I want to take you over to the studio sometime soon," I say as he sits back down. "Wow, we own a fucking recording studio now... You're amazing." He smiles as he pushes his hair behind his ear.

I smile back as I take him all in. He's wearing his black tank top, unbuttoned slim-fit black jeans, and that beautiful smile that always makes me melt.

"What are you staring at?"

"You. I'm staring at you. God, I've missed you," I say as he laughs once again.

He reaches for my hand and kisses the bird tattoo on my ring finger. "Baby girl, I missed seeing you too—and

WOW, your boobs look like they're going to pop outta that dress!" He adjusts his tight jeans as I giggle. *Same old Tyler.* He then shuts off the grill, places the food on our plates, and sits back down. "This is good," he says as he slices his meat and begins to eat.

I smile as I pick at my potato, then release a breath.

When we finish, Tyler leans back in the chair and lights up a joint to relax. "Want a hit, baby girl?" he asks, but I shake my head. "Really?" He registers surprise.

I sip my iced tea, wait for his hit to take effect, then say: "I'm really scared, but really excited to tell you something, Tyler!"

He looks over at me with concern as he blows out smoke and sets the joint in the ashtray. "I'm pregnant," I say, clapping my hands together.

Tyler's eyes dilate two sizes as he leans forward with his elbows on his knees, releasing a breath.

"Aren't you happy?" I ask. His initial reaction to any good news is lifting me up and spinning me around. I am hurt.

"Are you sure?" He stares at the ground, panic-stricken.

I nod my head as worry flushes through me. "Look, it's only the first trimester, I guess. I wanted to tell you in person. Only Trent and Mick know. I'm so excited!" I grin widely.

He says nothing for a moment, then mumbles, "Trent, huh?" He rubs his hand along his mouth, trying to digest everything. I just stare at him. He then stands up, shakes his head, walks into the place, and grabs his keys.

Oh, I hope the news doesn't make him angry or—worse yet—walk away from me. I sit there, paralyzed with disbelief.

Tyler opens the front door, walks out, then slams it shut, making the patio door vibrate.

He is walking away.

Instinctively, tears of fear begin to stream down my face as I figure by his reaction that I'll be in this alone. I tap my hands nervously on the arms of the chair, unsure what move I should make next. My gut churns. Tyler needs space, so there is no use in chasing after him. I close my eyes and exhale to try and soothe myself.

Twenty minutes later, I hear my cell phone buzz on the table next to me. I quickly answer it. "This is Alex." I hold my breath.

"Hey Alex, it's George from the *Metal Can*. Look, I have Tyler in here and I just served him," he says. "I know he's in AA, so—ummm—I thought I should just ring you," he says.

"Ah, shit, George," I huff. "I'll be down in a few minutes to collect him. Thank you for calling me," I say and click off the line. "Asshole went over to that damn watering hole down the street for a drink," I mutter to myself. I go inside, slip on my flip-flops, grab my keys, and head down to the parking garage, full of steam.

Walking into the smoky *Metal Can*, which smells of piss, an old country song drifting out of the jukebox, I nod my head toward the bartender as he points to Tyler at the other end of the bar. I release a breath and walk over to him as he leans his head against the palm of his left hand, smoking a cigarette, lost in his thoughts.

"Bet you needed one of these after the news, eh?" I

grab the empty glass, swirl the ice around, and shake my head in disappointment.

"Did your husband Trent need a drink after you told him first?" Tyler gulps the last swig of his drink down.

I roll my eyes and mumble, "Not my husband," as I rub my hand on his back. "Come on, Tyler, let's go home and celebrate." I squeeze his shoulders as he blows out smoke then puts out his cigarette in the ashtray. He glances over at me and apologetically shrugs his shoulders. I reach my hand out, take his hand, and walk him back to the Jeep in silence.

As I drive home, neither one of us has the courage to speak first. I just pout quietly to myself as I keep blowing air out my nostrils in a huff, stewing on how poorly Tyler is handling the news. *Why is he fixating on Trent? This is about my pregnancy.*

I pull into our parking space, turn off the ignition, jump out of the Jeep, and slam the door shut.

Tyler takes a step back. "I'm sorry, baby girl," he says softly. I ignore him and make my way to the elevator. "I said I was sorry," he repeats as he follows me. "I just need-ed a minute to digest the news," he confesses as we step into the elevator.

"In a bar?" I snap as I push the button with our floor number. "That's your reaction when I tell you I'm preg-nant? That's where you chose to 'digest the news'?" I make air quotes with my fingers. "You're unbelievable, Tyler. Instead of talking it through with me, your wife, you'd rather drown your sorrows in Jack Daniels again!" I shout. The elevator door opens to our floor and I brush past him. "Grow the fuck up!"

I shake my head as I put the key in our door, push it

ajar, kick off my shoes, and furiously toss the keys across the counter. I make my way onto the balcony and sit down, folding my arms in a huff as my eyes begin to water.

Tyler follows me and stands in the balcony doorway, stroking his bottom lip with his fingertips as he nervously watches me. "I said I was sorry, Alex. That was fucking stupid of me. Look, I had one damn drink. I'm just not sure how to deal with this sudden news flash," he says.

My eyes continue to water, and I notice a tear slip down his cheek as well.

"I wanted to celebrate with you and you just ruined it by walking out," I pout.

Tyler taps on the glass door and huffs. "Is my lovebird having a lil' chick?" he asks sweetly, knowing he's in the doghouse.

I chuckle and look back at him. He smiles warmly, walks over, squats down in front of me, and begins giving me little kisses on my forehead and both cheeks. I release a laugh and instantly forgive him for his stupidity.

"Oh, Tyler," I say as he pecks my lips while making chirping noises. "Oh God, I really should have told you first. I just got sick when we were painting and Trent had questions." I cover my mouth in shame. "I'm sorry." I muffle the words in my palm, then blow out a deep breath. "I'm not sure we can do this—I'm not sure what to do. I'm..." I pause as my confidence crashes.

Tyler shrugs his shoulders and looks up into my glossy eyes. "I'll never walk," he whispers. "We'll figure it out." He scratches his head and glances over at the flowerpot next to him. "I just need a little time," he mutters.

"Ty, we never talked about a family. It was just you and me, remember?" I ask as he looks back toward me. "But...I *want* a family," I say.

He nods, stands up, and slides into the wicker chair beside me. "I've never been through this either, Alex. Um, I don't really know the word *family*." He runs his hand through his hair and tenses. "Can I just have some time?" he asks again.

I nod my head as my eyes continue to water. "Okay," I whisper. He'll address this on his own terms. I just need to be patient with him. My thoughts float around my head as I remain quiet.

Breaking the silence, he questions: "Um, can we still have sex? Or am I going to hurt you?"

I laugh as I wipe my tears. "Of course we can still have sex. Is that all you're concerned about?" I smack his leg.

"I want to be with you right now," he says. "I miss you. The new studio business, being apart from you on tour, the lil' chick news—just...everything is overwhelming me at this very moment." He pauses. "I want you and I want you badly," he says as he adjusts himself in his tight jeans.

I smile, shaking my head. *He does have a lot to process. Bands and babies aren't usually a good mix. I just need to give him time.*

"I've reeeally fucking missed you," he whines softly as he bats his lashes.

"You have no idea how much I've missed you, Ty." I cave and stand up, taking his hand in mine. "Come on then," I say as the conversation swiftly changes from lil' chicks to sex which started this whole mess in the first place.

Walking into the living room, I push him onto a floor pillow, his back against the wall, and straddle him in my cotton dress.

"You won't hurt me, Ty," I say as I lean in and aggressively push my tongue into his mouth. He tastes like a mix of Jack Daniels and tobacco as I lick his lips then swirl my tongue with his barbell. I reach down between my legs and quickly unzip his jeans, releasing his hardened cock. I anxiously pull up my dress to my hips and slide down his shaft, longing desperately for him. *Forget the anger; weeks without him made me mad-crazy for him.*

"Oh, Alex," he pants as I hold on to his shoulders and slide myself along his length.

Using his fingertips, he slips my dress straps down, exposing my swollen breasts. He leans in and licks my nipples, which harden between his lips. He gently sucks as I push his hair behind his ears and watch him.

I feel his length deepen inside of me as I become overly aroused. I keep rocking back and forth on his hard cock, tossing my head back in euphoria. His mouth on me is all I need.

"I've missed you," I pant as he takes my breath away.

He clamps his hand down on my waist and pushes me a little harder onto his lap as I gasp, feeling the fullness.

"Oh, Alex, I need this, I need you," he cries out.

I lean into him and lick his neck. "I've needed you more." Tears roll down my cheek as I inhale his scent. *He is home.* I release a breath, lean my chest against his, and grip him tightly, working him over as he moans.

"That's it—be careful. I don't want you to be too rough," he says as I push harder. "I'm okay, Ty. I need you," I cry out as I continue to slide back and forth on him faster. "Baby, you're going to come," he says.

I bite my lip, flushing as I smile at him. *After what I've been through over these last few weeks, what I really need is to come.*

"Yes, that's it," I pant. "I'm…" I begin to orgasm as Tyler hardens, pushes deeper, and releases with me.

"Ahh," he moans, and I lick his lip and stare into his eyes. They are dark and dilated as I watch him finish.

He is so sexy. Taking it all in just overwhelms me.

"Wow, that wiped me out." I exhale as I kiss him once more and wipe my cheek.

"Me too. Do you want to go lie in bed and deal with the conversation shit later?" he asks, holding my hand steady as I get to my feet and pull my dress back down while he zips up his jeans.

I laugh and just roll my eyes. He needs to take the news in small doses. I can handle that. "Sure. I'll collect the plates, you go lie down," I say, helping him to his feet.

"No, let me help," he offers.

We put everything into the dishwasher, close the grill, shut the music off, and make our way into the bedroom.

"Oh, the bed has been so lonely without you," I groan as I step out of my dress.

Tyler suddenly stops me. "Lay naked with me, baby girl," he says. I smile, watching him remove his jeans. He pulls his tank top off, then crawls under the sheets. "Come here," he says.

I sit down on the bed, push up against him, and let him wrap his arms around me. I need this. I need him. I close my eyes and drift off to sleep.

CHAPTER
14

TWO WEEKS LATER

Tyler and I are back to our usual home routine. He seems happy; he keeps making little chirping noises to me every morning. That must be his way of letting me know that he is okay with the pregnancy. I hesitate to push it—there is plenty of time to plan. He needs to recover from the tour and get a handle on the new business that Trent, he, and I are about to embark on. I just have to wait for him to open up to me about starting a family.

"I think I want to take you over to the recording studio today," I say excitedly as I stand on my tippy toes, kissing him.

"Sure, lovebird, I have nothing scheduled in my day planner," he says, teasing me for reading mine neurotically throughout the week.

"Ooo, good! Let me grab my bag and slip on my shoes," I cheer, then pause and steady myself on my drafting table.

"Oh, baby girl, you all right?" he asks as he takes ahold of my arm.

"Just a little cramp, that's all," I say as I wipe a bead of sweat from my upper lip. "Put your shoes on," I direct

Tyler as I slip into mine.

We lock up, then head over to *Brimstone.* Pulling alongside the curb, Tyler shuts off the engine of the truck and gazes out the window at our new building.

"Girrrl, you did real good." He smiles.

"Thanks," I giggle. I turn to open the door, but Tyler stops me. "What's up?" I ask as I hold on to the door handle.

"Wait," he says, then swallows as he lowers his voice. "I want to make you happy. I do want to be a father some-day... I'm..." He pauses. "It's just—you've always been my whole world, Alex. I'm scared to bring a baby into it."

I bite my lip and smile. "This is about us and our world. We can do this," I say as I gently touch his cheek.

He nods his head. "I'm all in if you're all in, lovebird." He smiles and I feel relief that he is finally opening up to me.

"I'm all in, songbird," I say, repeating what he said to me the very first time I pledged my love for him on the loading dock. I glance over at the building and release a breath. "It's scheduled to be painted black," I say.

Tyler looks out the window at the motorcycle parked next to the front door. "Trent's here," he groans.

I roll my eyes. "Look, I'm sorry he found out before you, I was just excited and it slipped. I never did it in-tentionally. Anyway, y'all need to discuss what equipment you're ordering, so man up," I say, laughing. "You're a business owner now, Mr. Black!" I laugh again as he leans over and kisses me.

We hop out, and Tyler reaches for my hand and squeezes it. "Come on, mama bird," he says, holding my hand tightly in his.

I unlock the door and we walk in. "See all the rustic stars?" I ask, and Tyler nods his head. "Hello? Trent?" I call out.

Trent pushes the hanging plastic away as he steps into the "chill" space.

"The studio is behind there," I say to Tyler as Trent reaches out to shake his hand.

Reluctantly, Tyler shakes his hand. I glance up at Trent and mouth "sorry" as he pulls his hand back.

"Whatcha think, brother?" Trent asks.

Tyler's eyes widen as he looks around. He walks up to the pictures and just smiles as he looks over each one, glances at the couch, the rug, and nods his head in approval. "Alex, this place rocks," he says as he lifts my hand and kisses it again while still holding it tightly.

"Yeah, Alex, you and Mick really made something out of this 'intimate' space. The studio is behind the plastic," Trent says.

Tyler lets go of my hand and pushes the plastic aside. Trent and he tour the space as I stand there and release a breath.

"Oh," I whisper, rubbing my stomach as another kicking cramp causes me to hold on to the wall to steady myself.

"Check out the vocal booth," Trent hollers back, returning through the plastic and stepping in front of me. "Alex, you're all pale. Are you okay?" he asks.

I moan and grip his arm. He holds on to me while I try to steady myself once more.

Another cramp zaps me.

"Is it the baby?" he asks sincerely as my eyes begin to water. "Get Tyler, I need Tyler!" I cry out, grabbing my stomach. "Let me help you sit down," he says.

I lean over in excruciating pain. "No—get Tyler! I need my husband!" I push him, and finally he hollers, "Tyler, get in here!"

I start to cry as Tyler moves the plastic aside to see what is going on.

"Alexandria, you're bleeding!" he says nervously as he wraps his arm around me and sifts inside his jeans pocket. He throws Trent the keys. "Start the truck; we have to take her to the hospital!"

I grip him tightly. "Don't leave me, Tyler!" I panic as Trent opens the studio door and unlocks the truck.

"Baby girl, breathe. I need you to breathe." Tyler kisses the beads of sweat on my head that are forming as we slowly walk outside.

Trent rushes over, picks me up, carries me to the truck, and sets me inside. "Tyler!" I call out once more.

Trent pushes Tyler into the truck next to me then runs around to the driver's side and hops in. I lean my head on Tyler's chest as he runs his fingers through my dampened hair to try and soothe me. "I love you so much, don't leave me," I sob, clutching my stomach while Tyler keeps kissing my head.

Trent glances over at the two of us as he floors it to Baylor Hospital. He pulls up in front of the hospital and medical personnel meet us at the emergency entrance.

Tyler hops out and tries to pull me out of the truck. "My wife just started bleeding—she's pregnant!" he hollers as he watches the staff quickly set me onto a gurney. Trent grips his shoulder, but Tyler shrugs him off. "This is between me and my wife, asshole!" he snaps.

A staff member calls out what's her name? As everyone

starts running into the hospital. "Alexandria Black," he answers as he regains focus.

I reach out for Tyler's hand. "I need my husband," I cry out as the nurse taps my arm and tries to quiet me down.

"He'll be in once we take care of you, sweetheart," she says just as Tyler is pulled away by an orderly. I watch panic wash over his face.

"Alexandria, we're going to set up an IV catheter and I'm going to give you some fluids and medicine," the nurse says. "Doctor, she's losing a lot of blood. She's pregnant."

The emergency doctor steps in and begins to examine me. "It's okay, Mrs. Black, just relax. I need to take a look," she says as the staff members cut my pants loose then slip a drape over me. "Lightly sedate her—she had a miscarriage. Prep for an ultrasound and a D&C," she orders.

I close my eyes and everything fades to black.

My eyes struggle to focus as I stare at the IV pole, trying to decipher if I am awake or dreaming. I pull my hand up to my face, stare at the inserted catheter, and blink my eyes. I then look down and see Tyler. He is sitting in a chair pushed up against my hospital bed with his head down on my stomach as he sleeps. I slowly stroke his hair with my fingers as he opens his eyes. Immediately, tears begin to surface as he squeezes my hand and kisses it.

"I'm the one who's supposed to be lying in the hospital bed, not you," he whispers as he refers to his past drug overdose and tour bus accident. "How are you feeling?" He asks as he sits up and keeps kissing my hand.

"Numb," I answer as I recall the doctor saying the word

"miscarriage." "I was so excited but I failed," I whisper. Tears roll down my face as Tyler kisses my stomach and squeezes my hand a second time.

"I failed you, baby girl, I should have..." He pauses as he reflects for a moment. "When are you ever ready for that kind of news? I fucked up, not you." He flushes red and I know he feels bad for how he reacted when I told him I was pregnant.

"Someday," he mutters as he keeps kissing my hand. "God, I love you so much, Alex." He wipes his tears away with his fingertips.

"How ya holdin' up, Mrs. Black?" the emergency doctor asks me as she walks in and smiles at the two of us.

"I'm holdin'," I say sadly.

She takes out her stethoscope and listens to my heartbeat as Tyler backs up, wipes his eyes, and just watches the examination. The doctor then checks the machines and nods her head. "I can release you today. I'm going to send home some medication and you need to promise me that you'll rest," she says, looking over at Tyler. "That means you too, husband."

She smiles as she hands me a box of tissues. "Y'all can still try again." She taps my leg and flashes me a sympathetic smile. "I'm going to send my medical notes over to your doctor and you just be sure to follow up with her—you hear me?" she asks, and I nod my head. "Okay," she says as she instructs the nurse to release me.

I walk into our place, feeling depleted. Tyler locks the door while I look around. "I need a shower," I groan.

Tyler nods his head, takes my hand, and leads me into the bathroom. I stand there, helpless, as he turns on the water, strips down, then helps me out of my shirt and the green scrub pants I was sent home in.

"Come on, baby girl." He takes my hand and guides me into the shower. He washes my hair as I remain paralyzed under the water. He then takes the loofah and begins bathing me. I flash a slight smile as I pull him toward me and just hold him for a moment.

"Thank you," I whisper as he kisses my head.

Tyler washes his hair as I run the loofah over him. I then swipe a cloth rag between my legs. As blood stains the rag, Tyler gasps. "It's okay," I say.

He pulls me back into his arms and holds me for another minute while the water splashes off his back. "Let's get you into bed," he whispers. I let go while he shuts off the water, reaches for a towel, and covers me.

"Can you grab me a T-shirt and jogging pants?" I ask, wanting to dry myself off and fix my maxi pad.

He nods his head as he heads into our closet and pulls out a WHIP T-shirt and his joggers.

He returns to the bathroom and slips the tee over my head and pulls up the pants as I steady myself, holding on to his arm. He then brushes my hair out as I stand there sadly, staring at his reflection in the mirror.

"Okay, get in bed, baby girl." He kisses the top of my head and I do as I am told while he goes to get my medication and the heating pad.

When he walks back into the room, he hands me a glass of water to swallow the medicine, then leans down and plugs the heating pad in. I smile as he places the pad on my stomach, shuts off the bathroom light, then crawls into bed behind me. He wraps his arms around me as I release a breath. We say nothing more as I drift off to sleep in his arms.

The next day, I wake up in the fetal position. Tyler is out in the kitchen, talking on his cell phone. I sit up in bed, adjust the heating pad, and lean against the headboard as he ends his call. He then walks into the room with a tray and I smile.

"You're up, lovebird." He smiles back as he sets the tray down on the bedside table. "Here's some sweet tea to take your medication with and here is an English muffin and some fruit." He points to the plate on the tray as he leans in and kisses me.

I reach for the English muffin and take a bite as Tyler sets a napkin on my lap.

"I was talking to your mother." He rolls his eyes as I laugh. "She's stopping by this afternoon and bringing us something to eat," he says. "Oh, and Mick called as well. I just told him that you need to rest and to check on you in a few days."

I wonder for a moment if Trent reached out as well, but hesitate to ask.

Tyler blows out a breath as he sits down on the bed and pushes my hair behind my ear. "How are you?" I ask him.

His eyes tear up instantly. "It all happened so fast. The news, the hospital—it's a lot to wrap my head around," he confesses softly, and I nod my head in agreement. "I'm not sure if I'm ready to be a father, Alex. But we made a little chick..." He pauses as I giggle over the bird reference. "I want everything with you. Do you forgive me?"

I nod. "One day we'll be ready. In sickness and in health, right?" I ask.

He taps my leg. "In sickness and in health, baby girl." He flashes that beautiful grin once more and I know we are going to get through this together.

A few hours later, I wake from my nap and hear classical music playing. I pull myself upright and head into the bathroom, clean myself up, brush my teeth, and braid my hair.

"Baby girl, are you up?" Tyler calls out as I walk into the kitchen and pour myself some more iced tea. The sun is shifting west and the music is soothing, the door to the balcony open.

"It's comfortable here," I say as he walks up and kisses me.

Suddenly, there is a knock on the door. Tyler goes over to the door, opens it, and greets my mother.

"Hi, Mama," he says. He takes a dish and a bag from her hands and sets them on the counter.

"Oh, Tyler, give me a hug, sugar," she says as she steps into him and wraps her arms around him. She then sets her purse down as I walk up to her. "Oh, Alexandria, what are you doing out of bed?" she asks as she hugs me, steps back, then smooths out my braid.

"I've been resting for quite a while, Mama. I need to stretch my legs and get some fresh air," I say.

She glances around our place. "Very cozy. Nice album,"

she says, complimenting Tyler's choice of music as she walks into the kitchen. "I have a pot roast for y'all. Here is the bread, and I tucked a little dessert in there just for you, Tyler." She laughs as she fusses with the oven.

She always needs to stay busy; she just can't sit and visit. She pulls out the homemade bread and slices it, then sets the dessert on the counter. "Tyler, dear, set some plates for you two," she orders as I slide onto a counter stool and watch the two of them. "You're so thin, Tyler, you be sure to eat," she says.

I roll my eyes and Tyler sticks his tongue out at me.

She then pauses as the timer beeps on the oven and slides the dish in to warm it up. "Give it twenty minutes," she says. "Now you two have a nice, quiet dinner," she says. She walks over to me and hugs me once more. "I'm so sorry, dear. Jesus has his reasons."

"You're leaving?" I ask, surprised.

"Yes, I'll check on you later," she says as Tyler opens the front door and walks her out. "Wow," I say loudly. I turn on my heel and walk onto the balcony for some much-needed air.

When Tyler walks back in, he starts laughing as he closes the door behind him. "Wow!" he calls out.

"I just said the same thing!" I shake my head as Tyler nabs a piece of bread off the counter and meets me on the balcony.

"Are you hungry?" he asks, and I nod. "Good, we can eat out here," he says as he chews.

I turn and pull him toward me. "Thank you for taking such good care of me." I brush crumbs away from his lip. He smiles, then bends down and kisses me.

CHAPTER 15

A FEW DAYS LATER

I feel pretty good as my body begins to rebound. I already had my follow-up visit with my gynecologist this week and she told me that I was a healthy young woman and I still can carry on my own. She validated that cramping was a completely normal symptom of pregnancy and not to fear my body signals the next time around. She actually suggested that Tyler and I try again.

I stew on her suggestion as I stand in the kitchen, admiring all the flowers that Austin, my mother, and Mick sent me—it was a kind gesture. I then brush off the baby vibes as I put on our coffee. I pop my head back into the bedroom to check on Tyler. He is sound asleep on his stomach with our cat Beatle sleeping on his head. I giggle, then head back into the kitchen. I take out the eggs and fry the bacon. I set the breakfast counter with plates and our lovebird mugs that we received as a wedding gift.

"Good morning, baby girl." Tyler emerges from the bedroom, shirtless in pajama pants, scratching his head.

"Hi, songbird," I greet him as I flip the bacon and pour our coffee.

"You look better today." He smiles as he slides onto a stool at the counter, rubbing his eyes.

"I feel much better." I smile as I hand him a coffee. "Nova's swinging by in a little bit and you have a meeting, I believe," I say as I place an egg on the plate.

"Yeah, it's a band meeting about the video and then an AA meeting," he says as the toast pops up and I toss a slice on Tyler's plate.

"Video?" I ask.

"Oh, fuck, I'm sorry, baby girl," he apologizes. "Zack is having me, Trent, and Edward record a video for 'It's Done' over at the *Turn It Up!* theater," he says as I raise my eyebrows.

"That venue is so cool. I saw Black Rifle Coalition and the Deftones there," I squeal, setting the bacon out and sitting down next to Tyler.

"Deftones? When did you see the Deftones?" he asks as he pokes his egg with his toast. *Shit*, I think as I bite my bottom lip. "Oh, a while ago. You were in Los Angeles recording the film soundtrack or something and I went with Trent," I say nonchalantly as I butter my toast.

Tyler rolls his eyes. "Oh, was he in your life or was he out? How many times did y'all break up?" he teases. "It took me one time," he says as he holds up his index finger. "You said you wanted me and I was all in—I never left you," he says proudly, acting as if the competition with Trent is still in effect.

"And that's why I married you, Tyler." I lean in and kiss him. He drops the conversation.

❈

Midafternoon, Nova taps on my front door as she waits impatiently for me to answer. "Hi, girl." I smile as she steps inside blowing out a pink bubble from her gum.

"Hi, how are you feeling, girl?" she asks as she sets a bag and her purse down on the counter.

"I feel good. I feel back to normal," I answer.

She reaches out her arms and wraps them around me. "Why didn't you tell me you were pregnant?" She smacks my arm as I roll my eyes. "Mick told Edward, then he told Zack, now I'm standing at your door," she giggles.

"I was telling no one until I told Tyler first," I snap. "Well, Trent actually was the first one to find out as we were painting the studio." I feel my cheeks flush with embarrassment. "Look, I barfed and he was concerned. I was excited so I had to tell him," I huff with regret. "Can I get you something?" I ask to try and change the subject.

She spins on her heel and heads toward the balcony. "No, I just had coffee. Come sit with me," she says, and I join her. "How'd Tyler take the news?" She is dying to know.

I lean back in the wicker chair and sigh. "Well, pretty good for being Tyler. I mean, he had to put his head between his legs to catch his breath at first," I giggle. "Then he grabbed his keys..." I pause. "But I got him back." I blush with embarrassment. "Then he was so sweet," I say as Nova smiles. "You know, he never referred to it as a baby, he kept calling it 'lil' chick.'"

Nova taps my hand. "He was in shock, honey. We're y'all even trying?" she asks.

"Not at all. Tyler is so childlike himself sometimes, I'm unsure if I could handle two." I laugh as Nova nods her head in agreement. "He was so good with the hospital, with the recovery, I mean…" I pause. "He really loves me," I say.

Nova smiles. "Of course he does," she agrees.

"No. When I was bleeding, I called out, 'Don't leave me, Tyler.' Something inside of me thought he couldn't handle it—that he'd just bail," I confess, staring straight ahead, sounding as insecure as Tyler.

"Alex, honey, he adores you. You are his entire life. He's loved you for so long, nothing can or will ever stand between the two of you. I mean, look how unraveled he got just when he saw Trent kiss you at the party." She laughs. "He's not going anywhere, believe me," she states.

"I know he's a little immature, he constantly gives me pushback, but I love him so much, Nova," I say softly as she stands up.

"Wait, I have something to show you," she says. She goes inside and retrieves her bag.

Back onto the balcony, she tosses a magazine in my lap. "Your bird," she teases.

I pick up the rock magazine and smile at Tyler's picture on the front cover. He is in his black V-neck tee, bending forward, singing into a microphone with his platinum wedding band hanging from his neck, dangling down so everyone can see it clear as day in the photo.

"He mentions his wife and how 'she's the world to him' in the article too." Nova rolls her eyes as I bite my lower lip and flip to the article. "He's not shy about telling everyone he's your husband," she says.

I grin from ear to ear, feeling relieved. "Thank you, girl," I say. "No problem." She smiles.

❧

A FEW WEEKS LATER

Tyler is at rehearsal when I decide to throw on my long-sleeved, tight black Henley shirt, form-fitted black jeans, black heels, and head over to *Brimstone* to check if the sound equipment got delivered.

I pull up in front of the brick building and notice Trent's motorcycle as I shut off the ignition. I hop out of my truck, inhale the fall scent of burning leaves, and smile while I unlock the studio.

"Trent?" I call out as I move the plastic away from the studio entrance and look around. The new Neve console arrived and was set in place with bubble wrap still on it. Trent's KORG Triton is still packaged in the box on the floor while he sets up his Waldorf Q synthesizer.

"Hey," I say as he looks over his shoulder.

"What are you doing here?" He turns around. "Wow, you look pretty, Alex," he says, and, taken aback by the compliment, I feel my cheeks instantly flush. "How are you feeling?" he asks.

"Good, better, um—back to myself," I stutter. I look around at all the shipping supplies scattered around the studio.

"Tyler really has no idea how good he has it, huh?" Trent asks.

I dismiss the question. *Should have thought about that before you cheated, prick*, I think as I tuck a piece of hair behind my ear. "Well, I wanted to see if the equipment finally showed up," I say quickly, changing the subject.

"Oh, you could've just texted me. I mean, you didn't need to drive over," he says.

I shrug my shoulders. "I want to get out of the house."

I smile as I slide my hands into my back pockets. "It's most of the stuff you had set up in *Head Rush*," I say.

He grins. "You remember what equipment I had?" He laughs, seeming impressed as he shakes his head.

"I pay attention," I tease.

He checks his watch. "I'm taking off soon," he says as he sips from his bottled water just as there's a knock on the studio door.

"Hello?" a woman's voice calls out.

My eyes dilate two sizes as I turn around to see a petite girl with short black hair and piercings holding a motorcycle helmet.

"Oh, hi," Trent says, swallowing hard. "Liz, this is Alexandria."

I extend my hand and shake hers. "Hi, sugar, nice to meet you." I am friendly even though jealousy darts straight through my heart.

"Let me grab my keys and helmet and I'm ready to roll." Trent flashes her a grin as I shift my weight on my heels, watching him.

"I'll lock up, Trent, go ahead and take off," I say, blinking my lashes at him. "You sure?" he asks, and I nod. "Okay, Alex. I'll catch ya later," he says.

Liz waves, grabs ahold of Trent's arm, and they walk out together.

I stand there for a second, then head over to the couch and sit down, taking a deep breath. "Oh my God," I say aloud as I feel the strings of my heart being snapped. *It is the first time I've seen him with another woman since we've split.* I am just stunned at the betrayal of my heart. I immediately open my cell and dial Mick.

"Girl, where are you at?" he answers.

"Can you meet me at the *Broken Hearts Club* pronto?" I ask.

He giggles. "I'm in the neighborhood wasting time 'til Edward's through with rehearsal.

I'll head there now," he says.

"Good, I'll meet you there in a few minutes." I hang up, shake my head in disbelief, then lock up the studio.

CHAPTER 16

Walking into *Broken Hearts Club*, I release a breath, seeing Mick waving me over. An acoustic guitarist is strumming on the small stage as the candles on the tables flicker, lighting my path over to the booth. I slide in and greet him with a kiss.

"Girl, you look beautiful," he compliments me. "I mean, you're glowing," he says.

"It must be from the fury I feel from seeing Trent with another woman," I grumble as I motion for the waitress.

"Nooo!" he says, feeding off the band gossip.

"Just now! I saw him at the recording studio and while we were talking some little twit with a helmet strolls right into my studio!" I say loudly as the waitress sets down a wine glass, smiles, and pours me a glass from Mick's bottle. I mouth "thank you" to her then pick up the glass and take a large swig.

Mick laughs as he toasts me.

"Yes, he's seeing a chick! It feels so strange. I mean, why should I even care?" I pout as Mick taps my hand to settle me down. "I just reignited that bond that Trent and I once had. I feel like he is sincere with his apology and that I could trust him again. Now he's dating, never minding

142

to tell me, even after I told him about my pregnancy." Confused, I blow out my breath and wonder, *Are we truly friends or just exes?*

"Girl, when I saw my ex for the first time with someone new, I felt betrayed," Mick groans.

"Yes! I mean, he apologized, all those hurt feelings were buried, and then *bam*!" I shout. "The jealousy overcame me! Why?" I ask. "He left me twice and he had an affair behind my back. I mean, why do I care if he's seeing someone else?" I am shocked by this insecure feeling choking me. "I cried and cried over him—it was exhausting," I pout once more.

"He's sexy but he's a fucking traitor, girl," Mick says as he sips his wine just as the word '*traitor*' makes me think of the red spray painted word graffitied on his bedroom wall.

"Yes, he is," I agree as I sip more wine.

"Look, if he walked in right now, walked over to you, and pleaded his love for you..." He pauses. "Would you take him back?"

My mouth drops open. "Absolutely not!" I gasp.

"Exactly. Honey, no one compares to you. You are stunning—big tits, small waist, gorgeous face." He touches my cheek. "I mean, aside from being a knockout, you're so lovely, Alex. No one can deny that." Mick sips his wine and leans back.

"Why couldn't he leave with another dude? No offense." I laugh as Mick puts his hands up.

"No offense taken." He laughs with me.

"I mean, it wouldn't hurt this much," I confess.

"Girl, do you hear yourself? I know it's a jolt to the system when your ex finds someone new, but *hello*?"

He laughs as he shakes my arm. "You bagged the most sought-after lead singer—are you kidding me?" He laughs at my silliness. "You have Tyler, girl! If he was gay, you would sooo have some competition with me!" Mick tries to make me laugh as I shake my head. "God, he's so pretty," he whistles.

"I just feel like my crush asked someone else to the dance!" I say, amused by my teenage angst.

"Crush, yes. But Tyler, that's true love."

He set me straight as I suddenly feel like I am betraying Tyler somehow with my feelings. "I think I just miss Tyler. I mean, we haven't been intimate since before the whole hospital incident," I confide in Mick as he squeezes my hand. "I miss Tyler's touch," I whine. "Is he pulling away?" Mick asks with sincerity.

"No, just the opposite. He always needs attention— we're so protective of one another." I smile, then lean into Mick's ear and whisper, "Oh, and he fucks so much better than Trent."

"Now, that's what I want to hear more of; give me details! I know y'all are dirty!" "I never told Nova this, but I'll confide in you," I giggle, blushing while sipping my wine.

"What, girl? Give!" Mick nudges me.

"Granted, I was on cocaine at the time, but I slept with both Trent and Tyler together at WHIP's guitarist's lake house party." I bite my lower lip as Mick's eyes widen.

"No you did not!" He covers his mouth in surprise. "Wow, that would be something! You hussy!" He laughs as he pokes my side.

"Yes, I did. But I think that's the very moment I felt something for Tyler," I confess. "Yeah, that big dick!" he teases.

I shake my head. "No. I mean, I always play-kissed, held his hand, or danced with Tyler, but I never slept with him back then. Then the night of the party, when he was inside me for the first time, my emotions just overcame me. I mean, it could have been the coke, but from there on out I wanted him badly."

"Well, you nabbed him, girl!" Mick laughs, stunned.

"Oh, the whole evening was erotic. What woman in her right mind would turn down sleeping with the two of them? To kiss them, to touch them, to fuck them..." I pause as Mick starts rapidly fanning himself with his napkin.

"Oh, girl! I'm so jealous!" He laughs. "Trent is sexy and Tyler—whew! Maybe that is why the competition is so fierce between those two—they got a taste of something they liked!" He licks his lips as I sip my wine and release a breath. "Listen, who cares who Trent's banging now. It's always going to be second-rate to you, honey. Plus, he apologized, so let it go and move on," he says.

I know he is right. I feel relieved and drop it. *I just miss Tyler, that's all*, I think as I sip my wine and look around the club.

"How long are our boys rehearsing tonight?" I ask, checking the time on my cell phone. "They're wrapping up soon, so I need to go pick up Edward," he says.

"Thank you for listening to me vent." I blush.

"Oh, girl, I'm always here for you. Give me a hug," he says as he scoots closer and wraps his arms around me.

"Walk those long legs right over here!" I call from the balcony.

Tyler laughs as he locks the front door, kicks off his shoes, and walks outside. He bends down and kisses me while I sit in the wicker chair.

"Another one," I say, and Tyler smiles and gives me a second kiss. "God, I've missed you," I say as he straddles my legs with his. He leans in as I grab his neck, pull him closer, and moan for more. I lick his full lips then bite his lower lip as Tyler growls. "Oh, I miss your tongue!" I thrash my tongue around his. "I miss these lips," I say as I kiss them again. "I miss your touch, I miss you…" I pant as Tyler kisses me back.

"Baby, what's gotten into you?" He laughs as he pulls away. I wrestle with the button on his jeans as he just laughs again. "All right, my little sex-fiend." He grabs my hands to stop me as he stands back up.

"Yes, I want you," I flirt, trying to unbutton his jeans one more time. "Baby girl, can we have sex again? It's been so long… Is it okay?" he asks.

I stand up and put my arms on his shoulders. "Yes, we can," I whisper in his ear, and he lifts me up. I wrap my legs around him and he carries me off to our bedroom.

"I want it rough," I demand as he flashes me a grin and tosses me onto the bed. "Use the leather manacles!" I insist.

Tyler opens our bedside drawer and pulls out the leather cuffs. "Take off your clothes," he instructs as he stands there, casting a shadow over me on the bed while unlocking the cuffs.

I lick my lips, pull off my black Henley, and smile. I unbutton my tight jeans, wiggle out of them, and sit in the middle of the bed in just my black lace bra and panties.

"Man, you are one sexy woman," he compliments me as he stares for a few seconds, taking me all in. "On your knees," he orders, and I push myself up onto my knees in front of him. "Hold out your wrists." I obey, watching his expert hands buckle a cuff around each wrist slowly. He then leans in and whispers, "I own you."

I gasp as he slowly licks my bottom lip. He steps back, pulls off his T-shirt, and tosses it aside as my knees knock.

"Lay on your stomach," he says, and when I turn around and lay down, he kneels on the bed, pulls both my arms above my head, and locks the cuffs. He scratches his black-painted nails down my back until he unclasps my bra. He continues to scratch down my angel wings tattoo until he reaches my panties, then leans down and with his teeth grips the lace and pulls it down over my buttocks.

Goosebumps flare across my skin. He slides his arm under my abdomen and my back arches as my ass lifts. He cups my bare butt, then swiftly slaps it with his right hand as I gasp. He slaps it a second time. The palm of his strong hand sets me on fire.

"Ahh," I moan.

He grunts. "Do you want more?"

I nod my head. "Yes, Mr. Black," I answer, and he gives my ass another swift slap. *Oh how I crave his touch, no matter how rough it is.*

He slaps me once more, then grips my panties and pulls them completely off of me. He pauses and I hear him unzip his jeans and toss them aside. He opens my legs a bit wider and runs his tongue up my thigh, spreads my butt cheeks, and licks with his heated tongue. I squirm from the sensation the steel barbell elicits within me as he inserts a finger into my vagina. Pleasure begins to radiate through me as his finger is in my pussy while his tongue is in my ass.

"Oh my God!" I call out breathlessly.

"Do you like that?" he teases as I shift my hips. "I want more," I cry out.

He inserts a second finger and works me over. "Your slit is soaking wet, you bad girl," he growls.

My every need is to be fucked senseless by him.

He withdraws his tongue and his two fingers. He backs up, parts my folds, and slips his hard cock inside of me.

"Ohh," I moan as he lays on top of me and thrusts from behind.

"Alexandria, you cannot come 'til I say you can," he orders, and I bite down on my pillow while he pushes deeper. He slides in and out as I clench my thighs. "You make me so hard," he pants in my ear, nipping my neck. He reaches up and unlocks the cuffs and I pull my arms back. "I'm going to flip you over," he says as he slides out, grabs my hips, and flips me onto my back.

I immediately reach up and run my hands through his hair. "I want more," I gasp. "How bad?" he teases.

I open my legs wider and pant. "Fuck me, Tyler!" I cry out again—I have no shame. He rubs his hard cock against my trembling thigh, teasing me. "Come on, I want you, Ty!" I lick my lips as he bends down and slides his tongue in my mouth. "Ahh," I groan feverishly, licking his lips, then his neck.

"Oh, Alex," he moans as I suck harder.

"Fuck me," I demand, and he pushes himself back into me. I run my nails down his back as he fucks me rougher. *God, I love when he goes crazy on me,* I think as he pushes deeper.

"I get off on how hard you make me, Alex," he says.

"I can feel that! I want to come!" I am panting with both

pleasure and agony as I wait for his permission to come.

He slows his pace, runs his hand down the curve of my waist, then flicks my swollen clit. "You're so wet for me," he says as he rubs me with his finger and slides his cock back and forth, teasing more.

"I want to come for you, Mr. Black!"

He flashes me a grin, grabs both my hands tightly, and thrusts. He hits the right spot as this rockstar of mine rocks my world. The start of an orgasm ripples through my body as I clench around his hard cock, wanting more.

"Oh, Alex!" Tyler cries out. I clench tighter as he thrusts harder. "I'm coming, baby," he says breathlessly and I feel another orgasm ripple through me. Sweat beads along my neck as he licks me while he releases his pent up load.

A few moments later, we try to catch our breath as we come down after climaxing. "Oh my God, Tyler, you just made me come so hard—multiple times!" I laugh as I lick his lip.

"That was incredible—it's been too long," he says as he nuzzles his nose in my neck, flushing from the orgasm.

"I just needed you tonight," I whisper.

He emerges from my neck and looks down into my eyes. His dark eyelashes blink at me as he whispers, "No, I needed you more."

Tonight's conversation with Mick set me straight. *Trent? Ugh, I sooo moved on.*

"Hey Tyler, are you getting up?" I call toward the bedroom as I water my plants on the balcony. I hear nothing. I set my watering can down and make my way into the bedroom.

He is laying on his side with nothing but our satin

bedsheet concealing his nakedness. I bend down, push his hair aside, and kiss his neck. "Hey, beautiful," I whisper as he smiles. I kiss him once more. "Good morning," I say, sitting on the bed next to him. He just lays there as I let out a subtle laugh. "Baby, I bit your neck pretty good last night. That makeup artist is going to have to cover up a love bite." I push his hair back behind his ear, then lean in and kiss the mark on his neck once more.

He laughs as he opens his eyes. "No one's covering up anything," he says as I rake my hands through his tousled hair. "Ahh, that feels good."

"You have to be at the theater soon," I say. "Coffee's on, you just need to get your ass out of bed." I tap his sheet-covered butt as he stretches. I get up, collect his garment bag, and set it over beside his travel bag. Today is the video shoot for "It's Done."

"Are you coming with me?" he asks.

I roll my eyes. "Later. I'm heading to the theater with Mick," I say.

Tyler groans as he sits up and rubs his eyes. "I want to stay home and play with my bad girl," he teases.

I blush, standing at the foot of the bed, and shake my head. "Ooo, I think I'd like that too much. You know there's not one place left on my body that you haven't licked!"

He laughs as he runs his hand through his hair, knowing just what I am talking about. "Like I told you in Vegas, baby, name the place and the time," he flirts, and I smile.

"*Turn It Up!* theater is the place and eleven o'clock is the time," I say as I spin on my heel and walk back into the kitchen.

"Boo! You're no fun," Tyler whines as I pour his coffee and bring it to him in bed.

CHAPTER 17

Turn It Up! theater is closed today for the video shoot. Security is at the front door, only allowing the film crew, musicians, and their significant others as well as Zack from the record label to enter. The venue is strict, the schedule is tight, and both the crew and the band members have to abide.

"Ooo, look at the stage, girl!" Mick points to the main stage, which is draped under a thick black curtain. Tyler's microphone stand is set up in the center, Trent's black Steinway to the right and Edward's Stradivarius violin case to the left. There are black wrought iron candle holders scattered throughout the stage. The lights are dim and the stage crew is professional and quiet as they work.

"Okay, light the candles again. I need the band back up in two minutes!" the director calls out.

The sound engineer has the song queued up and ready to go as soon as the guys all take their places on stage. Trent walks out in his black velvet jacket, his black V-neck T-shirt, and black jeans, his hair shiny and layered. He takes a seat at the piano and stretches his fingers.

Mick looks over at me as we slide down in the maroon-colored auditorium seats and watch Trent.

"That feeling is punched, choked, and buried into the ground," I whisper as Mick chuckles and taps my hand.

Edward then walks out onto the stage and heads right over to his case, bends down, and pulls out his violin. He has his brunette hair styled into a faux mohawk, a black button-down dress shirt with a black vest, and his black jeans on.

Mick gasps. "Oh, baby, what did you do to your hair?"

Then Tyler walks out. He is wearing his tight black Henley shirt, his black dress scarf around his neck, and his black tight jeans. His hair is blown out and his long, feathered bangs swoop down across his eye. He has black eyeliner and black nail polish on as he stands in front of the microphone stand, adjusting it. *He is long, lean, beautiful, and all mine.* I bite my lower lip and look back over at Mick.

"Girl, I know what you are thinking!" He laughs.

"The scarf is sexy but he's actually wearing it because I bit the shit out of his neck last night!" I cover my mouth, trying not to disturb the set as I laugh.

Mick's eyes widen and he shakes his head.

Just then, the engineer turns on his microphone. "I'm going to start the track in a minute," he says.

The director gives him a thumbs-up. "Okay, gentlemen, we're going to shoot one last take, then it'll be a wrap."

Trent begins to play the opening verse. Then Tyler begins to lip sync to the words. "*There were times I let it fall through. There were times I cursed you. I know I left you alone. I know I used the wrong tone.*" He releases a breath as he glances away, then grabs the microphone and continues to sing, "*I wish I could change and go back. I wish I could put it all on track.*"

Just then Edward joins in on the haunting ballad. Tyler's voice goes up a few octaves on the playback as he pretends to belt out, *"I regret the tears. I regret dismissing your fears"*—all while holding onto the microphone with both hands and shaking his head. Trent plays the piano with pure intensity as Edward closes his eyes, rests his chin on his violin, and strings his bow.

Tyler pushes out the microphone with his hand, looks away, then pulls it back toward his mouth and sings, *"It fell apart, it's all gone. It fell apart, it's said, it's done."*

Mick and I gasp in unison—the guys are nailing it.

Tyler repeats the chorus, Trent and Edward play a solo, then the guys continue on with the last verse of the ballad before they all bow their heads in unison as the song comes to a close.

"And cut! Dudes, I know we got it! Thank you for the final take!" the director calls out, clapping his hands.

Tyler flashes a smile as the film crew joins in and applauds their hard work.

"Okay, guys," Zack hollers. "We all need a drink! We're all heading over to *GLAM* if anyone wants to join us."

"*GLAM*?!" Mick cries in disapproval.

I stand up and smooth out my leather leggings. "Yes! I love that lil' dive!" I squeal. "They always have cover bands playing eighties and nineties hair bands!" I raise my index fingers near my temples like devil horns as he rolls his eyes. "There'll be men in leather pants there!" I say, trying to persuade him.

He caves quickly. "Ooo—I'm in, girl!"

"Alex!" Tyler calls out as he jumps off the stage and struts up the aisle toward us. "Baby girl, you made it!" he says as he leans in and kisses me.

"Oh, those lips, Tyler!" Mick flirts, and Tyler blows him an air-kiss.

"Zack wants to head over to *GLAM*. I know you've got to be stoked!" he teases as he leans back in and softly bites my neck.

"I'm so in. You need to change, then I'll drive over with you." I smile as he kisses my neck a second time.

"Honey, I'll go get Edward and we'll follow you there," Mick says as he sashays away. I watch him walk down the aisle, then turn back toward Tyler.

"You looked gorgeous up there! I couldn't take my eyes off of you," I compliment him. He blushes and flashes me a sexy grin. "Really?" He releases a breath.

"Really," I say. "Are you hungry?"

He shakes his head no and takes my hand. "Come with me; I'll change and we'll split," he says, and I am amped up to head over to *GLAM*.

After getting our hands stamped, we walk into the smoke-clouded *GLAM*. The dive joint is packed with fans of metal bands. The clothes are tight, the hair is big, and the music is loud. The Guns N' Roses cover band is up and their music blares through the amplifiers.

Mick grips Edward's hand as he looks around, licking his lips. I turn to face Tyler, who changed into his Cinderella half-shirt with a black headband around his forehead and sunglasses on top of his head, looking like he was due up next on stage. He nods his head toward Zack, who is waving from a booth against the graffitied brick wall. I tap Mick's arm and motion for him to follow us. Tyler takes my hand and the four of us make our way through the crowd over to the booth.

"Hi, bitch!" Nova greets me, screaming over the music. She gives me and Tyler a once-over and nods her head in approval. "Scoot down," she orders Trent and Liz, and Tyler slides in, then pulls me in beside him. Mick slides in next to me and Edward follows suit.

"I have drinks coming," Nova says as she slips in across from me, holding Zack's hand.

Tyler pulls out a cigarette, lights it, then leans in to kiss me. I part my lips as he pushes his tongue in and circles it around mine. I gasp. "Amazing tits," he whispers, looking down at my thin white tank top and tight leather leggings.

I giggle. "You're making my tits hard with that headband, feathered hair, and tantalizing tongue," I whisper back.

He laughs, licks my lip, then inhales his cigarette just as Liz interrupts, "You guys are so affectionate," she says.

Mick laughs and taps my leg. "Oh honey, aren't they sexy? They are so in love." He winks at me as Tyler blows out smoke and laughs. "I can stare at them all night." He winks once more.

"I'm sorry. I mean, did you two just start dating?" Liz asks.

"Liz, he was my best friend, then my husband—now he's my everything," I say as Tyler smiles, leans in, and peppers my lips with kisses, then lifts my bird tattoo ring to his mouth and licks it.

"Obsessed-love is more like it," Nova teases as she helps the waitress distribute drinks around the booth.

I flash her a dirty look. *Nova and Zack could never understand my and Tyler's bond.*

"Does everyone know Liz?" Nova asks as she tosses cocktail napkins onto the middle of the table.

"Hi, everyone," Liz says. Her cheeks flush and she glances over at Trent, who is talking to Zack. "Imagine the children the two of them would have—they're both so beautiful," she says as Mick mumbles:

"Bitch." Trent glances over at me as Tyler kisses my head. "She doesn't know any better," I whisper to him.

Nova holds up her drink and addresses the booth. "To the video!" she says, and everyone raises their drink and repeats, "To the video!"

I gulp my drink down as Tyler sips his water. "You okay?" I ask him.

He grips my neck and thrusts his tongue back into my mouth one more time. "I'll just taste the alcohol from your tongue," he says, flickering his barbell in and out of my mouth, to my delight.

The cover band starts to play "You Could Be Mine" as the booth cheers. Tyler knows every single lyric, and I listen to him sing with amazement.

"Alex calls her truck Axl after this maniac!" Trent laughs.

I salute him for remembering, while Tyler puts his cigarette out and slides his hand over my thigh. Now that he is sober, he fights the urge with affection, and I just let him have at it.

"So, what's next with the single?" Mick asks.

The guys shrug their shoulders, so Zack intervenes: "Dudes, the tune is sitting at the top of the charts. Have you picked up a *Revolver* magazine recently?" He laughs— the guys always seem oblivious to how much their music is appreciated by their fans.

"That's pretty fucking cool." Edward nods his head

in surprise. "Did you hear that?" I ask Tyler as he lightly play-bites my neck. "I heard 'magazine,'" he says.

I laugh.

The band slows down their set with their ballad, "Patience."

"Oh, I know this song!" Mick calls out. "Come on, honey, we're going to dance," he says as he stands up and pulls Edward to the floor to dance.

I just lean back into Tyler's arms as I watch the two of them. Tyler nuzzles his nose in my hair and keeps kissing my ear and my neck softly. I relax, feeling his warm chest through the back of my thin top.

"Hey Tyler, do ya mind if I get an autograph?" a fan asks, slapping a band poster down on the table.

I notice Liz's eyes widen as she watches Tyler sign the poster.

"Cool—I dig the Coalition, dude, much more ballsy then WHIP," the fan compliments Tyler, simultaneously taking a jab at Trent. Tyler tosses the marker back.

Within a few minutes, a couple of other people have gathered around the booth, interrupting us and asking for autographs.

"Aw shit," Nova hollers as she looks around for Zack.

A large group of people jostles in Tyler's personal space, asking for autographs. He politely signs a few more, then Zack walks over with a security guard and asks the people to back up.

Tyler stands and pulls me to my feet. "We better bail, baby girl," he says, and I grip his hand as Zack walks us out the back exit.

❋

Driving back home, I can't stop staring at Tyler. I am so turned on. Watching the admiration the fans had for him while he signed autographs worked me up.

"I want to suck you off, right here, right now," I say as Tyler shifts gears. "Baby, you didn't have that much to drink!" He laughs.

"I don't need to have a drink to realize how much you turn me on," I say openly. "It's the fucking headband," he teases, and I nod my head.

"Pull over," I say eagerly as he looks at me with surprise. "I can't hold out!" I reach over and unbutton his jeans.

"Okay!" He laughs. "I'm taking a right," he says.

Soon, he parks the Jeep and I quickly unzip his zipper and grab his hard cock. I lean down and suck on the head as Tyler moans. I then push what I can handle of him into my mouth and begin to work his shaft up and down with my hand. I lightly grab onto his balls, gently tugging them as I suck harder.

"Oh, Alex," he groans, his head falling back against the driver's side seat.

I continue to slowly flicker my tongue while stroking him up and down, then suck as his veins pulse inside my mouth. His length extends as I begin to stroke harder.

"Baby, you're going to make me come," he gasps as I pick up my pace. Tyler pulls my hair but I don't let up. I use the lubrication of my saliva to stroke him faster as I feel him thicken in my mouth. I lick up to his V tattoo, then back down to his rock-hard cock and suck more.

"Oh god," he pants as I suck him off good. "I'm going to come, baby," he moans, and releases warmly inside my mouth and down my throat while gripping the back of my tank top. "Ahh," he cries out. I swallow and suck him once more as he exhales. "Oh, Alex," he laughs. I lick the excitement from his cock, then sit back up, wiping my mouth. "You never cease to amaze me," he says, euphoria written all over his face.

"You needed that, huh?" I laugh as he buttons his jeans and lights up a cigarette. "Oh, you taste so good—and you look so good!" I flirt, reaching for his cigarette to take a hit. "I couldn't help myself," I say as I inhale, then hand the cigarette back to him.

He laughs as he shakes his head as he blows out his smoke.

CHAPTER 18

The next day, I receive a text from Nova:

Your bird is getting too famous.

I laugh, then reply:

My songbird is handling fame just fine.

I pause to think about how well Tyler is actually handling fame. He seems so much more professional since he left WHIP. I am so happy for him—he deserves this.

"Baby girl, 'It's Done' is number one on the song chart listed here in *Revolver*!" Tyler calls out.

I roll my eyes, recalling Zack telling us that last night. "That's amazing," I say as I set my cell phone aside, then lean over my drafting table, and lightly bang my head.

"Baby girl, what are you doing?" Tyler laughs as he tosses the magazine on my table. "I guess *Revolver* requested an interview from me through the label." He smiles as I flip open the magazine and take a look at the chart.

"Mark my words, y'all will receive another award for this song." I nod my head as Tyler bites his lower lip and grins. "I mean, you wrote 'Betrayal' and that won an award, you wrote 'It's Done'—I'm just saying."

"None of this would be in my grasp if it wasn't for you," he says as he opens the balcony door and steps outside.

"Very true," I say.

"I'm going to head over to the edit suite to check out the video with Trent, do you want to come with me?" he asks, standing in the balcony doorway.

I stretch my arms and shake my head.

"Okay. I shouldn't be too long—editing bores me," he says, and I roll my eyes and watch him walk over to collect his keys.

"Take your jacket, songbird; the edit suite is always ice-cold," I say.

He turns and goes into the bedroom to grab his leather jacket, then walks back over to me. "I love you," he says as he bends down and kisses me. "See you in a few hours."

When he leaves, I release a breath, look back down at the magazine, and smile. I am so proud of him. *What did Nova mean last night when she called out the two of us for having an "obsessed" love at GLAM? What's wrong with protecting someone? Or not wanting to fail or disappoint them?* It made me a little irritated. I was only stating that Tyler and I had come a long way since we were best friends, then husband and wife, and now we are everything to each other.

I love how intense we are with one another—obsessed or not, I am happy. *But is Tyler a little too obsessed with me?* I wonder. He still has this lingering fear of abandonment and never wants to let go of me when people are around. Plus, the insecurity he feels about Trent is a little off-putting. I do know how to handle him though.

I huff and shake my head, dismissing Nova's rash judgment on our relationship as I get up from my drafting table and go outside on the balcony for some much-needed air.

A FEW WEEKS LATER

The chill of fall is in the air and my lungs burn while I run next to Austin on the Santa Fe Trail.

"Hey, soldier, slow down," I yell, and he laughs and jogs in place while waiting for me to catch my breath.

"How have you been feeling, sis?" he asks as I cough. "Ugh." I pause. "I'm all healed up," I say as I sip my water.

Austin stops jogging and lifts his Gatorade to his lips. "Are y'all going to try again?" he asks sincerely.

I shrug my shoulders. "Dude, I can handle a lot of roles, but mother? I'm not sure if I can handle that one." I laugh. "I should pay Mama more respect." I close the cap on my bottle and begin a slow walk. "I mean, I'm a wife, I'm a businesswoman, I'm..." I pause. "A mama?

Hum." I glance over at a woman on the path parallel to us, running while pushing a baby carriage. "Do you see me doing that?" I laugh again.

Austin nods his head. "I do. I'm sure the whole party scene is just getting old," he states. "I'm not sure we can or should do the club scene anymore. I mean, Tyler was mauled by fans the last time we were at *GLAM*." I laugh as Austin's eyes widen. "But I know it's still a fucking challenge for him being a recovering addict. Clubbing is the last thing Tyler and I need to be doing," I confess. "You know, Austin, he's a rockstar, he's a songwriter, and now he has the studio—I think that's all Tyler can handle at the moment," I say, a little saddened to find so many excuses not to have a baby. "It would be nice, though, to have the famous Tyler Black's baby," I giggle as Austin gives me a slight push. "What about you?"

He flushes bright red. "What about me?" he asks as he lets out a deep laugh. "You and Lilith. Are y'all going to get married soon?" I tease, poking his side. "We'll see. I do love her."

I nod my head in agreement. "Yeah, I like y'all together," I say, and he just grins and takes off running ahead of me. I guess the topic of love and babies is not his forte today. I shake my head and race to catch up with him.

After Austin drops me back off at home, I walk in and kick off my running shoes. "Ooo, I love when you're all sweaty," Tyler says as he leans against the kitchen counter, eating pretzels.

"You're such a pig." I smile as I unzip my running jacket. "Oh, Austin says hi," I say, walking over to the refrigerator to pull out a bottle of water.

"Your songbird's video got like a million hits!" he exclaims as he shoves another pretzel into his mouth.

"Are you fucking kidding me?" I ask.

He sips his water and points over to my open laptop. "Go take a look," he says, and I skip over to the drafting table and glance down at the open website. I push "play" and watch the "It's Done" video. Tears begin to fill my eyes.

"You look so beautiful," I whisper as Tyler walks up next to me.

"What the fuck do you see in me? You always say that—ever since I've met you, you've always called me beautiful."

He kisses the top of my damp head as I watch him singing in the video.

I scroll down to the recorded number of hits the video got and my jaw drops open. "Wow, do Edward and Trent know?" I ask.

"Of course they do—so does the rest of the band." He smiles.

"Well, all this publicity is good for Black Rifle Coalition. This video will only help y'all." I smile back as I look over at him. "I'm proud of you," I say, "but I need a shower." I groan as I close the laptop and head straight for the bathroom.

As I stand naked in front of the mirror, rubbing body oil all over my glistening skin, Tyler walks up behind me, picks up my hair, and drapes it over my shoulder. He leans in and softly kisses my neck. I stare at his reflection as a butterfly pirouettes in my stomach. He begins to trace his fingertips over my shoulders, down my waist, and over my hips.

"You're so breathtaking."

I smile while he admires my naked body. I turn around and face him as he leans in and slides his tongue inside my mouth. I gasp as he circles my tongue, then pulls out and lightly touches my lips with his fingers. He lifts my chin, looks directly into my eyes, and leans back in for another heated kiss. He trails his fingers down my neck, over my breasts, down my abdomen, and strokes my inner thighs.

"Ahh," I whisper, leaning back against the vanity.

He lifts me up and steps in between my legs. I pull at his drawstring and his pants hit the floor. I reach down and rub his velvety cock as he leans in and nibbles my ear.

"Make love to me right now," I pant, and he opens me

up and slides in.

"Oh, Alexandria, you feel so amazing," he whispers as I trace his hips and V tattoo with my fingertips, then wrap my legs around him tighter, pushing him in deeper. He brushes my hair off my shoulders and licks my neck with his warm tongue.

"Oh, Ty," I say as I close my eyes and lean my head back against the mirror. He gently pushes deeper as tears fill my eyes. I open them and see him staring back at me with tears in his. I bat my lashes as he leans in and flutters his lashes with mine. I sigh as I feel the dampness. "Ahhh," he moans as he slides in and out with ease. My nipples peak as he lengthens inside of me.

"I love you so much, Tyler," I whisper as he reaches for my fingers and tightens his hand around mine. "I'm so close."

He maintains his pace, sliding back and forth as he licks my tongue. I rake my fingers through his hair, pull him closer, and intensely roll my tongue around his as another tear slides down my cheek.

I moan and bite his lower lip while the sensation enraptures my body as he pushes harder. "Oh, don't stop," I say as the orgasm heightens and he starts to release inside me.

"I love you, Alexandria," he whispers as he closes his eyes and his skin flushes with goosebumps.

He is so beautiful to watch while coming inside of me—he overwhelms me. I exhale as Tyler opens his eyes. "Thank you," he says.

"For what?" I ask as I push his bangs behind his ear and listen. "For loving me the way you do," he says openly.

I wipe my eyes with my index finger. "Tyler, we have

been through so much together. I'll never love anyone the way I love you," I say, and he blinks his lashes and kisses my lips.

Later that evening, I am lying next to Tyler in our bed, letting my mind wander until he startles me by speaking.

"Do you want to try again?" he asks as he pushes himself up on his elbow.

I shift my body underneath the sheet and look over at him. "What?" I ask, wanting to be sure I heard the question correctly.

"Do you want to try again, baby girl?" he repeats, then bites his lower lip. "I feel I can handle a little bird. I was in shock when it happened the first time, but I want to experience everything with you." He smiles as he lifts my hand and kisses my tattoo ring finger.

"Rockstars have families too, you know." He sticks his tongue out and flickers his barbell as I laugh.

"Is the famous Tyler Xavier Black actually entertaining this conversation?" I giggle as Tyler rolls onto his back.

"Don't do that," he groans, exhaling and looking up at the ceiling fan. *Liz was right, we would have beautiful children. I mean his genes alone, my goodness*, I revel.

"I don't know, Ty. Everything is going so well—I mean, our plates are pretty full..." I pause as the question echoes in my head like subwoofers.

"I want a lil' chick with my lovebird," he whispers as he rolls his head in my direction.

I look at him, surprised; not that long ago he was

slapping my ass with a belt, and now he's talking babies? I am stunned.

"You won't even scoop the litter box and you're going to help with diapers?" I tease, and he plays-slaps my arm. "Hey, at least we're addressing the issue this time. The last time I was knocked up, you were panic-stricken. But…" I pause. "If you're in this with me, I would love to have a lil' chick with you." I laugh as I rub his cheek with my hand.

"Stop your pill," he says bluntly.

My eyes widen and begin to fill with tears at the knowledge that my husband wants to try. He leans over, kisses me softly, and says, "I love you, lovebird."

"Oh, how I love you, songbird." I smile and return his kiss.

CHAPTER 19

Another week skates by. I stay busy with design projects as well as coordinating a few bands to record over at *Brimstone.*

Suddenly, Tyler runs into the room, picks me up, and spins me around. "What? What happened?" I ask.

"You called it baby girl!" he hollers.

I laugh. "Called what?" I ask excitedly.

"Me and Trent are nominated for a songwriter award!" He puts his hands on his head, trying to digest the news.

"Oh my God, are you saying y'all are nominated for a *Verse* Award?" I put my hand over my mouth as he nods his head. "Holy shit!" I jump into his arms and he spins me around again.

"'It's Done' is nominated! I'm so fucking stoked!" He tries to catch his breath as I pepper his lips with kisses.

"You did it! You so deserve this nomination!" I squeal.

Tyler squeezes me tightly. "Zack just called me. I should probably call Trent," he says as he leans down and kisses me once more. His hands tremble as he shuffles his phone out of his pocket and dials Trent.

"Dude, did Zack call you?" He pauses. "Holy fuck, can you believe this?" he asks as he stands there, running his hands through his hair. "We did it, dude—I mean, this ain't no soundtrack bullshit, this is a fucking *Verse!*" he hollers as I stare at him, dumbfounded. "Yeah, call Edward, I know he'll be happy for us. Call me later." He hangs up, then glances back over at me.

"I told you that you were a good songwriter—do you believe it now?" I ask.

"I need a hit to calm me," he says, walking out onto the balcony and lighting up a joint.

I go into our bedroom, retrieve two sweaters from the closet, then go back outside. "Here, baby, pull this on," I say as I hand him the sweater.

He smiles, passes me the joint, and slips on the sweater. I sit on the wicker chair, inhale a hit, and just watch Tyler beam with excitement. He sits down next to me as I hand the joint back over and blow out smoke.

"The awards are in February," he says. "Fucking Las Vegas." He groans as he looks over at me.

"Good—when you win, I'm celebrating with you this time and not Roger!" I roll my eyes as Tyler laughs, recalling that time after the Billboard Music Awards when I was forced into celebrating with Roger while Trent fucked Tonya and Tyler was alone.

"Baby girl, your rockstar of a husband will book a private plane, we'll fly into Vegas, accept the award, then we'll fuck in the plane to celebrate as we're flying back home to Texas," he promises while I giggle. "I don't want to spend an extra five fucking minutes in that town!

We're in and we're out," he says, and I nod.

"Perfect—sounds like a plan," I agree. "Trent is not hitching a ride, either," I tease.

Tyler laughs. "The pilot, me, you, and the award. That's

it, I promise." He blows me a kiss and I smile.

"Listen, I'll call my parents and Austin, but you need to call your father," I say. He scowls. "Yes, Ty, your father needs to hear the news from you. Then call Gunner and Roger," I plead.

He growls at me as I laugh, stand up, and go in search of my phone.

An hour later, I wrap up my calls and am lying in bed when Tyler walks into the room.

His eyes are red and swollen and he looks spent.

"Are you all right?" I ask as he flops onto the bed and exhales. "I talked with my pop," he groans.

I run my fingers through his hair and ask, "What happened?" I continue to stroke his hair as I listen.

"We replayed the whole 'I'm sorry I wasn't there for you, kid' conversation," he huffs. "I asked him 'Why wasn't I worth the time?' and he fell silent." Tyler closes his eyes. "Why doesn't he ever have any answers? It's always the 'I'm sorry, kid' bullshit I get every damn time—I'm running in circles," he complains, releasing an exaggerated breath. "When we have a kid, I swear I'm not going to pull any of that shit," he promises as he opens his eyes and blinks his damp lashes at me. "Plus, talking about the miscarriage... it was just all too draining," he pouts.

I kiss his head. "He loves you, and he's trying his best, Ty." I try to comfort him as he rolls into the fetal position and offers nothing more. "Let's get some rest; the news exhausted us both. Call your friends tomorrow," I suggest. I switch off the light and wrap my arms around him.

"Good morning, my famous songwriting songbird!" I sing as Tyler stands in the kitchen and scratches his head. He still has on last night's sweater as he walks over to me and wraps his warm arms around me.

"Morning, lovebird," he says as he nuzzles his nose in my neck.

"I'm making you pancakes!" I step back and pick up the bowl of batter, continuing to stir. "Did you sleep okay?" I ask. As I pour a cake onto the griddle, Tyler grunts. I look over my shoulder.

He slides onto a stool at the counter and watches me pour coffee in a mug and set it down in front of him. He gives me a half-smile as I lean over and run my fingers through his hair.

"I know your father drained you last night, but the more you open up to him, the more your relationship will heal," I say as I turn back to the griddle and flip the pancake.

Tyler releases a breath and says nothing.

I set down two plates, utensils, and syrup on the breakfast counter. "So, are you heading over to *Brimstone* today?"

"I am. We are recording that band that Zack signed recently," he says as he takes a bite, and I smile. He always looks like a little kid when he eats my pancakes, all giddy and cute. I sit down beside him with my plate in front of me. "What's on your plate today besides pancakes?" he asks.

I laugh while I pour syrup. "Well, that band that y'all

are recording? I'm supposed to sketch a few designs out for their album cover and get it back to the label by mid-week." I take a bite, after which Tyler leans in and licks the syrup off my lips as I giggle.

"Man, Zack is keeping you busy," he says as he sips his coffee.

I nod my head happily. "*Brimstone* is keeping us busy as well. I'm so happy we decided to partner on it," I say as Tyler smiles.

"Could you believe all this would have happened for us back when I lived on the rehearsal space couch and you lived in that dump of a loft?" He laughs, reminiscing on WHIP's rehearsal space and my first place.

"I'm just happy I'm experiencing everything with you." I smile broadly. "I always knew you'd be a success once you pushed past the abuse," I say confidently.

He nods as he quietly finishes his breakfast.

In the afternoon, Tyler walks in and slams the door shut. I jump, scattering my charcoal pencils across my drafting table.

"Burr under your saddle?" I ask.

He flashes me a dirty look while kicking off his Dr. Martens. "Fucking Trent," he groans while he shimmies out of his coat.

Damn leather twins must have had another infamous spat, I think as I laugh to myself. "Do you want to talk about it?" I ask as I turn down my music.

He just shakes his head and with his pissy attitude walks into the bedroom and collapses on the bed.

"Never mind," I mumble, and I go back to work and let him sleep it off.

Later that evening, Tyler resurfaces and goes into the refrigerator, pouring himself a glass of water.

"Do you feel better?" I ask as I turn on my table light and my eyes adjust to see him standing there shirtless.

He walks over to me, shuts off the light, takes me by the hand, and bends me over the drafting table.

"What are you up to?" I laugh, but he says nothing, only unbuttons my jeans and pulls them off. I gasp.

He unbuttons his jeans, then kicks my legs wider apart. He grabs my hair, pulls my head back, and licks my neck. He sucks his fingertips, then roughly runs them along my vagina.

"Easy!" I say breathlessly.

He opens my slit and tries to push himself in as I grab onto the edge of the table in surprise. He thrusts and I feel my vagina tear a bit from the forceful entry. He leans down, pulls up my sweater, and bites my back.

"Ow," I cry out as he rams into me, trying to fully enter as the pencil holder knocks over and falls onto the floor.

I gasp for breath as he thickens. He pulls my hair back once more and lashes his tongue out, licking my mouth as he tries to push himself completely into me. I am dry and not enjoying this moment.

"Code black!" I holler. He pauses, leans back, and pulls out. "What the fuck, Tyler?!" I say as I turn around and look sternly up at him. "Take it easy." I push him aside, bend down, and pick up my jeans off the floor. "Talk to me.

What's going on?" I ask.

He shakes his head in frustration.

"I'm all for fucking out the stress, but baby, that really hurt," I say. "I wasn't ready..." I pause. "Do you want to hurt me, Ty?" I mutter, feeling a little off-put as he stands there with his eyes closed and pinches the bridge of his nose.

"Hey," I whisper. "Settle down. *That* is not our relationship. Maybe you handled Olivia a little rougher, but that's *not* our relationship, Ty," I repeat as I turn and walk into the bedroom, tossing my jeans into the closet, pulling off my sweater, and unhooking my bra. I feel Tyler's arms wrap around me.

"You have these moments where you kind of scare me," I say as I recall the birthday party makeup sex and when he slapped my face. He squeezes me tighter. "I'm well aware that we always push each other's buttons, but you just scared me tonight," I say, turning around to face him.

He leans in and gently kisses me.

"That's better," I whisper as he kisses me once more.

"I never realized I scare you," he whispers, embarrassed by his conduct. "Please don't leave me," he pleads as he presses his forehead to mine.

"I'm not leaving you, Ty, but you need to know that I'm not going to put up with shit like that again, hear me?" I release a sigh of frustration. "I love rough sex with you, but we need to be on the same pleasure page. That, out there in the living room—that was not pleasure for me. Do you hear me?" I ask again, and he nods his head. "We're moving forward; I want to keep this marriage strong before I bring a damn baby into it," I huff, then pause to calm myself. "Listen.

After everything Heston put me through, the one person in the world I always felt safe with was you, Tyler," I say. "Don't be like Gage, okay?"

He blinks solemnly in understanding. "Okay," he says.

I turn, walk back into the closet, and pull my jeans back on.

"Where are you going, baby girl?" Tyler asks as I put my sweater back on and slip on my shoes. He looks stunned.

"I need to get some fresh air," I say, huffing as I turn off the closet light, walk out into the kitchen, and grab my lovebird key chain.

Tyler sits down on the edge of the bed, releases a breath, and stares at the concrete floor. I walk out the door and head straight for my truck.

Pulling up in front of the studio, I notice Trent's motorcycle parked out front. I shut the engine off and just sit there for a moment, staring at it. Rain begins to tap on my windshield as I contemplate going inside. I put my head on the steering wheel, tears filling my eyes as I lightly bang my head.

"What am I doing?" I release a breath, then lean back in the seat. I wipe my eyes and tap my chest, which burns like I just smoked an entire pack of cigarettes. It's hard to breathe. I cry a little harder, trying to let it all wash out with the rain.

As I try to collect myself, I fish for a tissue in the glove compartment and blow my nose. I glance back outside at the motorcycle and notice Trent rolling the bike into the studio. His hair is dripping from the rain and his T-shirt clings to him as I watch.

I exhale and pause, then slap both my cheeks and start the engine.

Back home, I walk into the loft, and Tyler is lying on the bed. I toss my keys onto the counter, open the refrigerator, and grab a bottle of water.

"Baby girl?" Tyler asks.

I sigh. "Yeah?" I respond in a whisper.

"Thank you for coming back. I..." He pauses. "I really love you, Alexandria."

I swallow and bite my lower lip. "I'm sorry I compared you to Gage. I really fucked that up, Ty." I grimace.

"It's okay. Come in here, baby girl," he whines, and I laugh.

I set my water bottle down, spin on my heel, and march right into the bedroom. I crawl over him, lean down, and kiss him heavily. He dramatically exhales. I sit back, pull off my sweater, and toss it to the floor. He wrestles with my jeans, pulling them down and off of me.

"Make me feel safe," I say as I run my hand down his tattooed arm and pull his jeans down.

He leans up and licks my lip, then kisses it as I release a breath. He brushes the hair away from my face and kisses my forehead, my nose, my cheek, and whispers in my ear: "I'm so sorry baby girl. I never want to hurt you."

I swallow hard as I open my legs wide across his lap. He slowly enters me and I lightly tug on his hair in frustration. I rock back and forth, working him in as I lick his ear and begin to pant. As I become wet, I am able to accept him. *I am not in the mood for rough-housing tonight; this is a little more my speed.*

Tyler flips me over and gets on top of me. His cock hardens as he continues to thrust slowly. He makes love to me, easing in and out of me as I close my eyes. He wraps his arms tightly around me and I feel the warmth of his body radiate through me as I grip onto his hips.

"Oh, that's it," I whisper, finally letting my guard down as I ache for more. "Slowly," I say as he pushes deeper and moans. "Yes, that's it, Ty." I open my eyes and notice he is looking down at me.

He presses his full lips to mine, then pulls back. "I want to make a baby with you," he whispers as I grip his hips tighter and arch my back.

"You have no idea how much I need to hear that. Come with me," I gasp.

He smiles, exhales, then closes his eyes and rocks. I watch him, and the sight of him makes my knees weak as he slides back and forth.

"Ahhh," he cries out as he pushes harder, and I moan for more, squeezing his throbbing cock with my sex. I feel him harden one last time as he starts to come hard while I let myself go and begin to come with him.

"Oh, Tyler," I cry out, throwing my head back, enjoying my orgasm.

"Alex," he whispers, and I can feel him releasing all inside of me. "I'm so sorry," he whispers as his body presses against mine.

I run my nails lightly over the skin on his back as he tenses up. He pulls out and rolls over onto his back, reaching for a cigarette and lighting it.

"I know you are." I snag the cigarette from his hand

and take a hit before handing it back to him. "Do you want to talk about what happened at the studio?" I ask.

He shakes his head. "I have bigger things to focus my energy on than fucking studio projects." He flashes me a grin and I forgive him, knowing exactly what he is referring to as I blow out the cigarette smoke.

CHAPTER 20

A FEW WEEKS LATER

I stand in the bathroom, tapping my fingernails on the vanity, and wait for the pregnancy test to marinate. No fucking period, I'm tender, I'm nauseous, and I want to strangle my husband. I pause and inhale deeply...I'm pregnant. I shake the test and read it once more, laughing, then lean against the vanity and bite my lower lip, smiling.

"Are you okay, baby girl?" Tyler asks as he stands in the doorway, scratching his head. I glance up at him and show him the test. "What's that mean?" He grabs the test from me and tries to read it as I let out a subtle laugh.

"It means you knocked me up," I say.

He laughs and tosses the test onto the counter, picks me up, and swings me around. "You and me?" he asks. "A lil' chick is in the nest?"

I laugh as he kisses me excitedly. "Oh, I'm so happy!"

I feel relieved. We did it. If there's one thing I can give back to him to show him how much I truly love him—this is it.

"Now, I'll call the doctor today and get a full check-up, but I want to be sure everything is okay before I start spilling the beans to everyone. I want to wait a few weeks. I need to be confident my body can handle a bird," I say nervously as Tyler chuckles.

"You can do iiiit," he sings sweetly, leaning back in and kissing me again. "All in," he whispers as he kisses my head.

"All in," I whisper back.

Later that evening, I pull on a sweater, walk out onto the balcony, and inhale the chilled November air. I lean back in the chair and just daydream about us starting a family.

I have to grow the fuck up someday, I think as I laugh and pull my knees into my chest.

Tyler seems so at ease with our decision, which pleases me to no end. The studio is profitable. My design work is consistent. The band has another gig lined up. And my husband is up for an award—this is everything I've ever wanted.

I then feel a wave of anxiety fill my chest as I try to slow my breathing from the onset of a panic attack. *I can do this; my body won't fuck it up again.* I breathe in through my nose and out through my mouth, trying to settle my destructive train of thought. I just have to get through the first twelve weeks or so.

I breathe out once more and check the time, then get up and go into the kitchen to stir my homemade Texas chili. I hear the key turn in the front door and my heart flutters.

"Hi, mama bird," Tyler says as he shuts the door behind him and kicks off his Dr. Martens.

"How was the rehearsal?" I ask as he walks over, stands in front of the Crock-Pot, and inhales. I lift a spoonful to his mouth for him to taste.

"Oh my God, that's so good, baby girl." I smile and put the lid back on.

"The rehearsal kicked ass. This New Year's Eve show is going to blow their minds!" he howls. "Oh, I told the band no Trent on this gig either." He pulls his sweater off and tosses it toward the bedroom.

I pull the hem of his cotton T-shirt down and kiss him. "Y'all still haven't kissed and made up?" I tease as Tyler rolls his eyes. "Y'all have kissed before," I giggle. "I witnessed the both of you kissing twice!" I poke his side, making kissing sounds, and he blushes.

"What? Blow me," he says as he turns around and pops a squat on the floor pillow. "The first time was when the three of us werc on the dance floor together and the second..." I pause and giggle once again. "When we were at the lake house party," I tease. "We were on coke." He stretches out his legs, looking uncomfortable as he takes a ride down memory lane with me.

"Uh-huh," I say as I make another kissing sound with my lips. "I don't like kissing men," he pouts. He folds his arms in a huff.

I just laugh. "Don't tell that to Mick—he has a mad crush on you," I tease again. When he flips me the middle finger, I drop it.

I shut off the Crock-Pot, reach for two bowls, and fill them with my chili. I get out the corn chips and pour some in a basket. I walk over to Tyler and hand him his dinner, then grab my bowl and the basket of chips and sit down on a floor pillow next to him. "It's like a little picnic," I say as he laughs and scoops his chili with a chip. He smiles as he eats.

The next morning, I am praying to the porcelain god as I flush the toilet and lean back.

"Ugh," I pout as I wipe my dry-as-a-desert mouth.

"Ew, baby girl. Can I get you anything?" Tyler asks as I toss my damp rag at him. He steps back and walks away.

"I swear I don't know what's worse—morning sickness or a fucking hangover," I moan, disturbed by the wake-up call.

Tyler returns, laughs, then hands me a ginger ale and sits down on the floor.

"Thank you," I whisper as I sip and look over at him. He is in his Talking Heads T-shirt and black joggers as he leans against the door. "Are you waiting for me to throw up again?" I ask as he laughs.

"I'm just here if you need me," he says.

I smile then wipe my mouth. "I think I'm all right," I say as I try to stand up.

"Wait, I'll help you," he says, hopping to his feet, taking my hand, and pulling me up.

"I need to lay down," I groan, and he nods his head and follows me back into bed. "Ahh." I push the pillow under my head as he rolls over and holds me.

A few hours later, I wake up and Tyler is out in the other room on his cell phone. I sit up and check the time.

"Energy sucker," I mumble as I tap my stomach and smile. I hear Tyler end his call as he walks back into the room.

"How ya holdin' up?" he asks. I flash him an irritated look. "Okay, well, I'm heading over to my studio, can I get you anything?" he asks.

I shake my head no. I do not feel well. I want to be left alone.

Tyler walks over and kisses my head. "Love you," he says.

"I *must* love you more," I growl, and he smiles, rubs my belly, and kisses my head once more.

After Tyler leaves, I make my way into the kitchen and place some bread into the toaster.

I then walk over to my day planner and review my projects. Everything seems to be in order. I just need to invoice a few clients, the label for the recording session, and we would wrap for the holiday break. I check my cell and read a text message from Austin:

Parents are on their cruise. I'm spending the holidays with Lilith and her family in Arizona. Call me if you need anything. Love you.

I smile, then reply:

I'm wrapping up projects. Tyler and I are off through the holiday break, ooo I hear the cabin calling! LOL. Love you, soldier.

Just then, my toast pops up. I pull out the butter and my iced tea from the refrigerator, eating my toast while standing at the counter. I start to feel better and decide that after my shower I will invoice the record label, then meet Tyler at the studio—I need to get out of this place.

❧

Pulling up to *Brimstone*, I smile as I shut off the ignition and glance up at our freshly painted building with its new sign. It is official; we are in business. I open the door, step out, then lean back in and grab Tyler's red flannel shirt off the seat. I lock the truck and make my way into the studio.

"Hi, Alex," Trent greets me, wrapping cables in a white muscle shirt and black jeans. I glance around. "Where is everybody?" I ask.

He smiles. "We're done—you can invoice Zack now." He laughs. "Already taken care of," I say proudly as he registers surprise.

"You are efficient!" He laughs again. "We're just cleaning up, then I'll lock the place down for the break." He tosses the cable aside.

"Oh, come here," I say. I step into him, reach my arms out, and pull him into a hug. As I inhale his familiar scent, I squeeze him tightly. "Congratulations on being nominated," I whisper, and he squeezes me a little tighter as I turn my head and kiss his warm cheek.

"Thank you," he says as he lets go and smiles at me.

I hear the back door close as I take a step back from Trent.

"Hey, lovebird, what are you doing here?" Tyler asks as he walks over and kisses my lips. "Hi, songbird." I kiss his lips once more as Trent laughs at our pet names.

"Cute," he teases as he tosses the rest of the cables in a plastic bin and walks away.

I roll my eyes, then hand Tyler his flannel shirt. He throws it on as I push his hair off his shoulder. "You need a haircut," I say.

He runs his hand through his thick black hair. "I just

need to put all this shit back; we finished the session," he says, and I smile.

"I heard. I already invoiced Zack," I say, but he ignores me. Tyler pays no mind to the business aspect of the studio—it bores him. He feeds off the creative side and I let him have that.

Trent covers the sound console as Tyler unplugs everything.

"Can I help with something?" I offer as the two of them shake their heads as there seems to be a method to their madness. I just lean in the doorway and watch until they finish.

"Well, I'll be in Louisiana for the break," Trent says.

"Well, we'll be Dallas, so if you need us to take care of anything, just let us know," I say.

He nods his head. "I think that about does it," he says as he puts his hands on his hips and looks over at Tyler.

"Okay." I reach out and grab Tyler's hand as I rattle the keys, letting Trent know I'd lock up.

He reaches down for his helmet, then extends his hand to Tyler. "Good work today, Ty," he says as Tyler shakes his hand in return then walks out.

I squeeze Tyler's hand a little tighter as he glances around the studio then hits the lights.

We walk out hand in hand as I lock up.

"Meet you at home?" Tyler asks as we walk toward my truck.

"Wait." I pause. "Here, sit in the back of the truck with me," I direct, and Tyler walks with me to the bed of the truck and we hop up. Legs dangling, I ask, "Are you really ready to start a family or are you just acting happy to please me?"

"Mama bird." He blushes, caught off guard. "I'm really happy." He smiles. "I've loved you ever since the day I met you. I married you. Now, I want a family with you," he says.

I let out a sigh of relief. "After the rocky start with the first pregnancy, you really were wonderful, Ty." I pause. "You actually surprised me. So, thank you." I smile back. "I want this for us. I feel like I let us both down when I couldn't hold the first birdie, but I'm trying real hard with this second one. Tyler leans over and kisses my head.

"I got a checkup, I'm eating well, my stress level is low, and I just want to put all my energy into *our* family. It just feels right. I have friends, I have Mama, Daddy, and Austin, but you, Ty, you have always been the closest to me, so I know we can do this together." I exhale as Tyler squeezes my hand.

"I'm all in, lovebird," he says, and I smile.

"I'm all in, songbird." I squeeze his hand back. "Oh," I jump out of the truck bed, "my parents are on a cruise. Austin is heading to Arizona. How about you and I go hide out in our cabin next week?" I suggest.

He hops down and closes the bed of the truck. "I'd love that," he says as he leans in and kisses me.

"Good, I'll get everything in order for us. We need this." I smile as Tyler helps me into the front seat and I rev up Axl.

"Meet you at home?" I ask as he shuts my door and waves.

CHAPTER 21

The following week, I have the pet sitter booked, the bags packed, invoices done, and the computer shut down. I am ready for a little getaway from all the noise of the city.

"Hey, are you ready to go?" I call toward the bedroom as I zip up my computer bag. Tyler walks out in his form-fitting black thermal shirt and black jeans, and I smile at him.

He pushes his hair back with his sunglasses and searches the kitchen junk drawer for our keys.

I just pause for a moment and take him all in. *I love him*, I think as he glances up at me and busts me for staring.

"What?" he asks.

I laugh. "Nothing," I say as I sling the computer bag over my shoulder.

Tyler walks over to the front door, opens it up for me, then bends down, grabs our bags, and locks up.

Pulling into the cabin, I release a sigh as I look around at all the trees that are bare from the change of season.

Tyler parks the Jeep and jumps out. "Ahh, we're here!" he says, stretching as he admires our wedding gift. "I really love this place," he says.

I nod my head. "Me too," I agree, pushing my braid off my shoulder and adjusting my tight cream sweater.

"Ooo, we can use the fireplace now!" Tyler calls back as he steps onto the porch and unlocks the front door. It was too hot for the fireplace during his surprise birthday party, but today it couldn't feel more perfect.

I follow Tyler in as calmness washes over me. I look around in appreciation. Everything is clean and back in order after the birthday party.

"Oh, you better bring the groceries first so I can put them away," I suggest, and he turns and goes back outside to collect the food and our bags. I walk over to the radio, switch it on, and begin to sing classic rock songs as I open the cabinets.

Tyler walks in and places the groceries on the counter as I start to unpack.

"Why don't you light a fire?" I ask as the sun seems to be setting for the day. I open the refrigerator and stock the shelves then wash my hands in the farmhouse sink while daydreaming out the window.

"Oh, I just love this place," I say as he walks up behind me and wraps his arms around me.

"Fire's lit—when do we lose the clothes?" he teases as he kisses my neck. "Something about this place gets you so sexually worked up," I say as he laughs. "It's you. Just you alone gets me all worked up."

I blush as I turn around. He leans in and kisses me. My heart pounds as his warm tongue slowly flickers around mine.

"Now?" I giggle.

He ignores my question as he pulls my hair tie out and unravels my long braid. He runs his fingers along my sweater, grabs the edge, and pulls it over my head while my 'friend' chain dangles between my cleavage. I reach for his thermal shirt and, following suit, pull it over his head while his 'best' chain scrapes against his chest. He shuffles around in his jean pocket and takes out a pair of tiny metal clamps and sets them on the counter beside us.

"Oh, you brought gifts," I note as he leans in and licks my shoulder, unfastening my satin bra. I gasp heavily as he slides it down my arms and tosses it to the floor. He reaches out and lightly tugs on both my nipples, making them erect. "Oh," I gasp again.

He smiles as he leans in and licks the left nipple, squeezes it, then licks the right. I shift my weight against the sink as Tyler reaches around my back, flips on the faucet, and fills his hand with water. He then rubs the cool water across my breasts and sucks my nipples harder. I moan as he picks up a metal clamp and clips it onto my hardened nipple. I inhale, making my chest rise as he clips the other one on. *Oh, the sensation drives me wild.*

"I like that, Mr. Black," I whisper as he slips his hand inside the band of my stretch pants, moves my satin panties aside, and inserts his finger. I grip onto the counter's edge as I try to steady myself.

"That's what I want to feel," Tyler whispers back as he inserts a second finger. "You're so hot for me," he says.

I nod my head eagerly. He leans back into my breasts and licks up my cleavage, then over the clamps as I squirm with anticipation. He flicks his heated tongue into my mouth as his fingers dance. His rhythm is on point and I squeeze my legs together while he plays with me.

"No coming yet, baby," he says as he withdraws his fingers and snaps my waistband, making me clench my abdominal muscles. I pick up his hand and suck on the fingers. His haunting dark eyes dilate while he watches me. "You're such a tease," he says as he pulls his fingers away and licks my bottom lip, letting out a deep laugh. He tugs my pants down, lifts me up onto the sink, and opens my legs. He turns the faucet back on and soaks my pussy, then leans in and finger-fucks me once again.

"Oh!" I cry out just as he bends down, spreads my lips, and sucks on my wet-soaked clit. Gripping the counter, I pant as I watch him between my legs, performing oral sex, and *ooo*...he is good.

"I want to fuck you. Is that okay?" he asks sweetly as he drags his tongue over my hood, up my hip, and back to my breast. He flicks his tongue on the clamp once more as I pull his hair, nodding my head *yes* in ecstasy. Tonight I did want to fuck him. He's reading my signals just right as he guides me off the sink.

"I want you to fuck me slow from behind," I cry out, and he pauses in surprise.

He gently bends me over the kitchen counter and I feel the metal nipple clamps tap against the cool granite. I release a breath. He then unfastens his tight jeans, pulling them down to his pubic hair. He leans forward, licks my ass cheek, then squeezes them both. He steps back and slowly pulls his hard cock out. I gasp as he strokes himself. He then spreads my legs and slowly inserts the head of his cock.

"Oh, Ty..." I moan.

"You make me so hard, Alex," he says as he traces his

black polished nails down my angel wing tattoo, sending shivers down my spine.

"Fuck me slow." I look back at him as he flips his hair out of his face, spreads my folds, and slowly slides the rest of the way in.

"I love how wet you get when you're turned on," he says as he grips my hair with his fist and play-bites my neck.

"You turn me on—you do this to me," I pant as he holds my waist and thrusts cautiously inside of me, making sure he isn't applying too much pressure.

He stretches me as he fucks me slowly while I spread my arms out over the cool counter, submitting to him. I heat up as he hits my G-spot, making me tremble with pleasure. I can feel my excitement lubricating his hard cock as he easily rocks in and out.

"Tyler…" I whisper. "Tyler, baby I'm going to come—I can't hold out," I warn as euphoria starts to overwhelm me.

"That's it, come all over me," he says as he bites my shoulder and continues to slide in and out. Unselfishly, he lets me finish my intense orgasm. My legs go limp as noodles. He withdraws his cock, then leans over to whisper in my ear, "Now get me off, baby."

I smile and eagerly push myself up off the counter, turn around, and face him. I delicately pull the clamps off of my sensitive nipples one at a time, roll his nipples between my index finger and thumb, then clamp them onto him.

"Holy fuck," he says. I've never used them on him before.

I giggle, then tease his nipples with my tongue as I pull his hair back and suck on his neck. I feel his hard-on against my leg as I pull his leather belt out of the loops of his jeans, then push the pants down to his ankles. "Bend over, beautiful."

I smile, snapping the belt as he laughs and shakes his head. "No, Ty, bend over," I repeat. He swallows hard and bends over for me just like he did when I used the flogger on him.

I lick up his spine, step back, and swing the belt, making a *slap* noise against his butt cheek.

"Holy fuck!" he cries out as I swing it again against his flesh. I reach around his hip and stroke his erection. "Ahh, again," he moans. I step back and swing the belt a third time, then stroke his cock feverishly once more as my fingers begin to tingle.

"Follow me," I whisper into his ear, and he pushes himself up from the counter, exhales, then follows me to the fur rug in front of the fireplace. I lay back on the white fur and motion with my finger for him to join me.

He bends down, casting a shadow over me, leans in, and lashes his tongue into my hungry mouth. I spread my legs, grab his stiffened cock, and slide him back into me. I then reach my hand around and insert my finger gently inside of him.

"Now fuck," I order as he gasps. "Come on, don't pull that 'awe shucks' bullshit with me." I bite his neck and push my finger in a little bit deeper. He begins thrusting as I slide my finger in rhythm. "I know what you like," I whisper as he leans closer and licks my neck, panting heavily.

"That's it," I say as I feel him lengthen even more inside of me as he pushes his pace. I am getting so worked up again. I open my legs wider, letting him easily slide back and forth. I suck his bottom lip and push my finger in and out while he releases warmly inside of me.

"Oh, I feel you coming hard," I whisper again as I push his hips and begin to orgasm for the second time, quivering all along his pulsing cock.

"Oh, Alexandria," he cries out as I am getting him off good.

Once he finishes, I exhale, pull my finger out, and throw my head back in exhaustion. "Oh, Tyler, baby, you are trouble," I groan.

He laughs and rolls over onto his back. "I need a fucking cigarette after that," he says breathlessly as I laugh.

"Trouble," I repeat.

The two of us sit on the cabin's wooden porch step, wrapped in a throw blanket as Tyler smokes his much-deserved cigarette.

"I know you're bruised." I laugh as I glance up at the evening sky.

Tyler blows out his smoke and shakes his head. "Baby girl, you gave it to me good!" He laughs as I reach over and rub his ass.

"I distinctly recall you telling me you were a masochist." I play-bite his shoulder. "With you, Alex, it's so much more. I mean, I always thought I was a dominant until I fucked you." He bites his lower lip as he flicks ash off his cigarette.

"That's because you trust me," I say as I pull the blanket close. He nods his head, agreeing with me. "I never pushed it that far until I had sex with you," I say as he raises his eyebrows. "I mean, Gage was dominant, but no passion;

Trent was..." I pause.

"I'd rather not relive your sexual past," he whines, and I quickly bite my tongue. "Well, I'm very aware of your past, Mr. Black." I run my fingers through his hair. "You

are by far the best lover I've ever had," I say as he smiles and inhales his cigarette, allowing me to stroke his ego. "Well, I'm famished," I huff.

"Let me feed you, mama bird," he teases as he pulls me to my feet. "Hey, I didn't hurt you in there, did I?" he asks as his voice cracks a bit, and I shake my head. "I mean, I was making love to you slowly, trying to please you." He swallows as he brushes my hair out of my face and looks into my eyes for confirmation.

"You were perfect. I love pleasing you too, Tyler—I'd do anything for you," I say as he blinks his long lashes back at me. "I want to make you happy. I'm so afraid to disappoint you," I whisper.

He protectively pulls me close to his bare chest. "I'm the one that was always the constant disappointment. You loved me no matter what I did, remember?" He releases a breath as he squeezes me tighter. "You, wife..." He pauses. "You make me so unbelievably happy." He steps back and taps my belly.

"Feed me," I say, and he takes my hand and leads me to the kitchen.

After we eat, Tyler sets our dishes into the sink, then holds out his hand. "Let's go get some rest, mama bird," he says.

I follow him upstairs into the loft area, strip off my clothes, slide into his T-shirt, and crawl into bed.

❃

The next morning, I slowly open my eyes and try to focus on Tyler next to me. He is laying on his stomach, naked, long, silky hair splayed over his face, the comforter just barely covering him.

I gasp as I notice the bruises. Man, seeing the red welts on his backside still makes me squirm. I feel my stomach grumble for a moment as I exhale.

"I couldn't love you any more than I do at this very moment," I whisper as I sift my fingers through his locks, watching him sleep. I lean my head back on the pillow and daydream about us becoming a family. The feeling seems so surreal. Was I actually going to have a little bird? I giggle as I watch the ceiling fan rotate.

"Oh, my ass!" Tyler groans.

"You asked for it," I say, laughing, rubbing my sore breasts. "What happened to just making love traditionally?" I question as he runs his fingers slowly up my arm.

"I can do that. You should feel my morning wood." He laughs as he throws his long leg over mine. "Was it okay to have sex?" he asks with concern.

I smile and look over at him. "Yes, baby, my doctor said that it was okay to have sex.

Actually, she advised me to do it as long as I felt well enough." I laugh, thinking how wanting to throw up comes and goes throughout my daily routine. He rolls over and smothers my belly with kisses. "Ty!" I holler out. "Stop!" I laugh as I run my hands through his locks.

"She said it would reduce stress, improve my mood, help me sleep, and..." I pull his hair and poke his chest. "It'll help me bond with you."

"Oh, so, since we're medically advised to have sex, let's

make love 'traditionally,' as you say." He laughs as he air-quotes with his fingers then sticks his tongue out at me. I just smile. He then pushes himself up and flashes me a sinful grin.

"Ty, what are you doing?" I laugh as he crawls up to get on top of me, forcing my legs open with his and inserting his morning erection. "Oh my God," I say as he nuzzles his face into my tousled hair and thrusts. "Oh my God, Ty..." I gasp as he keeps a slow, steady rhythm. *He feels incredible.* I am completely breathless.

"Oh, Alex," he whispers as he slides back and forth. I bite my lower lip, grabbing his buttocks.

"Ow, easy, baby!" He laughs as he tenses his glutes. I giggle, release my hands, and run my nails lightly up and down his back. "Ah, that's better," he says as he grows harder and pushes deeper. "I'm going to come like this—this is..." He blows out a breath, groaning with utter plea-sure. "Oh, you're close too, baby, I can feel it," he whispers.

I exhale and squeeze him tighter, feeling his cock pul-sate as he releases within me. "Oh, Alex," he cries out as I close my eyes.

"Oh, Ty," I moan, releasing with him. *Wow, he can still make me come so quickly sometimes; it is unbelievable.* I try to catch my breath.

"Baby girl, you made me come so fucking hard!" He laughs as he pulls out and rolls over onto his back.

I just lay there with my legs spread, feeling satisfied. "Good morning," I greet him. He laughs again. "Yes, it is."

CHAPTER 22

A few hours later, I am preparing homemade soup for lunch as Tyler lays on the couch. I stir the pot and glance out the window at the bare trees.

"I hope we have a boy," Tyler says suddenly, and I smile and look over my shoulder at him. "I'm telling you, Alex, I won't pull any of that shit my pop pulled with me," he says.

I turn around, wiping my hands on a dish towel. "I know you won't. Give him or her all the love you've never received. You know what it's like firsthand to be abused and abandoned, so make it right this time around." I smile as I watch him stare up at the rustic chandelier, processing everything.

"I want to give *you* everything," he says, and I smile. "I was such a fuck-up for so long, but..." He shakes his head and puts his hand on his forehead, in deep thought.

"But you pulled through. You've grown up, Ty. You've really made a good life for yourself," I compliment him.

He smirks. "Good life for us. We're good, aren't we?" he inquires.

I lean over the counter, looking at him. "We're better than good. We can and will provide for this lil' bird—we can do it," I say with a sigh. "I'm so ready to move on with you, Ty. I'm really happy about this decision to start our own family."

"I'm all in, my beautiful wife. We promised we would never leave each other." I smile, relieved we are still in this together.

After we eat lunch, I feel wiped as I slip on Tyler's sweater, grab my book and a glass of water, and head upstairs to the loft area. Tyler follows me, pulling off his shirt and crawling back into bed alongside me, dozing off as I try to read. I feel a little crampy and recall the doctor telling me it was perfectly normal as I shift underneath the throw blanket. I toss my book onto the floor and close my heavy eyelids.

An hour later, I wake up in a pure sweat. I sit up, pull off my sweater, and reach for my glass of water on the bedside table.

I look over my shoulder at Tyler in a deep sleep beside me. I grind my teeth for a moment as cramps start to vibrate throughout my stomach and lower back.

"Perfectly normal, my foot," I grunt. I then feel a wave of nausea as I dab my damp upper lip with my fingertips and hold my stomach. The symptoms feel all too familiar. "Please don't do this," I whisper as I gingerly stand up and exhale.

I slowly walk over to the bathroom, walk in, shut the door, and lean against it. "Please, body, don't betray me," I whisper once more as I feel my jogging pants dampen. I look down and my pants are once again stained with blood. I pull them down, rush over to the toilet, and sit down as I feel the pregnancy begin to pass, gripping the sink next to me as a heaving cramp passes through me.

This can't be happening, I think as tears surface and my breathing becomes heavier. I glance down and see the vast amount of blood and swallow hard. *I'm such a fucking failure.* Tears begin to stream down my face as I wipe my eyes in disbelief. *I'm not disappointing Tyler. This can't be happening.*

I feel panic flush through me as I shake my head, wiping my dripping nose. I feel another cramp roil through me as I sit there. I take a deep breath, then start to clean myself up and flush the remains of the miscarriage down the toilet. I stand up and feel suddenly weak, gripping the sink once again to steady myself.

I take a minute, then reach into my bag, step into a clean pair of cotton underwear, stick the maxi pad to it, and grab ahold of my stomach. I release a few breaths, then pull up the panties and adjust my tank. I walk over to the sink, wash my hands, then rinse my face a few times. The cool water begins to soothe me.

Glancing at my reflection in the mirror, I am disturbed. *Fucking failure,* I think again.

I blow air out of my nostrils as anger flushes through me. I begin to cry, stepping back and sitting on the edge of the bathtub. I glance at my overnight bag, then lean down and shuffle my hand around inside, searching for the Valium. I shake my head in disappointment as I flip off the lid and pour the entire contents of the bottle into my mouth. I gag on a few pills floating down my throat when Tyler's voice startles me.

"What the fuck, Alex?" He rushes over to me and pushes my head downward. He shoves his fingers roughly into my mouth and down my throat, gagging me. I vomit the pills into the bathtub. "How many did you take?" he hollers as he fishes around my mouth feverishly, searching for any remaining pills. "Did I get them all?!"

He gags me a second time, and I grip onto the side of the porcelain tub and puke again. "Don't you leave me, Alex!" he calls out as he turns on the bath water and rinses out my mouth. "I'd be so lost without you; don't you leave me!" He is crying as I cough and wipe my mouth.

"Ugh," I say as he pulls me back upright and slides me off the edge of the tub, onto the cold tile floor.

He slides down next to me and just squeezes me tightly as I begin to bawl. "You're my whole world, beautiful girl—stay with me," he says, sobbing as he sways and runs his fingers through my hair, trying to soothe me.

I grip him with my trembling hands. "What happened?" he asks nervously.

"I'm a fucking failure, Ty!" I cry out. "I lost our baby again. I don't understand. I'm so heartbroken." I cry even harder.

"Shhh, you're okay, baby girl," he whispers as he holds me, wiping his own tears away with the back of his hand. "You're okay," he repeats.

"Why us?" I ask as Tyler kisses my head, then I mumble, "I'm sorry." He shushes me. "Beautiful girl, you're okay," he whispers again.

I close my eyes and let him hold me.

"Here, baby girl, drink this hot tea," Tyler says.

I sit up in bed and take the steaming mug from his

hands. "I'm sorry, Ty."

"I'd fall apart without you. We need each other. What were you thinking?" he asks in a low tone.

"I..." I fumble for the right words. "You have everything. You're famous, you're up for an award—you have everything," I repeat. "And I'm just empty." I let out a depressed huff.

"All that is bullshit. I have nothing if I don't have you." He swallows hard as he tries to hide his disappointment in me.

"I wanted to give you this," I say as he flashes a slight smile and kisses my head. "This baby was just something between us—not the band, not the studio, but *us*." I sniffle as I wipe my nose.

"I appreciate that," he says. "But I need you. I can't live without you. Why did you try and leave me?" he asks as tears begin to stream down my face once again. "You promised you'd never leave me. I mean, all these years it's been just you and me, baby girl," he whispers.

I pleaded for him not to leave me during my first miscarriage; he's pleading for me not to leave him during my second—we can't handle much of anything without the other.

"I'm sorry, Tyler, please forgive me," I cry. "Maybe something was wrong—that's probably why my body got rid of it." I try to sip my tea, attempting to rationalize the situation.

He releases a breath, takes my mug from me, and sets it on the bedside table. He leans me back on my pillow, then walks around to the other side of the bed, lays down next to me, and wraps his arms around me. "Just close your eyes, baby girl," he says, and I drift off to sleep in his arms.

The next morning, I open my eyes and notice that Tyler isn't lying next to me. I wipe my eyes, sit up in a panic, and look around the loft for him. I notice the front door is cracked open. He's sitting out on the wooden steps, smoking a cigarette. I swallow hard as I stare at him for a minute, then go into the bathroom, clean myself up, and make my way downstairs.

I stand at the screen door and continue to watch him. He looks like he is a million miles away in thought. I open the door and sit down next to him, but he continues to stare straight ahead, pretending not to notice me.

He blows out smoke, stomps on his cigarette, and asks, "Ready to go home?" I nod my head and go back inside the cabin to collect our things.

Arriving home, we unload the Jeep and make our way into our flat. Beatle and Beethoven greet us upon entering, and I smile and bend down to pet them.

"Can I get you anything?" I ask Tyler as he carries the luggage into our bedroom. He shakes his head as he opens the bag and begins to pull out all his dirty clothes. "Just leave them in a pile, I'll get to it," I say.

Tyler ignores me. He walks over to the washing machine and starts a load as I stand back up and walk into the laundry room.

"I said I'd get to it," I mutter, but Tyler just pushes past me and goes back to unpacking his suitcase. "What's the matter with you?" I ask.

He shrugs his shoulders as he sets his bathroom essentials on the vanity.

I walk into the bathroom. "So you're not going to talk to me now?" I am surprised at his attitude.

"I'm just in a mood," he says as I rub his back with my hand. He shoves me off with his shoulder then walks out.

Okay. I guess I'll leave him alone with his mood. I turn and begin to unpack my own things, then decide that ignoring him isn't an option for me.

"I thought we were okay," I snap, hanging up my leather jacket in the closet. "We're fine," he mumbles.

"Then stop with the attitude," I say.

He flips me off, then walks toward the balcony door.

"Fuck you too," I yell, slamming the bedroom door shut and sitting down on the bed in a huff. Once again, his emotional roller coaster is giving me whiplash. "I'm the one who's bleeding over here!" I holler, clutching my stomach tightly.

Suddenly the bedroom door flies open and Tyler stands there, staring down at me. "I'm hurt too, you know." He flashes me an irritated look.

"Well, getting angry doesn't solve anything!" I retort. "Oh, and suicide does?" He hits the door with his palm.

I tear up once again. "I know you hurt... I'm so sorry. My emotions are all over the place too, Ty," I whisper as he shakes his head.

"I lost the lil' bird too and you tried to leave me." He pauses. "You promised me that you'd never leave me," he whispers.

"I love you, Tyler," I say as he huffs in frustration. "I panicked. I'm sorry..." I hesitate. "Say we'll be okay," I demand, standing and pushing him against the door. "Say we'll be okay."

I wrap my arms around him as a wave of tears glosses over his eyes. He squeezes me back and begins sobbing. I cry with him as we slowly slide down the bedroom door onto the ground, just holding each other tightly.

"Say we'll be okay," I whisper as I squeeze him tighter.

"We'll be okay," he says as he rubs his damp eyes against my shoulder.

CHAPTER 23

FIVE WEEKS LATER

Tyler zips up his wardrobe bag as I swing the Jeep keys around my fingers, smiling. "What time is the sound check?" I ask as he pushes his hair back with his sunglasses and shoves his cell phone into his jean pocket.

"In an hour, so I need to get going because I'm cruising by to pick up Edward," he says, looking over at me. "Are you still heading over to the venue with Mick?"

I nod my head. He leans down and kisses me, trying to take the keys from my hand. I won't let them go; I just keep kissing his lips, and he laughs.

"I love you," he says.

I smile and release the keys. "I love you more," I say as I walk him to the front door, lock it behind him, and lean against it.

Tonight is the New Year's Eve concert with Black Rifle Coalition and the REVENUE splitting the bill. They performed this gig last year at a private event at *Club Chamber*, but this time around it's at the *Turn It Up!* theater, a much larger venue.

I check my watch and rush off to the bathroom to hit the shower.

There's a knock at the front door and Mick yells, "Hey, sexy girl, let me in!"

I laugh and open it. He stands there, tall and slender like Tyler, his blond hair slicked back. He adjusts his black jacket and spins around.

"How do I look?" he asks.

I give him a once-over. "Dashing!" I say as he smiles and leans in for a hug.

"What's this?" he asks as he smooths out my satin black dress. "I like the dainty spaghetti straps, the low-cut back, and ooo—those heels!" He nods his head in appreciation.

I giggle. "I'm bra-less and pantie-less tonight!" I tease as he smacks my butt. "You hussy. Tyler has got it so good, girl!"

We laugh as I walk over to the kitchen drawer to find my lovebird key chain. "Let's go!" I say, and Mick picks up my clutch as I lock up.

Arriving at the all-too-familiar venue, we park and slip in through the back entrance. The security guard checks his list and waves us in as Mick rolls his eyes and takes my hand.

"The green room is upstairs," he says, pointing to a set of elevators. We walk past all the REVENUE's gear as I smile at my logo plastered on their banner.

"I can't believe they're playing a gig with these vandalizers," Mick whispers.

I laugh and press the button for the elevator. As we reach the second floor, the elevator door opens, and immediately we are in the midst of a crowd.

"Who are all these people?" I ask with surprise.

Mick looks around in awe. "Girl, they're reporters, friends of both bands, fans..." He pauses. "Drama." He play-slaps my butt, and I laugh.

"You feed off the drama," I chastise him.

He nods his head in agreement. "Oh lord, honey, look at that man!" he says. "Tyler, he is just too fine, girl!" He laughs as I look over and see Tyler shooting the bull with a group of people. He has on his tight black pants with the leather patches on the thighs and a pair of braces hanging off of them. He rocks a black form-fitted Henley T-shirt with all the buttons open, exposing his chest, and the sleeves pushed up, flashing his ink. His black hair is blown out and feathered, black eyeliner lining his beautiful brown eyes.

I stand there, watching in appreciation, as Mick laughs at me.

"You go say hi to your bird—I'm off to find Edward. We'll meet up in VIP!" He releases my hand as I nod my head.

I shift my weight in my heels, watching Tyler. People just walk right in front of me, but I don't let them break my concentration.

A moment later, Tyler's eyes meet mine and his face lights up as he shakes a man's hand then pushes his way through the crowd over to me. He holds my neck, leans down, and slides his tongue into my mouth. I gasp as he pulls his tongue out, kisses my lips, and whispers, "You look stunning." He smiles.

"It's for you," I whisper back as he runs his finger under the strap of my dress.

"I'm a bit anxious with all these people around. Come, follow me," he says, taking my hand and pulling me into a private dressing room, locking the door behind us.

"Is this where you get dressed?" I ask.

He laughs. "It's where I'm getting *undressed*," he says, and pulls me over to a black velvet love seat next to a dressing mirror. He sits down, unbuttons his pants, and pulls me onto his lap.

"Wow, Ty, you're all wound up!" I laugh, but he says nothing—it's been weeks since we had sex at the cabin and he *is* wound up.

He slides my dress up to my hips, then takes out his hard cock, opens my slit, and slips in.

"Oh, Tyler!" I say, the crowd outside the door drowning out my cry.

He pulls down my dainty dress straps, baring my breasts to him. He leans in and sucks on my peaked nipples as I throw my head back. I rock back and forth on his lap as he sucks harder. I push his bangs aside and lean in toward his neck.

"Oh, Alex," he says as he thrashes his tongue into my mouth and pulls my hips harder.

I run my nails over his exposed chest as his mouth opens and he starts to pant. "Fuck me, Ty," I say, and he pushes deeper while looking directly into my eyes. "Fuck me. Fuck me, rock god," I say.

I run my hands through his hair, then lick his pouty lips as I clench my thighs. He rubs my hips once more, then grips my butt cheeks and inserts his finger into my ass. I moan in surprise. *Hey, that is my move.*

"Oh, make me come like you do," I pant as he pushes deeper with his finger and I slide back and forth. "Tyler, baby, that's going to make me come," I warn.

He sucks my shoulder, marking me as he groans. "You are soaking my cock, Alex—I mean, I can't..." He inhales deeply. "I can't hold out too much longer," he warns.

I maintain my rhythm as he blows out his breath slowly, trying not to orgasm. "Come on, come with me," he says achingly, unable to hold out.

I let go and quiver all along his pulsing cock.

"Good girl," he whispers as he lets go and begins to come inside of me. I clench my glutes, accepting it. I am coming hard with him.

"Oh, my Alex!" he groans as we finish together.

After climaxing, we both exhale and start laughing with relief. I lift up as he pulls out and grabs a nearby T-shirt to wipe himself off. "You are so wet." Smiling, he gently wipes me off too.

I slide off his lap and stand up, adjusting my dress. "I can't control myself around you!" I laugh as I lean into the vanity mirror and fix my smudged makeup.

Tyler stands up and adjusts his pants. "Now I'm ready to fucking kick ass tonight," he says as he flips his hair back off his face and grins at me.

I smile at him in the mirror as I fluff my lashes. "Happy New Year," I say, turning around as he steps up to me.

He traces the bite mark he left on my shoulder, then leans in and kisses me. "Happy New Year, wife." His smile makes me melt.

We're startled by a bang on the door and Gunner hollering, "Yo, Ty, the REVENUE are on, and dude, aren't you supposed to sing backup for one of their tunes?"

Tyler's eyes widen as he cracks the door open. "Shit, dude, I almost forgot. I'm heading down now," he says as I giggle and wave to Gunner, who shakes his head, clearly sensing we just had sex.

Standing backstage, Mick walks up to me and rolls a bottle of water across my shoulder bite as we hear Tyler singing backup vocals for the REVENUE. "Does that man have any control?" He laughs as I lick my lips. "Hussy," he says. The crowd suddenly realizes that it is Tyler Black singing, they go crazy, screaming and whistling for him.

"Do you hear that?" I ask Mick as my eyes widen with surprise.

"Girl, they love him more than the REVENUE!" He laughs.

We listen to the song as the stagehands begin to roll Black Rifle Coalition road cases over to the stage entrance.

"They're up soon," Mick squeals as Edward walks up behind him and kisses his neck. "You call me the hussy?" I tease as Edward taps Mick's ass and walks over to his guitar case.

We then hear, "Tyler Black, everyone!" as the fans scream once more, showing their appreciation for Tyler. He walks off the stage and heads straight over to me and Mick.

"Whatcha think, baby girl?" he asks as I hand him my water bottle and he takes a sip. "That's what you recorded in Los Angeles after you finished the film soundtrack, right?"

I ask, and he nods his head. *That feels like a lifetime*

ago. "You sound killer, Ty." I smile as he returns the water bottle. "Mick and I are going to sashay over to VIP—good luck up there, songbird," I say.

He flashes me a smile, then leans in and kisses me.

The crowd never simmers down after the REVENUE's set as they all start to chant: "Black...Rifle...Coalition!" I feel the butterfly awaken in my stomach and begin to break dance as I look around in awe from VIP.

Austin slides into the row and hollers, "Where have you been, Alex?" Mick nudges me, then says to Austin, "Hussy."

Austin just rolls his eyes. "I miss Tyler! I wanted to say hi but I guess y'all were too busy." He laughs as he shakes his head.

"Yes, they were getting busy, all right!" Mick rubs the love-bite on my shoulder as my cheeks flush red.

"I knew y'all would last—you've always loved him," Austin says, and I smile. Suddenly the house lights dim as the crowd keeps on cheering.

"Are you fucking alive out there?" I hear Tyler ask on his megaphone. The crowd erupts as he walks out on stage. "I said, *are you alive out there, motherfuckers*?!" he screams, and the crowd roars. "Let me hear you welcome the band," he says as he put his boot up on the amplifier and smiles at the crowd. They all start to chant:

"Black Rifle Coalition, Black Rifle Coalition, Black Rifle Coalition..."

"That's what I'm fucking talking about," Tyler hollers as Vincent beats on the drums. He then tosses the megaphone, grabs his microphone stand, and holds it out over the crowd.

"Black...Rifle...Coalition!" the fans chant once more as

Gunner, Edward, and Lilith join in rocking their introductory song.

"Wow!" I scream as Austin whistles through his fingers.

All of a sudden, the band stops as Tyler slams his microphone stand down and belts out a long metal scream before the band kicks back in.

Austin shakes his head; that's his favorite part of the set.

Tyler picks up the stand and sings: *"I won't lay in your shadow. I'm always pushed aside.*

I'm sick of controlling my anger." He pauses, then goes up an octave. *"Just go away and leave me behind!"*

The crowd goes crazy.

Mick rolls his eyes. "Girl, that shit is too much!" He waves the crowd off.

I laugh, then stare back at Tyler. He is amped. Preshow sex did him some good. I blush as I recall calling him a *rock god* in the throes of passion. After everything we've been through over this holiday break, I have never felt closer to him.

I shake my head, unable to grasp the notion of leaving him. What was I thinking, trying to check out at the cabin? Tears suddenly start to surface and I fan my hands quickly to try and dry my eyes.

"Are you okay?" Mick asks me with sincerity, and I nod my head while wiping my nose. "I need some air," I say.

He takes my hand and hollers over to Austin, "Girl time, we'll be right back." Austin nods his head, then goes back to banging it.

Mick pulls me outside onto the loading dock to get some much-needed fresh air.

"This is where I professed my love to Tyler," I sigh as I wipe my eyes, remembering how I laid my heart out on the line to him. I had no idea what I was in for that evening when I spilled the beans to him, telling him how much I loved him. Now I can't imagine my life without him.

"What's going on?" Mick asks.

Tears surface once again. "I had another miscarriage," I mumble. "Tyler really wanted to try this time and my body betrayed me. I ate a mouthful of pills to check out and Tyler gagged me. I'm so ashamed." I begin to hyperventilate as Mick steps in and hugs me tightly. "He's so good to me—how could I leave him? What was I thinking? Oh, Mick, I love him so much!" I cry out.

He holds me close and we sway together.

"I'm so sorry to hear that," a voice interrupts us.

I step back from Mick and look over my shoulder.

Roger is standing there, evidently drunk. "I wish Tonya loved me that much," he groans. "I still can't wrap my head around the affair. Look, I'm really sorry for your loss, Alex," he says as Mick waves him off, irritated.

"It's okay, Mick," I say as Roger steps up to me and wraps his arms around me, reeking of alcohol. I continue to cry, knowing he is hurting as well. "How are you holdin' up otherwise?" I ask.

"As good as expected. I mean, my wife actually left me and..." He shakes his head as I lean in and graze his five-o'clock shadow with my fingertips to calm him..

"Tyler and I are always here for you," I say as Mick flicks my arm, warning me to knock it off.

"Tyler's a good man—you did well dumping that bastard Trent," Roger slurs as he turns, tosses his liquor bottle aside, then goes back inside the venue in a huff.

"Be careful there," Mick says. "I'm sorry, honey. Tyler loves you so much. Maybe y'all aren't ready for children; maybe the universe has another plan."

I release a breath. "Maybe. I haven't told anyone," I confess as he brushes my hair off my shoulders.

"I won't say a peep," he promises.

I let out a sigh of relief. "Thank you," I whisper, and he smiles empathetically down at me.

"They'll be wrapping up the set soon, then I have a little private New Year's party planned for just me and Edward!" He laughs as he smacks his palms together and rubs them mischievously.

"Ooo! Well, let's get out of here, then!" I holler, wiping my teary eyes once more. I wrap my arm around Mick's waist as we make our way back inside the venue.

"They're you two are!" Austin yells as roadies push BRC road cases past us. "The band is finishing up. Are y'all staying for the afterparty?" he asks.

Mick and I both shake our heads no.

"Boo. Well, then, call me this week," Austin says as he kisses my cheek.

We then hear: "Happy fucking New Year's, Dallas!" The crowd roars, then starts their chant for Black Rifle Coalition again.

Within a few minutes, Tyler makes his way backstage and hands his microphone off to a stagehand. "Lovebird, whatcha think?" he calls out as he struts over to me, sipping his water and dabbing the sweat off his face with a hand towel.

Mick nudges my arm. "Oh, I love when you're all wet, Tyler!" he teases, to which Tyler flashes him an uncomfortable grin. Mick then turns to me and says, "I'll see ya, girl," as he makes a telephone gesture to his ear for me to call him as he walks away.

"Hi, songbird! Oh my, the crowd chanting y'all's name was exhilarating!" I cheer as he leans in and kisses me.

"You liked that, huh?" He laughs.

I nod my head. "Um, Houston...I think we have a problem," I say. Tyler's brows furrow. "We do? What's the problem now?" he groans.

"Well, I was out on the loading dock a minute ago with Mick, and Roger was out there tanked," I say, swallowing hard, waiting for Tyler's reaction.

"Again? Shit, really?" he asks furiously, and I nod my head. "Well, we better take him home," he huffs as he tosses his used towel aside. "Let me tell the band. I'll grab my gear then we'll get him on outta here," he says.

I just stand there, wide-eyed, nodding my head.

CHAPTER 24

"Don't puke in our Jeep," I say as I look in the rearview mirror at Roger swaying in the back seat.

"I don't puke. Hey, dude, do you have any coke?" Roger asks. I roll my eyes as Tyler shakes his head. "Remember how fucked up we got in Vegas, dude?" He laughs as he taps on my seat, jolting me forward.

"You know I don't snort blow anymore," Tyler says as he glances over at me, then looks out the passenger-side window.

"Oh yeah, that's cool," Roger says. He leans his head back, laughs to himself, then starts to nod off.

"I swear, if he pukes..." I groan, but Tyler flashes me a dirty look. "Do I turn here?" I ask.

"Yeah. He's like the third house down on the right," he says.

I pull up in front of a modest house. *I can't believe I am at Tonya's house.* I blow out a breath as I shut off the engine.

"Roger, wake up," Tyler says as he steps out of the Jeep and pushes his seat forward. "Dude." He taps on Roger's leg. "You're home. Let me help you out." He grabs Roger's arm and guides him out of the back seat. I slam my door shut relieved he didn't barf.

We walk up the sidewalk leading to his porch when a neighbor startles us as she calls out, "Hey, asshole, I'm not an all-night babysitter. You better get your fucking kid!"

I stop in my tracks as the woman in disheveled clothing and house slippers walks a little boy over toward us.

"He's yours," she says as she pushes him toward Roger, who looks down at the child and says, "Fuck Tonya."

I gasp.

"Whoa, take it easy," Tyler says as he walks Roger inside the house.

I just stand there and look down at the child. He must have been all of three years old, with chestnut hair like Tonya and big green eyes like Roger.

"Who's that on your pajamas?" I ask. "Batman," he says.

I squat down to take a closer look. "Batman is my favorite!" I say, and he smiles, then rubs his eyes. "Daddy is going to go to sleep. Are you sleepy too?" I ask him.

He nods his head.

Just then, Tyler walks back outside. "He passed out," he says, scratching his head, then glances over at the child. He walks down the porch steps and squats down in front of him. "I'm Tyler—do you remember me?" he asks, and the kid smiles, remembering his father's friend. "Tell me your name again," Tyler says.

"Tristin," the boy says softly as Tyler shakes his little hand.

"Ahh, that's right." He smiles as Tristin takes a step forward and hugs Tyler. "Thanks, buddy," he says. "Can I take you inside?"

Tristin nods his head and Tyler lifts him into his arms

and carries him into the house.

Tristin twirls Tyler's hair in his little hand as he stares at him. I smile to myself and follow them.

As we walk through the filthy house, I shake my head in disgust. We walk past Roger's room. Listening to his obnoxious snoring, I roll my eyes.

We open a door and see a twin mattress in the middle of the floor, one blanket, a few superhero toys scattered around, and a dim night-light plugged into the wall. Tyler sets Tristin down and adjusts his too-small Batman pajama shirt over his exposed belly.

"Get in bed Bruce Wayne," he says as Tristin giggles and hops into bed.

I pull the single blanket over him, then run my hands through his hair. "Good night," I whisper.

He rolls onto his side. "Night-night," he whispers.

Tyler and I walk out and close the door behind us. Tyler shakes his head in disbelief. "We can't leave him here alone while Roger sleeps off the alcohol," I say.

Tyler looks around. "Look at this fucking place; it's a fucking mess," he says.

"Let's go sit on the couch and just wait 'til Roger's sober," I suggest, and Tyler takes my hand and leads me to the living room couch.

A few minutes later, Tristin walks out into the living room and stands in front of Tyler. "I'm hungry," he says.

I lift my head and check my watch. "Did you eat dinner tonight?" I ask, to which he shakes his head. "Hum," I say.

Tyler stands and picks up Tristin. "Let's go into the kitchen," he says as we walk into the kitchen together. Tristin points to a yellow cereal box on top of the refrigerator. "Cereal?" Tyler asks. "Ooo, this is my favorite kind, I love Cheerios!"

Tristin smiles and Tyler grabs the cereal box as I shuffle through the cabinets, looking for a child's bowl. I then take a spoon out of the kitchen sink and wash it while Tyler sets Tristin down at the table and pours a little cereal in the bowl. He then turns and opens the refrigerator, takes out the milk, and smells the carton. He checks the date.

"Is it fresh?" I ask, tapping my foot.

"It's okay," he says as he pours a little milk into Tristin's bowl and I hand him the spoon. I begin to collect all the dishes on the counter and start washing them.

"How is it?" Tyler asks as he pours a handful of Cheerios into his own palm and tosses it back into his mouth as Tristin laughs.

"Baby girl, you don't need to do the dishes," Tyler says as he glances over at me and takes a seat at the table.

"Yes I do." I flash him a look of concern.

Tyler looks back at Tristin. "Is that good?" he asks again as he steals a Cheerio from his bowl and Tristin giggles. "You really were hungry," he remarks, watching Tristin eat the entire bowl of cereal.

"Done!" Tristin hollers.

Tyler laughs. "Good job, buddy," he says.

Tristin jumps down from the seat, walks over to Tyler, and tries to crawl into his lap.

Tyler lifts him up and sits him on his lap while Tristin plays with his silver hoop earrings. I just smile, then turn off the kitchen light and run my hands through Tristin's hair as he closes his eyes. Tyler continues to rock him back and forth as I motion for him to follow me back to

Tristin's bedroom, where he bends down and sets Tristin in his bed, then covers him up. I pick up a stained teddy bear and set it next to him as he yawns once more and begins to drift off to sleep.

We both release a breath. Tyler takes my hand and leads me back to the living room.

The next morning, I am wearing Tyler's leather jacket over my satin dress, leaning on him as he sleeps upright with his head against the couch cushion. Roger casts a shadow over the two of us as he kicks Tyler's boot.

"What the fuck are y'all doing here?" he asks in his deep southern voice.

Tyler, startled awake, stretches his arms, then kisses the top of my head. "Dude, we brought you home after the show. You were pretty fucked up," he says as he rubs his eyes and tries to focus.

"Really? I don't remember shit. I must have passed the fuck out," Roger says as he scratches his five-o'clock shadow.

"Tristin is in his bed sleeping," I say.

He grunts. "I'm making coffee, y'all want some?" he asks.

I shake my head. "Should I give Tristin a bath?" I offer as he turns and walks toward the kitchen.

"Nah, I'll handle that shit," he says.

I look over at Tyler. *Is this the same guy that drew me a bath in Vegas?* His demeanor has changed.

"Let's take off, baby girl," Tyler says, tapping my leg, and I agree. "Hey, dude, we're taking off," he calls out.

Roger walks back into the living room and reaches out his hand to shake Tyler's. "Sorry for all this," he says as Tyler returns the handshake.

"Call me, dude. Catch ya later," he says as he takes my hand in his and walks me out to the Jeep.

Driving home, I crack the window and let out a long, deep breath. "Roger is a fucking hot mess," I say as Tyler runs his hand through his hair in frustration.

"This whole mess is what's getting to him! The affair, Tonya bailing on him, then the fire…" He pauses and looks out the window. "You know he is responsible for the fire," he says.

I nod my head. "I feel so bad for Tristin," I say.

Tyler looks over at me. "Stay out of it, baby girl," he warns. I release another breath and pull into our parking garage.

Walking into our place, I lock the door behind me, kick off my high heels, and stretch my aching feet.

"Ahh," I moan as Tyler removes his leather jacket from me. "Thanks, Ty. Hey, I'll make some coffee while you go jump in the shower," I offer as he blinks his tired eyes and kicks off his boots.

"Thank you," he says and walks away.

I stand there for a moment, then make my way to the coffee maker and fix the coffee. As I take out mugs for the two of us, I just stew on last night.

I feel a little saddened for Roger, but he *did* act like an asshole. He was drunk, pissed off at his wife for leaving, and ignored his kid. The storyline was parallel to Tyler's: the mother left, the father became a drunk and took it out on the kid. My stomach turns as I think about Tristin at the house alone with Roger.

I take out the milk and sugar and lean against the counter. *Tyler was so sweet with Tristin.*

I smile and shake my head.

"What are you thinking about?"

Tyler startles me, and I look over at him standing there in his joggers, cotton T-shirt, and wet hair.

"Feel better?" I ask as he slides onto the stool at the counter. "You were so cute with Tristin," I say.

Tyler smiles. "One day we'll have a lil' bird," he says as I reach out my hand and squeeze his hand.

"One day," I say.

ONE WEEK LATER

"Baby girl, the *Verse* Awards are in a few weeks. I'm booking the private plane now," Tyler says as he types away on my laptop.

"Really?" I ask, standing in the kitchen putting dishes away.

"I told you that since the awards are in Las Vegas—and you and I don't want to hang out in Las Vegas—that I'd book us a private plane. I told you your rockstar husband will fly in, accept the award, then fly out. In the meantime, I'm fucking you in the plane to celebrate on the way back to Dallas!" He laughs. "Wait, I'm confused. Do I address myself as a rockstar or rock god?" he teases.

I flush with embarrassment and bite my lower lip. I sounded like such a *WHIP-ette* calling him "rock god" when we had sex in his dressing room.

He laughs again as he types in his credit card information.

"Oh, how exciting! I need to text Nova and see if I can borrow the dress she wore for the Billboard Music

Awards!” I call out as I lean over the counter to grab my cell phone.

“Trent can fly coach—I’m not taking his ass with us,” Tyler grunts as he continues to type.

“We have to at least make a plan with him to walk the red carpet together. I bet he brings Liz,” I groan.

Tyler ignores me. “Okay, it’s all set. Two pilots, no stewardess, no alcohol.” He smiles. “It’ll be just you and me, baby girl,” he says, and I squeal with excitement.

“Just you and me,” I repeat. “I finally get to go to an award ceremony on your arm for once.” I wiggle my hips, typing out my text to Nova while Tyler smiles at me.

CHAPTER 25

LAS VEGAS

Tyler stands in front of the mirror, adjusting his black-on-black, pin-striped, form-fitting jacket, smoothing out his slim-fit pin-striped pants, then straightening out his black bird-print scarf. As he runs his hands through his feathered locks, he calls out, "I'm so happy I don't have to wear the same fucking outfit as Trent. I mean, WHIP looked cool and all at the Billboard Music Awards all matching, but this outfit makes me feel more like me." He laughs.

I stand next to him at the mirror, adjusting the black sequin dress that Nova got married in.

"You look beautiful," I say. "I mean, just *beautiful*," I compliment him.

He flashes me a grin in the mirror, then turns around. "Baby girl, you fill that dress out so much nicer than Nova." He whistles as I pull my hair over my shoulder and lean down to pick up my high heels.

"What time is the car picking us up?" I ask as I slide on my shoe.

Tyler checks the clock on the bedside table. "We better get going," he says.

I collect my clutch, then go out to grab my lovebird key chain from the kitchen. "Do you have everything?" I ask as Tyler walks out of the bedroom and reaches for my hand.

"I do now." He squeezes it and I smile.

Walking onto the private plane, the two pilots greet us, state that we are in for a smooth flight, then watch us as we select our seats.

"Ooo, leather!" I squeal, rubbing my hands along the black leather seat. Tyler looks over at me and smiles. "Are you nervous?" I ask, but he shakes his head. I reach over and take his hand in mine, kiss it, then release a breath as the plane begins to taxi.

"Thank you for coming with me," he says.

"Of course. Oh, I texted Trent to meet us at the red carpet entrance so that we'd go in together," I say, to which Tyler nods his head. "Just relax—it's a quick flight." I remind him, sensing he is a bit nervous even though he's clearly trying to hide it from me.

Arriving at the *MGM Grand Garden Arena*, I feel squirrels boxing in my stomach.

The driver pulls alongside the entrance of the venue. "That's where the red carpet begins," he calls back to us as he points to other musicians walking along and posing for pictures.

I look outside the window and spot Trent. "Good, there's Trent," I say as Tyler fusses with his dress scarf.

The driver walks around the sleek vehicle to open the door for us. "Just text me when you are ready to be picked up, sir. I'll be in this same area," he says as Tyler steps out and hands him a hefty tip. The driver salutes him with his cap. "Thank you, sir," he says with a smile.

Tyler reaches back into the car, takes my hand, and helps me out.

As I step out, I wave to Trent and Liz. Trent is dressed in a form-fitting black suit with a V-neck T-shirt underneath exposing his inked chest. He rocks his man-bun and eyeliner as usual. I just smile as I watch him reach for Liz's hand and walk over to us.

"Wow, you two are stunning!" Liz greets us as I squeeze Tyler's hand.

"Thank you. How exciting is this?" I ask as she adjusts her black minidress, which matches her short, slicked-back hair.

Trent leans in and kisses me on the cheek, then shakes Tyler's hand. "Y'all ready to head in?" he asks as a security guard comes over and guides us to the red carpet.

Adoring music fans and photographers line the entrance behind a velvet rope as we walk the red carpet.

"Oh my God, there's Tyler Black!" one fan calls out, and suddenly flashbulbs are going off.

He smiles, sticks out his tongue, and gives them devil-horns, then squeezes my hand tighter. Trent and Liz follow behind us until we reach the backdrop displaying "*Verse* Awards" on it. Tyler and Trent are professionals by now; they let go of our hands and walk over to the press to pose for a few pictures.

"They look good, don't they?" I ask Liz as she stands there, bright-eyed, nodding her head. I suddenly have a flashback of the Billboard Music Awards, when WHIP was posing all together. Then there were five of them—now there are only two.

My stomach turns as I release a breath, thinking about how Tyler punched Gage Heston on the carpet in my defense. *He always loved me.*

I smile as I lick my lips, staring at him. Tyler steps away from the photographers and holds out his hand for me. I accept it, and he pulls it up to his mouth and licks my ring finger. I giggle.

We walk inside the familiar venue, where a hostess greets us and directs us to our seats.

Walking through the venue, I gaze around with excitement as fans cheer and wave signs for their favorite artists from two tiers up. We scoot down the row of auditorium seats and sit down next to the band that is up for the "Rock Band of the Year" award. I select a seat between Tyler and Trent. Liz immediately starts chatting with the band next to us. She is giddy and she is cute. The nominees in front of us turn around and introduce themselves. Trent begins to chat with them, but Tyler just leans in and kisses me on the lips.

"I wanted to do just that the last time you and I were here," he whispers as I kiss him back and adjust his dress scarf.

"Hey, isn't that Jack White?" I ask, pointing to one of our favorite musicians, still taken aback by the presence of famous artists even though my husband is quickly joining their ranks. I smile as I glance back up at Tyler, proud of him, and I lean in and kiss him once more.

Just then, the house lights flicker, letting the audience know that the ceremony is about to begin.

"Here we go," Tyler says as he releases an anxious breath.

A well-known nighttime talk show host walks out

on the stage as the crowd cheers. He begins his opening monologue, but Liz keeps chatting with the rock band. Trent tries to silence her by tapping her leg. She turns toward the stage and begins to giggle, then laughs loudly at the host's jokes. Tyler and I just look at each other and shake our heads.

All throughout the ceremony, Tyler seems calm, quietly sitting and watching the award show. I glance over at Trent, who seems a little bit more nervous than he was at the Billboard Music Awards, fidgeting with the rings on his fingers. He catches me staring at him and flashes me a grin. I smile back and bat my eyelashes.

An hour into the event, last year's "Songwriter of the Year" walks out on stage as the fans cheer for him.

"Holy shit, this is it," Tyler says as he shifts his weight in his seat, then glances over at Trent.

The gentleman thanks the fans, then starts into a "what makes a good song great" speech. I just hold my breath. He then runs through the list of nominees one by one, followed by their hit song and a fifteen-second clip of their video. I tap Tyler's leg when they show him singing on the big screen—he is so beautiful.

The announcer then draws in a deep breath as he opens a large gold envelope.

"And the winner of this year's *Verse* 'Songwriter of the Year' Award goes to..." There's a dramatic pause. "Tyler Black and Trent Van Zant for their hit song, 'It's Done'!" he hollers.

Tyler releases a breath, then leans over and kisses me a few times. Trent stands up, hugs Liz, then turns to me, pulls me to my feet, and kisses me on the cheek. He steps around me and grabs Tyler, pulling him into an embrace.

I hear him whisper, "We did it," as Tyler steps back, turns, and starts walking down the aisle with Trent following behind him.

Liz stands there cheering as I wipe my eyes and release the breath I was holding while the audience claps.

Tyler and Trent walk up the stairs to the main stage, make their way over to last year's winner, and accept the *Verse* Award. Tyler hands it over to Trent and motions for him to speak into the microphone.

Trent steps up, looks at the award, and says, "It's been a challenging time for Tyler and I, but I'm so happy I was able to work alongside my creative brother again. I want to thank Tyler Black, our record label, and, of course, our fans. Without the fans and the million hits y'all gave us on our video, this wouldn't have been in our reach—so thank you." He smiles as fans whistle, then Tyler walks up to the microphone. The fans don't let up with their screaming as he smiles, shakes his head, then speaks.

"I want to thank Trent Van Zant for composing this piece, Edward Perry for his amazing talent on the violin, and my wife, Alexandria Black—for always believing in me. Thank you," he says, nodding while everyone claps.

Music begins to play as the two of them are directed off the stage.

"They did it," I mumble, shaking my head, and Liz flashes me a smile. I am so proud of the two of them.

"Mrs. Black?" a seating host asks. "Yes?" I answer.

"I'm here to take you backstage; follow me," he instructs, and I stand up, motioning for Liz to come with me as we follow the seating host.

Walking backstage, the host directs us to the press tent, where the award winners have been shuffled in to take pictures and partake in a quick interview. I peek inside and see Trent and Tyler holding up the silver *Verse* Award and posing for a picture together.

"They're in the tent," I say to Liz, and she nods her head as she tries to absorb all the chaos.

Tyler emerges from the tent soon after, runs over to me, picks me up, and swings me around. I giggle and he sets me down and begins peppering my cheeks and lips with kisses.

"Oh my God, I'm on real fucking high right now!" he says as I squeeze him tightly. "We got the big V," he says, sticking out his tongue, and I return the gesture and laugh.

"I called it, songbird!"

"You did, lovebird—you did," he says, giving me props as he grabs the award from Trent's hand and shows it to me.

"Oh, it's gorgeous!" I shout as he lights up like a Christmas tree. He is so happy; so proud of himself.

Other musicians begin to walk over to Trent and Tyler and congratulate them as I stare down at the heavy-weighted silver award in my hand. I can't believe it. These two have come so far. They're constantly at each other's throats, but creatively they are geniuses. I smile as I hand the award over to Liz so she can get a closer look, and I watch Tyler beam with excitement as he laughs and carries on with Trent.

"So, are the two of you coming out to celebrate with me and Trent?" Liz asks.

I chuckle, remembering how my last celebration went down in Las Vegas. I ended up in a wedding chapel for an impromptu wedding, then in a hotel room with swingers. I shake my head. "Noooo, sugar. Tyler and I are flying back to Dallas tonight," I say.

"Hey lovebird, I texted the driver—let's head out," Tyler says as Liz hands the award over to him.

"You kept your promise," I say happily as Trent rejoins us.

"This is going to look so badass on display in *Brimstone*," he says as Tyler tries to hand him the award. "No, you hang on to this, brother."

"Well, congratulations," I say once again as I step in and hug Trent. He hugs me back, then hugs Tyler. "I'm ready to celebrate!" I smile at Tyler and lick my lips, knowing damn well Trent picks up on it. He lost out on celebrating with me last time because of Tonya.

"I'll see y'all back in the big D," Trent says as Tyler and I take each other's hands and head for the exit.

Stepping back onto the private plane, Tyler takes a seat in front of me across from a small table. He sets the award down on the table and just shakes his head in disbelief.

"Congratulations, sir," the pilot says as he glances down at the *Verse* Award.

"Thanks, dude," Tyler says. He shakes the pilot's hand, then watches him walk back into the cockpit and shut the door.

"Nice hardware," I tease as Tyler looks back over at me and laughs. It is evening outside as I gaze out the window at the bright lights of Vegas. "Sayonara!" I say as I flip off the city.

Tyler laughs and removes his suit jacket. The plane begins to taxi for take-off as I grab the award off the table and click a seatbelt around it next to me. "I'm so proud of you," I say to Tyler.

He leans back in the leather seat and releases a breath. "You pushed me to listen to Trent's apology, then pushed me to write and record that song, then pushed, pushed, pushed..." He pauses as he smiles to himself. "I have everything because of you," he says, blinking his eyelashes in gratitude.

"And I'll *keep* pushing you." I smile back as he lifts his finger and motions for me to come over to his seat. I unfasten my seatbelt, stand up, and walk over to him. I lean down into his personal space.

"Closer," he says, and I pull my dress up and straddle his lap. "Ah, that's better," he whispers, moving my hair off my shoulders and leaning in to kiss me.

I part my lips as he closes his eyes and slowly licks my tongue. "Umm," I say.

He opens his eyes and just stares at me. "I love you. I really love you," he says, and I lose my breath as my heart melts at his openness.

I sigh and blink my false lashes a few times back at him, then thrust my tongue into his mouth as he leans back in the seat.

"Now I want a celebratory fuck," he says.

I laugh and brush his long bangs out of my way as I lean forward and lick his pouty lips. I unbutton his pin-striped dress pants, pull out his endowed cock, and stroke it.

"Oh, Alex," he moans quietly as I slowly slide down from his lap and kneel between his legs. I insert his hard cock into my mouth and begin sucking. His fingers rake through my hair as I lick the entire length, then push it back in. I flicker my heated tongue around the head a few times, suck it, then engulf his shaft within my mouth repeatedly.

"Ahh..." he cries out as I cup his testicles, tug, and slide my finger into his rectum. He gasps as I simultaneously suck and finger-fuck him. His face flushes as he watches me. I can taste the pre-cum on my tongue as I lick him, then suck harder. "I need to fuck you." He is breathless.

I keep my pace slow with my finger as I lick over his V tattoo, then trail my tongue back down to his cock. "You turn me into the biggest slut for you," I say softly.

He groans as I work him over. "Baby, get on my lap." His voice aches. "I need to be inside you," he cries out, nearing orgasm.

I keep at it for a few more strokes, then let go of his cock and retract my finger. I push my sequin dress up and drop my lace panties. He pulls me onto his lap, parts my slick folds, and enters me.

"Oh, you are so warm," he says as I am taken aback by how hard his erection is. I release a breath, then squeeze my muscles as I rock him up and down. He thrusts his hungry tongue into my mouth as I pull his hair, craving more. I roughly circle my tongue around his barbell as he picks up his pace. He holds my hips down as he pushes deeper. I try to take all of him in as I lose my breath.

"You are unbelievably hard tonight, Tyler," I pant as his dark eyes meet mine.

He pushes deeper, concentrating. I lift my hips, then slide back down, fucking him hard repeatedly.

"Oh yeah, fuck me just like that," he says as I continue to thrust. "Get me off, baby," he pants.

I push back down, squeezing him as I ram my hips harder. "Come on, Ty," I plead, then cry out as I ride him, nearing climax. "Don't stop," I beg as he braces my hips steadily on his cock and starts to spurt inside of me. His orgasm overwhelms me. I tremble on him, releasing all my pent-up past celebration tension.

"Oh, Tyler," I whisper, lifting my hair off my neck and closing my eyes as euphoria washes over me.

He licks my dampened neck as he softly bites it and whispers, "I don't know what the hell you just did to me, Alex, but my body will never be the same."

I laugh, then wrap my arms around him and whisper, "Congratulations." I can feel him smile against my skin as he bites me a second time.

The next morning, I glance over at Tyler sound asleep on his stomach and just stare at him for a moment, taking him all in. His feathered black hair is once again flopped over his eyes. His pouty lips twitch as he dreams. His inked ivory skin glows as the morning sun peeks in. I lose my breath, reminding myself that I love feeling this way. I never feel more loved than when I am with Tyler—my best friend, my husband, my everything.

"Baby girl, I can feel you staring at me again," Tyler groans.

I giggle. "Good morning, songwriter of the year," I whisper as I push his hair out of his eyes.

He chuckles. "A fucking *Verse*! I still can't believe it," he says. "I can," I gloat with a smirk.

"Thank you for being my slutty date last night," he teases as I giggle once more.

"You rock god," I tease back. "You always turn me into

a slut—what gives?" I ask as I lightly scratch my fingernails down his back.

"The private plane was so fucking worth the extra expense." He laughs.

I lick my lips. "I never had sex in an airplane until you," I say. "Mark that off my bucket list of where to fuck the famous Tyler Black," I tease as he growls at me. "Breakfast?" I ask, and he nods his head. "I'm on it," I say as I slide out of the sheet and head toward the kitchen.

"Oh, we have dinner plans tonight with my parents—they want to treat you for the award," I call back, and he groans. "Don't do that! You have to go. Then I think Zack is meeting us over at the recording studio to bullshit with y'all and take a look at the award," I say as I prepare coffee. He groans a second time. "Is that all I'm getting out of you today, groans?" He groans once more and I just shake my head.

CHAPTER 26

Walking into the upscale restaurant, I spot my handsome father at the hostess stand, checking in on our reservations in his dinner jacket and Stetson.

"Hi, Daddy!" I call out.

He turns around and flashes me a grin. "Hi, Alexandria, how have you been holdin' up, sugar?" he asks.

I smile. "I'm holdin', I guess," I say as I release Tyler's hand and give my father a hug. "And you, Tyler! I'm so proud of you, son," he says as he holds out his hand.

Tyler smiles, then shakes his hand firmly.

"Oh, there you two are!" Mother calls out, returning from the powder room. "Alexandria, what a pretty white cocktail dress. Oh, and there is our award-winning son-in-law! Come here, Tyler, let me give you a hug!" she says as she pulls Tyler into her arms. "You're so handsome in this black dress shirt and matching scarf," she says as she actually compliments him this time around instead of telling him he is too thin.

"Hi, Mama," I say as I reach for Tyler's hand and squeeze it back into mine.

The hostess walks over to us and instructs us to follow her to our reserved table. My father rounds us up and the four of us follow the hostess. The restaurant is full of Dallas's elite as my mother struts behind my father, holding her head up high as we pass the piano player and arrive at our table. Tyler pulls out my chair as my father pulls out my mother's and we all take a seat.

"I'd like this bottle of wine," my father says, pointing to the drink menu. The hostess nods her head. He then looks around at the packed dining room and chuckles. "We're in the club." He smiles. "Our boy is famous; we're now in the club."

My mother rolls her eyes. The waiter approaches our table, shows my father his wine selection, then opens the bottle and begins pouring wine for everyone.

Tyler whispers in my ear, "Is it okay if I have one glass, baby girl?"

I nod my head. My parents do not know Tyler's history with addiction, and right now, with him being the center of attention, I do not want to embarrass him by bringing it up.

"To Tyler!" My father holds up his glass. "We're so proud of you, son—congratulations," he says, and I feel tears in my eyes as we all toast.

"To Tyler," my mother says happily as she sips.

I set my glass down. Tyler nuzzles my neck and kisses my cheek. Even in front of my parents, he isn't ashamed of showing his affection for me.

"Excuse me, folks, I just want to come by and say congratulations."

My eyes feel like they are going to pop out of their sockets when I hear that all-too- familiar voice.

I look up and see my ex, Gage Heston, standing there.

"Congratulations on winning the *Verse*, Tyler," he says.

He adjusts his tie, then reaches out to try and shake Tyler's hand.

Oh lord, don't start anything here. I huff, squeezing both of Tyler's hands in mine so he is unable to shake this demon's hand. Tyler growls under his breath.

"Oh, Mr. Heston, how are you, darling?" my mother asks, fawning all over him while I flash her a dirty look.

He pulls his manicured hand back and turns around to face my mother. "I'm well, ma'am. I just heard the good news about Mr. Black from his record label. Are you celebrating tonight?" he asks.

I shake my head, beginning to fume. My father picks up on my signals right away and interrupts them.

"Look, it's nice of you to come by, Mr. Heston, but I'd like to get back to celebrating with my daughter and her husband privately—you understand," he says sternly as I release a breath.

Gage's eyes dilate as he registers surprise at the abrupt news of our marriage. He always hated Tyler. "Oh, I see," he says, sucking in a breath. "Well, once again, Mr. Black, you've done good for yourself." He looks down at the two of us holding hands, then shakes his head.

I say nothing as he turns and walks away.

Tyler leans in and kisses my head. "It's okay, baby girl," he whispers as I reach for my wine and down a few sips to try and brush off the encounter with Gage.

My father taps my hand to settle things down, then changes the subject. "So, what are y'all having to eat tonight? What looks good?" he asks.

I smile at him, then look down at the menu.

Wine turns into dinner and the mood is lightened by

my father and his hilarious military tales. Tyler laughs as I quietly eat my salmon. When the piano player begins playing a familiar ballad, Tyler wipes his mouth on the linen napkin and takes my hand in his.

"Let's dance, baby girl," he says. "Excuse us," he says to my parents as we both stand up.

My father stands as well, flashing us a smile as we make our way over to the dance floor.

Tyler pulls me into his chest, kisses my cheek, takes my hand in his, and begins to sway with me.

"Thank you," I whisper as he kisses my lips. I know he can sense I am upset over the presence of Gage and he knows exactly what calms me. I hold him tightly as I gaze up at him, paying no mind to any other couple on the dance floor. I love him for that.

When the song comes to a close, Tyler kisses my lips once more, takes my hand, and walks me back to our table. He pulls out my chair as I sit and kisses my cheek, then takes his seat next to me.

"Well, kids, I took care of business; we can get on out of here," my father says.

Tyler reaches across the table and shakes his hand. "Thank you, sir, for dinner; I truly appreciate it," he says.

I lean over and kiss my father on the cheek. "Thanks, cowboy," I tease. My father laughs, then tips his hat. "Yes, thank you for a lovely evening." Mother smiles over at the two of us. "Congratulations, Tyler," she says.

We depart the restaurant and part ways outside at the valet station.

I keep my hand on Tyler's leg as he shifts gears, making our way down to *Brimstone.* "Let's just stay for a little while, Ty, I'm kind of spent from two days of celebrating," I confess as Tyler looks over at me and smiles. "Thank you for going to dinner tonight—it means a lot to me and my parents," I say.

"I like your parents; it was nice to be together. I just wish that cocksucker Heston didn't show his fucking face," he grunts.

I laugh. "Well, Daddy made sure he knew damn well that you were my husband and I think that hit him harder than when you sucker-punched him on the red carpet!" I laugh as Tyler nods his head in agreement.

"I wanted to clock him once more tonight, but I kept my cool in front of your parents," he huffs.

"Well, that asshole doesn't have a *Verse,*" I say proudly.

Tyler laughs as we both glance back at the award in the back seat.

Pulling up in front of *Brimstone,* Tyler turns off the Jeep and looks over at me. "Ready?" I ask.

"Ready," he says, reaching back for the award.

"Wait, come here," I say, and he leans into me from the driver's-side seat. "Let me taste you," I flirt.

He grabs my neck, pulls me toward him, and thrusts his tongue into my mouth.

I moan softly. "Baby, let's just leave the award here on the sidewalk for Zack and go home and make love the rest of the night," I plead while he keeps peppering my lips and neck with kisses. "Come on," I tease as I lick his lips and run my hands through his hair.

"I want to go back onto the plane," he says, and I laugh while tugging on his hair. "Oh, Alex, look what you do to me," he says, taking my hand and rubbing it over his dress pants along his hard-on.

"That's what I want to feel." I continue to play-bite his pouty lips.

"You know I will just push up this lil' white dress and have my way with you right here, right now, if you don't control yourself," Tyler threatens playfully.

I groan and pull myself away. "Shit. Let's go do this. Can we continue this later?" I ask as I check my makeup and fluff my hair in the visor mirror.

"Let's go, my lil' tease," Tyler says, adjusting himself in his pants.

We open our doors and hop out. Tyler makes his way around to the passenger side and takes my hand, the award in his other hand.

We walk into the recording studio and immediately hear:

"Surprise!"

We both shake our heads and laugh. Zack pops a bottle of champagne as Nova runs over to hug Tyler.

"Oh my God, you looked so good on television!" she squeals.

Tyler blushes, then looks around and nods to his bandmates, Mick, Austin, Trent, and Liz. "Hey, thank you for recognizing me when you accepted the award, dude, that was totally cool," Edward says appreciatively.

Mick leans in and pecks Tyler's cheek. "Yes, thank you for giving my man a shout-out. Trent didn't say shit." He rolls his eyes as Tyler hands the award over to Edward.

"Dude, it's a *Verse*! You so deserve this!" Edward shouts excitedly as he admires the award.

Gunner then swipes the award from Edward's hand and nods his head in appreciation. "It's fucking heavy," he says, curling it like a weight.

"Hey, hand it over to Zack," Tyler says, and Zack accepts it and holds it up in the air for everyone to see.

"Our boys did it! Woo-hoo, so proud of you two!" Zack whistles as he glances over at Tyler and Trent.

Austin walks over and stands next to me. "Your husband did real good on this one," he says, and I nod my head. "But this wouldn't even be in his grasp if it wasn't for you." He puts his hands on my shoulders and looks directly into my eyes.

"Thanks, soldier," I say shyly as he hugs me. "Hey, I just had dinner with the parents," I say when Austin releases me.

"Oh yeah, how'd that go?" he asks.

"Daddy had his Stetson on, Mama flaunted her arrogance, and they both were *very* proud of their son-in-law. You know, the one that Mama slapped?"

Austin laughs as he nudges my arm, remembering the moment I introduced Tyler to her as my husband. "She's proud," he says.

I roll my eyes. "Proud? The same woman who told me musicians were no good and that rock and roll was the devil's music?" I roar as Austin sips his champagne and shakes his head.

Lilith joins us and salutes me with her champagne glass. "Congrats, girl—you have to be so excited for Tyler!" she says happily.

I smile at her. "I am. I'm proud of him when he just takes out the garbage," I say, to which she giggles.

Zack hands the award to Trent and hollers, "Okay,

gang, Trent is going to put the award on display!"

Trent walks up to the shelf in the middle of all the pictures of WHIP and Black Rifle Coalition hanging on the wall and sets it down next to their Billboard Music Award for all of us to admire once more.

"Yeehaw!" Tyler hoots as everyone starts clapping while Austin whistles.

Soon after, Trent receives a phone call and excuses himself, stepping outside the studio to take it. Our friends continue to sip champagne and salute the award. This is a gigantic stepping-stone for Trent and Tyler, and even for Black Rifle Coalition and our intimate little recording studio. Everyone is on cloud nine.

"I need a cigarette, baby girl," Tyler says, the only one not drinking champagne. "I'll go with you." I grab a loop of his pants and follow him outside.

Tyler fishes in his pockets, pulls out a pack of smokes, lights up a cigarette, inhales, then releases a breath.

"Better?" I ask, knowing that all the celebrating was making his head swirl. "Better," he says, taking a second drag.

Trent is over by our Jeep, pacing the street as he talks on his cell phone. We just watch him as we lean against the black brick building. Trent soon hangs up and shakes his head as he walks over to us.

"What's up, dude?" Tyler asks, blowing out smoke.

Trent reaches up and takes Tyler's cigarette from him, inhales, then hands it back. "Roger got busted," he says.

"What? Are you sure?" I ask as I wave the smoke in another direction.

"Yep. The police officer handling the arson case called me to notify me that the suspects were arrested and that means Roger and a few dudes from the REVENUE. They got busted for burning down *Head Rush*. They have nothing on vandalizing my apartment, but fuck it," he says. "They arrested those assholes." When Tyler shakes his head, he says, "I'm sorry, dude, I know Roger is a friend and all, but they played with fire and they're getting fucking burned," he says.

Tyler inhales from the cigarette once more, then drops it and stomps it out. "You started this shit," he mumbles. Trent looks up at him with disgust. "You and that fucking bitch Tonya— not Roger, dude." Tyler flashes him a dirty look.

"Fuck you, Tyler," Trent says, irritated.

"Whoa! Hang on, you two!" I try to intervene, things quickly getting heated. "No—fuck you, Trent! My buddy is now going to jail because you couldn't keep your dick in your pants," Tyler says as Trent pushes him against the wall. "Stay out of it, you asshole," Trent snarls.

I open the studio door and call out, "Help, guys!"

Gunner and Austin come running out just as Trent grabs ahold of Tyler's neck.

"Whoa! What the fuck, dudes?!" Gunner pulls Trent away as Austin grabs Tyler. "Settle down. What the fuck happened?" he asks.

Tyler huffs, trying to pull his arm out of Austin's grip. "We moved past all that bullshit, Tyler," Trent says.

Tyler flips him off. "Yeah, keep telling yourself that! Once again, I'm pulled into your bullshit!" he hollers.

Trent glares at him and shakes his head.

"Go cool off, Trent," Gunner says, pushing Trent aside.

The gang is all standing in the doorway, watching us as Zack tries to regroup everyone. "Show's over, folks, get back inside," he says.

Nova laughs. "Damn leather twins," she huffs as she rolls her eyes and looks over at me. "You all right?"

I nod my head, then reach for Tyler's hand. "Come on inside, songbird," I say, but Tyler exhales and just stares at Trent starting up his motorcycle and speeding off. "Nova, you better give Liz a lift home," I suggest, and she nods her head.

Everyone begins collecting their things and saying their goodbyes to Tyler and me.

I hug Zack, hand him the champagne bottle, and smile sarcastically. "I've got this," I reassure him as he kisses my cheek and gathers Liz and Nova.

"I'll talk to the REVENUE's manager and we'll chat later," he says as he walks out of the studio.

After everyone is gone, I lock the door and walk over to Tyler, who is sitting on the couch, staring at the floor.

"Ty, you had a wonderful few days; don't let this ruin everything," I say. "Roger knew this would bite him in the ass sooner or later." I release a breath as I sit down next to him and rub my hand along his back.

"I know, but I was right. I mean, Trent brought all this shit on," he says.

I groan, not wanting to relive Trent's infidelity. "Yes, he did. But you do not need to get involved," I say as he looks over at me.

"When it comes to anything with you, I'm involved. He hurt you," he says stubbornly, trying to slow his breathing by inhaling through his nose and exhaling out of his mouth.

"I have nothing to do with Trent aside from business," I say with frustration.

"I want to take this *Verse* Award and shove it up his ass," he says, and I laugh as he leans into me and starts kissing me. "I love you so much, Alex; I'm so protective of you," he reminds me as he throws my words right back in my face. I told him in the past that I was protective of him and now he won't let up as he defends me whether it has to do with Trent, Gage, whomever, he promises to protect me.

I smile and try to let it go. "Look, just because Trent skirted around behind my back does not mean I'm involved in this any longer," I huff. "This is between Trent, the REVENUE, Roger, and Tonya—not me," I say.

Tyler scratches his head, then nods.

"Good. Now let's just go home," I say, the conversation exhausted. We stand up, glance over at the award on the shelf, then hit the lights.

A few days later, Tyler is at band rehearsal when I finish up another design project, close my laptop, and let out a drawn-out breath. My cell phone rings, startling me, and I snag it off the drafting table and pick up.

"Hi, Zack, how ya holdin' up?" I answer as I rub my eyes.

"Hey, Alex. Listen, I just spoke with the REVENUE's manager. He told me that three of the guys have charges pending against them—Roger being one of them," he says.

I shake my head. "Shit," I mumble.

"In Texas, arson is a second-degree felony. They're all getting a fine tossed their way plus fucking prison time," he says.

I groan. "Oh, Tyler won't like that one bit. But between you and me, Zack, they get what they deserve. I mean, the REVENUE has been bad news since the start." I let out a breath of frustration. "We're all aware of the drama they bring, and the further I can keep Tyler away from them, the better..." I pause. "I mean, I really like Roger—I know he's Tyler's friend and all—but he was hurt by the affair just as much as me and he was married at the time. I mean, he could have gone about things a different way. I don't know."

"Don't get yourself so worked up," Zack says. "You have moved on with Tyler. Roger is not your problem, and neither is Trent." He pauses. "What a mess... I just wanted to give you a heads up with what's going on with Roger, that's all," he says.

"Thank you. I really do appreciate it. I'll explain this all to Tyler," I say softly.

"Good. You just focus on Tyler. I'll touch base with you soon, hon—you take care," he says and clicks off the line.

I begin rubbing my temples. *Oh boy.* I have to tell Tyler about his best friend's impending incarceration. I shake my head, trying to settle all the chaos swirling inside.

A few hours later, Tyler walks into our flat and kicks his Converse off at the front door. "Hi, baby girl," he says as I walk over to the balcony door and open it.

"Hi, songbird. How was your vocal lesson and practice?" I ask him. "Same shit." He laughs as I roll my eyes.

"Sweet tea?" I offer, and Tyler nods his head and follows me to the kitchen, taking a seat at the counter. I pour both of us a glass, then set his in front of him and he smiles and sips it.

"Listen, I spoke with Zack earlier," I say. Tyler's eyebrows raise. "Roger and two other REVENUE dudes are being charged for burning down the recording studio. In Texas, arson is a second-degree felony. They're all getting a fine plus fucking prison time."

I huff and Tyler shakes his head in disappointment, but before he can say anything I continue, "You and I are staying out of this. Roger has an attorney and Zack is keeping us up to speed, but I think that's the extent of our involvement. Agree?" I ask, and he runs his hands through his hair and nods. "Good. Now, can I feed you?"

He motions with his finger for me to come to him. I walk around the counter and stand in between his long legs as he sits on the stool. I bend down and softly kiss his lips.

"I love you," he says as I lean in and kiss him a second time. "I love you more," I say, feeling relieved.

CHAPTER 27

A FEW DAYS LATER

I am sitting on the balcony, relaxing and smoking Tyler's joint, wearing a tank top and sweatpants when I hear my cell phone ring. I blow out the smoke, set the burning joint in the ashtray, and walk over to the drafting table to grab my cell phone. I look at the number flashing across the screen but don't recognize it. I think, *What the hell,* and answer it.

"This is Alex," I say.

I hear a man coughing on the other end of the line. "Oh, hey there, Alex. Umm, it's Roger," he says.

"Roger? Where are you calling me from?" I ask.

"Prison," he says. "Listen, I spoke to my attorney about a few things and we're trying to get all my affairs in order and..." He pauses, then releases his breath nervously. "Are you alone?" he asks.

"Yes," I say, sitting on a floor pillow and leaning against the window, wondering what the hell he is calling me for.

"Alex, my parents have passed on. I have no family here. The attorney cannot track down Tonya since she bailed. I'm out of options here," he groans.

"Options for what?" I ask, hoping he isn't going to beg me for bail money.

"Tristin," he says, and my mouth drops open. "Child Welfare took him the night I was arrested. They want to place him in permanent foster care, but the thought of him bouncing in and out of homes frightens me. I don't want to fuck him all up. I mean, Child Welfare Services said I was neglecting him and..." He pauses. "I really fucked shit up for me and my family. This whole damn affair really took a toll on everyone. Tyler is my only true friend. I know you and him are stable. You make enough money. Tristin needs a good home environment—would you consider taking him?" he asks.

I swallow hard. My heart pounds as I remain silent, processing everything.

"I remembered that you guys were trying for a family. Well, I spoke to my attorney, and a friend or an acquaintance can adopt through an independent adoption as long as they meet the requirements and all that shit," he huffs.

"Roger," I say, tears surfacing as I recall my two former miscarriages. "I have to talk to Tyler, but I would absolutely look after Tristin if that's what you think is best for him," I say.

He releases a sigh of relief. "I'm giving you my permission. I just can't imagine Tristin in foster care. I mean, that's my lil' dude and all, but I cannot physically take care of him. It has to be this way. I will be rotting in here for quite some time, and Tonya..." He grunts.

"She never took interest in the kid—he was a mistake in her eyes, and he's always been dumped on the neighbor. His mother bailed and I was a drunk and now I'm a fucking prisoner." He coughs.

I think of Tyler's family storyline and it breaks my heart. "Tell your attorney to get ahold of me. I'll talk to Tyler," I promise, and Roger dramatically exhales.

"Whew. Thank you, Alex—really, thank you," he says. I hear a security guard tell him to wrap it up. "I gotta split," he groans.

"I'm sorry you're going through all of this, Roger," I whisper. "Me too," he replies, then hangs up.

I sit there, frozen, and think about Tristin.

An hour later, I am sitting back on the balcony, trying to process everything that Roger asked of me. *Was this the right move? Should I adopt someone else's child? Am I ready to take on a child?* I really want my own child with Tyler. I have so many questions floating around in my brain that I don't even hear Tyler come home.

"Are you okay?" he asks, standing in the doorway in his black tank top, black jeans, and bare feet.

I nod my head and wipe my eyes.

He walks out, takes a seat in the wicker chair beside me, lights the joint, and exhales. "You *sure* you're okay?" he asks.

I look over at him. "I spoke to Roger," I say, still stunned by our conversation. "You did?" he asks, handing me the burning joint.

I take a hit, lean back, and blow out the smoke. "He wanted to see if you and I would take on Tristin," I say as I keep staring forward. "He's with Child Welfare Services at the moment.

Roger doesn't want him in permanent foster care so he

asked if we would care for him." I shake my head. "Tonya bailed. Roger is a drunk."

"Huh," he says as he leans back and taps the chair's armrest. "Why us?" he asks.

"Well, Tristin has no other family. The attorney cannot locate Tonya and the kid is always with the neighbor," I say, waiting for Tyler's reaction. "Plus, Roger said you were his only true friend."

"Fucking Trent. I told him we would be pulled back into his bullshit," Tyler huffs. "What do you think, baby girl?" he asks as he looks over at me.

"I..." I struggle to form words. "I think we should do it," I say. I couldn't believe what came out of my mouth.

Yes, I want to help this child. Yes, I want to help Tyler's friend. Yes, I want to start a family.

"Yes, Tyler. I think we should do it," I say confidently as he reaches for my hand and squeezes it.

"Tristin is a good kid; he deserves a loving home. I mean, we'll figure it out—we always do," he says.

"Are you in?" I ask, wanting to be sure he is with me on this decision. "I'm all in," he says, and I release a breath as tears surface once again.

I look over at Tyler and see wetness trailing down his cheek as well. "I love you," I whisper.

"I love you more," he whispers back.

Later that evening, I lay in bed in my nightgown, staring at the ceiling, digesting everything. I can't turn my mind off as I think about Tristin.

I feel Tyler's hand rub up and down my arm—he's not

getting much sleep either. I look over at him as he pulls my hand up to his mouth and kisses it. I blink my lashes at him as he begins kissing my palm, my wrist, my inner arm, and trails his lips all the way up to my neck.

I let out a breath. He kisses my ear, then my lips. He slides over me, between my legs, and softly kisses my lips once more. He licks my tongue with his, then circles around it a few times as I quietly moan. He pulls the lace straps of my silk nightgown down and softly kisses my shoulders as I close my eyes.

He rolls his head over my exposed breasts as I run my hands through his hair, my nipples peaking. He licks one as I push my head back into the pillow. He sucks the other one, and my breathing becomes ragged, longing for more. He licks across my chest, up my neck, and slides his heated tongue back into my mouth. He tastes so sweet as he kisses with so much intensity.

"I want to make love to you," he whispers, and I gasp. He is showing his gratitude once again through sex because I agreed to take on the adoption and help out his best friend.

He slowly pushes my nightgown up to my hips as he lightly pecks at my neck.

I open my eyes and watch him as he opens me up with his warm fingers and enters me. "Oh, Tyler," I moan, losing my breath as he begins to gently thrust in and out of me and I am overcome with emotion.

"I love you so much, Alex," he says as he looks into my watery eyes. He kisses each eyelid, my nose, then licks my lips. I feel him push deeper and I quietly ache for more as I squeeze his back with my fingertips. He slides his tongue back in as I lick his warm barbell.

"Oh, Tyler." I pant heavily as I pull him closer to my chest and wrap my arms around him. He keeps thrusting in and out as I shuffle my legs, allowing his thickness to fill me. "Ty, baby, you feel so amazing," I whisper, still unable to catch my breath. "I need to feel close to you tonight."

He brushes the hair away from my eyes. "Alex, I need you so bad," he says, thrusting harder as I slide up the satin sheet.

"Don't stop, baby, keep making love to me," I cry out. I feel him ease in and out of my slickened sex gently.

"I love you," he says again, and I can *feel* just how much as his cock hits my G-spot. He moans as he pushes deeper. "Oh, I love how I can feel that you are about to come," he gasps.

It is unbelievable how close we've become with one another. I relax as I take all of him in and my body begins to release on his hardened cock.

"That's it—oh, Alex," he moans as he keeps his rhythm, letting me enjoy the orgasm fully, trying to hold out for me. I quiver on his cock as he picks up his pace, releases a breath, and then lets himself go. "Oh, Alex. Oh, you feel so..." He can't complete his sentence as he starts coming inside of me.

"Oh, Tyler," I say, feverishly kissing him as he climaxes.

After he finishes, he puts his head on my shoulder and squeezes me. After everything we've been through, I have never felt closer to him. He releases a breath in my ear and holds me a few moments longer.

I don't need to say anything; I already know.

❧

The next morning, Tyler is still sleeping as I slip out of the sheets and make my way into the bathroom. I pull my hair into a braid, brush my teeth, and go out to make coffee, anxious to get ahold of our attorney and discuss our adoption decision. I turn the coffee pot on, spin around on my heel, and bump right into Tyler.

"Good morning," I greet him with a smile as he leans in and kisses me.

"Morning, my lovebird," he says. "Did you get any sleep?" He jumps up on the counter and takes a seat.

"I did. Thank you for last night; it was a pleasant surprise. I didn't realize how much I really needed you," I say appreciatively, and he smiles, his cheeks flushing as he leans over and kisses my head.

"I know you want to call our attorney and start on all that shit—and please do. But I want to head down and talk to Roger myself, if that's okay with you?" he asks.

I raise my eyebrows. "Of course. Should I go with you?" I ask, taking two mugs out of the dishwasher and setting them on the counter.

Tyler shakes his head. "I think I need to do this alone. You just call the attorney," he says as I step in between his legs and rub my hands up and down his thighs nervously.

"Are we ready for a lil' bird?" I ask.

Tyler smiles. "A little bat!" He laughs, and I recall him calling Tristin "Bruce Wayne." "Let me feed you, then you can head down there. I don't think anyone should know what we're up to until we have a little more information," I suggest. Tyler nods his head in agreement. "I'll start on your eggs."

"Baby girl—this is one thing we can do for Roger, and I want to help," he says, and I smile.

"Well, he'll know we're going to give it a try, but..." I pause.

"No buts, baby, we'll just try," he says confidently. My stomach swirls with joy.

After Tyler finishes his breakfast, he showers and heads down to the jail to visit Roger. I put all the dishes into the dishwasher, pour a second cup of coffee, and dial our attorney.

CHAPTER 28

A few hours later, Tyler returns, exhausted. He flips off his shoes and goes to the refrigerator for a bottle of water.

"How'd it go?" I ask anxiously as I stand up from working on my laptop.

Tyler takes a sip of his water and shakes his head. "That place is a fucking pit," he says. "Roger looks like shit but felt relieved when I told him we would try to adopt Tristin."

"He hasn't changed his mind, has he?" I ask.

"Nope. He is adamant about Tristin having a good home. His home environment was a fucking mess. The kid's pajamas didn't even fit him. I mean, it was winter and the kid was barefoot!" Tyler huffs.

I nod my head. "I know. I was there. But listen," I say softly as Tyler stares at the floor. "We can change all that. You've really come into yourself, Ty. You would be such a good daddy," I say.

He bites his lower lip, looking up at me. "Think so?" he asks.

"Yes," I say. "He'll be ours. We can always try again in the future, but let's just take this one step at a time. With everything you and I have been through, we can handle this—believe me." I smile as he nods his head, then continue, "Now listen, I spoke to our attorney." Tyler's eyes light up with curiosity. "He set us up with one of the partners who specializes in adoption. He contacted me right away and—whew, he got straight to the point on how this all goes down," I say as I shift my weight back and forth.

"Since Roger is incarcerated and has agreed to the adoption, he just needs to sign a consent form giving up rights and responsibilities. In the meantime, we have to complete a home study," I say.

"What the fuck is that?" Tyler asks, worry flashing across his face.

"No test." I laugh, knowing Tyler hated school. "Well, we have a shitload of documents to sign, financial statements to send over, copies of our birth certificates, marriage license, and health records," I say, and Tyler immediately looks a little panicked. "Yes, I asked him about your history of abuse, but all your health records are clean, your rehabilitation is complete—the attorney had no need to worry about that. We have to provide autobiography statements, and they need to do an inspection of the home, then interview us," I say with a heavy sigh. "It's a lot, but it can be done," I say confidently.

Tyler frowns. "Roger told me Tristin is in foster care."

"That's how the system works, baby. I mean, the attorney said he can push this through as quickly as possible," I reassure him. He says nothing, just stands there, processing everything. "Let's just start nesting."

I laugh as he looks at me strangely. "What the hell is that?"

"Let's set up the second room for him. Let's put all that shit in storage downstairs and just move forward like the adoption is on its way. I mean, the attorney said there was no reason it wouldn't work out," I say, and he smiles. "Maybe we should tell our friends? Hmm... Let me just tell Mick, then we'll go from there. Should we start gathering all our documents?" I ask.

"Absolutely," he says. He walks over to the floor pillow and pops a squat.

"I have so much already on the computer that I'll create a file, then we'll go from there," I say.

Tyler nods his head. "I love how organized you are." He laughs as I sit down next to him, and we get to work.

That evening, Tyler and I complete everything. I am exhausted and hungry but elated by how focused we are.

"We just need references," I say. Tyler looks over at me as he rubs his tired eyes. "I'll ask Zack first since we do the most business with him. Why don't you turn on the grill? We need to eat," I suggest.

He stands up, stretches, and goes out to turn on the grill. I am so grateful he is giving me no pushback; we signed and completed everything the attorney requested. I love him for that. He is not backing down—he says "All in" and keeps his word.

As we eat our fajitas out on the balcony, I can't stop smiling. "His room should be Batman-themed," Tyler suggests.

I giggle. "Let's do it! I'm going to order him a bedroom set from IKEA, then I think you and Austin should pick it up and put it together," I say, and he sips his iced tea, nodding his head. "I'll call Austin and tell him the news.

I'll call Zack tomorrow about the references—he can tell Nova. Then I'll call Mick to help me decorate. You can tell the rest of the band. I'll call my parents in a few days, but I think our lil' circle of friends will be happy for us," I say with a hint of insecurity.

Tyler smiles. "Fuck them if they're not. I mean, it's our nest—it's our life. So, whether they're on board with it or not, we're still moving forward with this," he says, and I am taken aback by his lack of worry about our friends' opinions.

"You know, you're right, Ty. It's our nest, our decision." I smile back, then bite into my fajita.

Tyler wakes up early, puts on the coffee, then throws on an old Tom Petty and the Heartbreakers T-shirt with his ripped jeans so we can get to work on cleaning.

"Hey, mama bird, are you getting up?" he asks as he stands over me, casting a shadow. "Hi, daddy bird." I laugh as I sit up and rub my eyes. "Last night wore me out," I say. Tyler hands me a coffee mug. "I'm ready to clear out that room and get to work on the Batcave," he says as I giggle and sip my coffee.

"Let me order a bedroom set, text Austin to pick you up, and I'll start packing the room,"

I say.

Tyler leaves the room, then returns with my laptop and sits on the bed next to me. "Pick one out," he says excitedly.

I open the computer, go onto the IKEA website, and select a child's bedroom set with a toddler bed. *He is not sleeping on the floor like at Roger's house.*

"What about this one?" I point to a picture, and Tyler smiles. "He'll love it—I'm sure of it!" He laughs and kisses my head.

I text Austin and Mick and tell them about our decorating mission for today. Everything is moving forward and I can feel the excitement vibrate through me.

A few hours later, I have the second bedroom all packed up and I hear the front door open.

"I'm in the Batcave!" I holler, to which Tyler laughs.

"Austin is here with me—where should we start?" he asks as I walk out into the living room.

"Come here, sis," Austin says, opening his arms and motioning for me to come in for a hug. He wraps his arms around me tightly and laughs. "I'm so happy for y'all. I promise to be the best uncle ever," he says as I squeeze him.

"Thank you for picking up the bedroom set. Please just help me bring boxes down to storage, then unload the bedroom set and start putting it together," I instruct.

Austin nods his head. "Let's go, Ty," he says as he heads toward the back bedroom. Tyler leans in and kisses me on the lips, then goes to the bedroom to help Austin.

When we are done loading our storage unit downstairs, I order a pizza as I watch the two of them begin to build Tristin's bedroom set.

"Knock, knock!" I hear Mick outside in the hallway and run over to open the door. "Girrrl! Always something going on with you! Listen, I stopped by the children's store in Uptown and the seedy little comic book store down in Deep Ellum—and look at everything I scored!" He raises a handful of bags.

I grab a few from him and bring them inside. "Wow! Mick, that is so thoughtful of you!"

I say.

"I need details—are you knocked up?" he asks quietly.

I stick out my tongue, and he laughs. "Here, let's take these bags into the back room," I say. "No, I'm not knocked up. I wish I was, but no," I huff. "We're trying to adopt Roger's kid, Tristin," I say.

He covers his mouth in surprise. "Roger and Tonya's spawn?" he whispers, and I nod my head. "Whyyy?" he asks as his eyes widen and he shakes his head in disbelief.

"As you know, I'm having trouble in the baby department and this child needs a loving home. His mother bailed and his father is a drunk in prison," I explain.

Mick lets out a deep breath. "That story sounds all too familiar, girl." He waves his hand like he's swatting away a bug. "Did you tell Trent?" he asks.

I shake my head, still feeling guilty for spilling the beans about my first pregnancy to him. This time around, it is between me and Tyler, not Trent.

"I get it—you do what you need to do," Mick says as he leans in and hugs me. "Well, Auntie Mick is here to help. So, where do we start?"

I point to the paint cans on the floor and he laughs out loud.

❧

A few hours later, the room is painted, the furniture is brought in, and Mick and I set up the Batcave as I tell him the story of the night Tyler and I brought Roger home drunk after their New Year's show. He thinks the Batman theme is absolutely fitting as he shuffles through his shopping bags and begins pulling out superhero items to hang on the wall.

"I found these metal prints at the comic book store!" he hollers with glee.

I smile at him. "They're perfect!" I say happily as I take one from his hands and run my fingertips over Batman.

We hang the prints, put the new matching sheet and comforter set on the toddler bed, then plug in the Batmobile lamp. I stand there, elated, looking around the room as Mick goes out into the hallway.

"Daddy Tyler and Uncle Austin, what do y'all think?" Mick calls out, and the two of them walk into the room, wiping pizza grease off their mouths.

"Are we good or are we good?" I ask as Mick hugs me. "Oh, that lil' man is going to love this!" Austin says.

"Think so?" I ask. Tyler leans down and kisses me on the lips. "Thanks. Why don't y'all throw the boxes out then go relax on the balcony? I think we're done here," I suggest, and he and Austin make their way back out to the living room.

When there's another knock at the door, I open it quickly.

"Hey, mama bird!" Nova sings as she drops her shopping bags and leans in for a hug. "Zack told me everything! I've digested it and I really think y'all are making the right move," she says.

Tears surface in my eyes as I hug her tight. "Come,

Aunt Nova, you need to see what Mick and I did!" Excited, I pick up her shopping bags, grab her hand, and pull her into the back bedroom.

"Holy Batman!" she squeals.

I laugh with relief. "It's his favorite superhero," I say as I watch Nova walk around the room and run her hands over the comforter and the stuffed Batman toy, beaming.

"I want one," she says.

Mick laughs. "What, a stuffed Batman?" he teases. "Well, Auntie Mick has to take off, girl. Call me and let me know when I get to meet this little Tristin," he says as he hugs me.

"I love you, Mick, thank you," I say as he blows me an air-kiss and makes his way out to say goodbye to Tyler. I turn to Nova and smile.

"Okay, Alex, I found so many cute threads for three-year-olds, all the way up to six! I mean, I don't know how quickly lil' birds grow, but I've got you covered!" she says as my mouth drops open.

"Tyler calls him a little bat," I chuckle, but Nova ignores me as she opens the drawers to the dresser and the closet door, then begins putting away the children's clothing.

"Look, I got some rock band T-shirts too!" She laughs as she folds Metallica, Beastie Boys, and Journey shirts into the drawer. "I also bought superhero pajamas—and just look at these slippers!" she squeals as she tosses Batman slippers at me.

I catch them and sit down on the floor, watching her work with amazement. "Wow, you went overboard! You are such a good friend," I compliment her.

She smiles and keeps working.

Later that evening, Tyler and I walk Austin and Nova over to the front door.

"Please promise to call me as soon as y'all know something," Nova insists, and we nod our heads. "I'll throw a 'welcome to the family' celebration at the cabin for y'all if you want, so we could all meet him together!" she offers excitedly.

I hug her, then Austin, letting him squeeze me a bit tighter as I know he is thrilled for me and Tyler. He turns and hugs Tyler, then walks Nova out.

When we close the door, we both release an exhausted breath and lean against the wall. "Oh, I sooo need a shower and bed," he groans.

"I'll join you," I say, and we hit the lights and turn in.

CHAPTER

29

A FEW WEEKS LATER

The thorough home inspection and grueling interviews are complete. The documents are signed and processing for approval. Roger's attorney took care of everything on his end, and Tristin is ready for adoption. The social worker keeps communication open with our attorney on when or if we can bring Tristin home from his current foster placement. Per Texas law, the adoption can't be finalized for six months, and will require a scheduled hearing in front of a judge.

My head swirls with legal mumbo-jumbo as I tap my fingers on my drafting table and review the last email my attorney sent over. As I scratch my head, my cell phone rings.

"This is Alexandria," I answer quickly, recognizing the law firm's phone number. "Hi, yes, Mrs. Black. I sent an email with one last request for you and Mr. Black," the attorney says. "I need you two to sign an adoption placement agreement. It's a document that includes the consent to adopt. By signing this document, you two are agreeing to the placement and to caring for Tristin. You are also promising to follow all the necessary requirements to finalize the adoption," he adds. "Any questions?"

"Umm," I stammer, trying to process the information. "Does this mean we are approved?" I ask.

The attorney lets out a low laugh. "Yes, Mrs. Black. Sign the form and get it back to me as quickly as possible. Then I'll schedule a time for you to pick up Tristin here at the law office," he says.

Tears fill my eyes.

"Aside from this form, I have everything I need from you and your husband.

Congratulations," he says.

I shake my head as my heart pounds in my chest. "Wow. Thank you again for all your hard work. I'm so happy with how efficient y'all are." I release a breath. "Y'all are worth every cent!" I laugh. "So, I'll just sign this form and get it back to you. Then I'll talk to my husband and we'll schedule a time to meet. Thank you again with all my heart."

I say goodbye and hang up, then sit there for a moment and just let relief wash over me. I release another breath, then get up and walk into the bedroom. I stand in the doorway, watching Tyler nap, and smile before walking over to the bed and tapping his shoulder.

"Ty," I say.

He rolls over and checks the time. "Baby girl, I crashed," he says.

"Ty," I say again, and he sits up and looks up at me. "We got approved." I grin broadly. Tyler's eyes widen as he jumps to his feet, picks me up, and spins me around. "We did?! Wow! We got ourselves a lil' bat?" He laughs as

I begin to cry, sets me down, steps back, and looks into my eyes as tears surface in his. "We really did it, lovebird," he says.

"We sure did, songbird," I say softly as Tyler wraps his arms around me and holds me.

The next day, I send the last of the signed documents over to the attorney. He schedules a pickup time for Friday at the law offices downtown. Tyler has band rehearsal tonight, so he is going in early to share the good news with Black Rifle Coalition.

As I clear my calendar for the weekend, I read a little note I made to myself to print and drop off invoices at *Brimstone*. I collect the paperwork, set it into a folder, and change into my tapered jeans and white Henley. I pull my hair back into a braid, then grab my bag and keys and head over to the recording studio.

Arriving at *Brimstone*, I notice Trent's motorcycle parked out front. I shut off the engine, gather everything, straighten my jeans, and head inside.

"Hello? Trent?" I call out as I toss my bag onto the couch and look around the studio. "Hey, Alex, whatcha doing here?" he asks, setting aside his headphones, pushing out his chair, and gets to his feet. I look him over in his U2 T-shirt, black jeans, and layered messy man- bun hanging off his neck.

"I have copies of invoices for you to review," I say as I hand him the folder.

He smiles, takes it from me, then sets it down on the console. "I haven't seen you since the little award surprise gathering with our friends," he says.

I nod my head. "I have been swamped," I say with a sigh.

"Yeah? Well, I shot Tyler a text and apologized for that evening but got no response," he says solemnly. I bite my lower lip and run my hands over my shirt. "What's up? Are you all right?" he asks.

I shake my head. "Trent, umm..." I pause. "Tyler went down to the jail to see Roger," I say, to which Trent's eyes widen. "He knows what Roger did was wrong, but Roger asked a huge favor from us," I say, feeling a lump rise in my throat.

"What? Pay his fucking bail?" He laughs, pretending to organize the folder I just handed him.

"No." I draw in a breath. "We're adopting Tristin," I say, and he sets the folder back down and looks over at me. "Yes, I know you know who Tristin is." I did not need to expand on his mistress' son as he shakes his head.

"Look." He pauses. "I don't blame Tonya for the affair. I blame myself. I was weak. I fucked up. Everything you and Tyler have..." He hesitates again. "I wanted it all with you, Alex," he confesses.

Tears start to surface as I feel frustration rush over me. I reflect for a moment, wondering what my life would have been like with Trent instead of Tyler, then dismiss it immediately. *He could never be the man Tyler turned out to be*, I think.

"Well, it all happened for a reason. I mean... Actually, I don't know what the fuck I mean!" I laugh awkwardly. "I forgive you. Hell, I even forgive Tonya. I moved on with Tyler and now we're adopting Tristin. I don't care how this all really came to be—all I care about is that the child has a loving home," I say.

Trent nods in agreement. "That's really big of you," he says.

"It's a huge commitment, but Tyler and I decided that we were not backing down. My attorney handled everything, so we can pick him up on Friday," I say. "I just don't want any weirdness from you when you see Tristin with Tyler. Can you promise me that?" I ask.

Trent glances away.

"Can I ask that of you?" I repeat. "You owe me." Trent nods his head.

"Thank you," I whisper as I turn to grab my bag. "Alex," Trent rasps. "You're a good woman," he says.

I nod my head and walk out.

That evening, I sit on the balcony with my sweet iced tea and call Austin, Nova, Mick, and my parents to share our excitement regarding the adoption approval. Tyler is passing the good news along to the band tonight, so there's only one final person to contact. We have so many loving people in our lives that I know Tristin will soon feel the love too. I decide to dial my father-in-law.

"Um, hello?" a deep, southern voice answers.

"Mr. Black?" I ask. I click on speakerphone and lean back. "Yeah, this is him," he says.

I feel my stomach turn. I'm not quite comfortable talking to him just yet, but I need to take the bull by the horns and tell him what the hell Tyler and I are up to.

"This is Alexandria—Tyler's wife," I say.

"Oh, doll, how are you?" He chuckles and I feel a bit of relief.

"I have some news to share with you. I know you knew about my previous miscarriages and how Tyler and I were trying to start a family. Well, I want to tell you that we've elected to adopt," I say excitedly.

"That's wonderful news!" he says, and I smile.

"A dear friend of Tyler's fell on hard times and we're going to adopt his son. His name is Tristin and he's three years old," I say matter-of-factly.

"That's something else—wow," he says in disbelief.

"Now, I'm calling because I want you to know that you are welcome into this child's life.

I want you a part of Tristin's life as much as Tyler's," I say.

He gasps softly.

"Alex, who are you talking to?" Tyler interrupts me suddenly, and I jump and clutch my heart as I look over at him. He must have come home from band practice early; I didn't hear him sneak up behind me.

"Hold on for one second, Mr. Black," I say as I wave Tyler over and point to the wicker chair. He blows out his breath, flashes me a stern look, and takes a seat. "Sorry, Mr. Black, Tyler just walked in. I want him here as I share the good news with you. Again, we want you to know that you are welcome into this child's life. We want you a part of Tristin's life as much as Tyler's," I say again.

Tyler shifts his weight in the chair.

"I..." Mr. Black pauses. "I would love that, Alexandria," he says. "Tyler, I'm sorry I haven't been able to answer all your questions. I mean, you asked me why you weren't worth my time, and I haven't stopped stewing on that. I promise to give you as much time as you want from here on out. I want to be there for both you and Tristin." He pauses. "Are you okay with that, Tyler?"

Tyler bites his nail in deep thought. "Yeah, Pop, I'm okay with it," he says, and I release a breath.

"Wow, my son is going to raise a son," Mr. Black says proudly.

"Yes, he is. Thank you, Mr. Black. We pick Tristin up Friday, but we need a few days for just the three of us together to have him settle in. We are still strangers to him, so I do not want to frighten him by introducing too many people at once," I say.

"I understand, doll," he agrees.

"We'll call you soon and let you know a good time for a visit," I say.

I can hear the smile in his voice as he answers, "Thank you, guys, I would love that.

Tyler, you have guts to take shit head-on—a quality I've never possessed."

"Don't say that. You're trying real hard with me, Pop, and I need to respect that," Tyler says.

As my eyes widen, I glance over at him and smile. "Look, we'll speak with you soon with more details, okay?" I ask Mr. Black.

"Okay," he says. "Thank you for opening your lives up to me—I'm really excited to meet Tristin." He pauses. "And Tyler, I truly love you," he says softly.

"Okay, Pop." Tyler's eyes began to water. "We'll give it a try here, I promise," he says as he exhales deeply.

"Talk with you soon, Mr. Black," I say. "Okay, doll, good night," he says.

I hang up and look over at Tyler. "Thank you," I say. "Are you okay?"

He nods his head. There is no need in dissecting the phone conversation. I now know he will allow Mr. Black back into his life as well as Tristin's, and I am pleased. I want him to finally let go of all that anger and heal the hurt.

Leaning back in the wicker chair, I feel proud of us. Tyler and I are going to change this boy's life. My friends, the band, and our families are all supportive. Even Trent and Roger are on board. I feel overcome with joy and I just smile and sip my tea.

"I'm going to get something," Tyler says, standing up.

I prop my feet up on the metal railing to block him, and he flashes me his beautiful smile. "Kiss me first," I demand.

After he leans down and softly kisses my lips, I put my feet down and let him pass.

A few moments later, I hear his footsteps, then a colorful bouquet of flowers appears in front of my face.

"For you, lovebird," Tyler says, and I gasp. "Thank you for handling all of this shit," he laughs.

"Oh, they're lovely!" I cheer.

Tyler leans down and kisses me once again as I take the bouquet. "I also picked this up!" he says excitedly, handing me a small black box with a black satin ribbon around it.

"What's this?" I ask, surprised by the sweet gesture.

"Open it," he eggs me on as he bends down between my legs and watches me.

I untie the ribbon, remove the lid, and see two sterling silver bat charms. I burst into laughter. "Really?" I pick one up and study it.

"One's for my necklace, one is for yours!" he says happily, and I giggle while he removes the necklace from around my neck. He unclasps it, slides the silver bat charm next to my "friend" heart and wedding ring, then slips it back over my head.

I reach for his necklace, unclasp it, slide the other bat charm next to his "best" heart and his platinum wedding band, then slide it back around his neck and kiss him.

"This is too perfect!" I say as I smother his lips with kisses. "I love you," I whisper. "I love you more," he whispers back.

CHAPTER 30

FRIDAY

"I can't sleep, baby girl; I'm too excited," Tyler says as he flops his leg over mine.

I lay naked on my stomach, eyes closed, and groan. He begins to kiss my back and I feel his morning erection rub against my bare skin.

"I love how you get when you're excited about something." I laugh as I adjust the pillow under my head and don't budge.

"Baby, I want to fuck you," he whispers, trailing his fingertips along my butt cheeks. I groan once more, my eyes still closed. "It's too early," I mumble.

"Never too early for a fuck." He laughs as he pushes my legs open a little wider, slides in between them, and starts to lick my pussy from behind, leaving me powerless.

"Ahhh, really?" I moan as he licks up one fold, spreads my lips, and flickers his barbell inside of me a few times. "Wow, that tongue gets deep," I say, laughing into the pillow.

"Baby, you want deep, you're going to get deep," he

teases as he licks down the other fold, then slides his finger in and slowly finger-fucks me.

"You're relentless," I say. I turn my head and look back at him between my legs.

His black feathered bangs hang in his face as he concentrates. He slides in a second finger, and I clench my cheeks. "Well, it's working!" He laughs, likely feeling the wetness on his fingers.

"Ahh, that does feel fucking good, Ty," I say as I grip the pillowcase.

He leans forward and begins to trace his tongue up my spine, moves my long hair out of the way, and slowly licks my neck.

"That tongue is amazing," I compliment him.

He laughs in my ear, then sucks on my earlobe as he presses his chest against my tattooed back. "Can I fuck you now?" he asks directly in my ear, and I nod my head. He opens my legs a bit wider, opens my slit, and slides inside of me. "That's better," he whispers.

"Oh, Ty," I gasp, breathless as his warm mouth presses against my neck, kissing me as he pushes slowly back and forth.

"Didn't you say a minute ago that I go deep?" He laughs as he licks my shoulder blades. "I can handle it," I say, and he presses his palms into the sheet and thrusts deeper inside of me with his raging hard-on. "That's fucking deep," I pant as his erection stretches me.

He runs his nails down my bare back, then presses his chest against me once more as he pulls my hair back. "I love fucking you," he says as he works himself up. "Baby girl, you are so tight." He pushes harder as I close my eyes and bite my lower lip. He picks up his pace, leans back, and slaps my ass.

I cry out as he slaps it again.

He pushes my legs wider, scratches my cheeks with his nails, and thrusts. "I want to feel that pussy coming on me," he pleads as he rocks me harder. "I'm making you incredibly wet, Alex. I love when you're this wet." He bites my neck.

I keep panting while taking him all in. "You got me worked up this morning..." I pause as I try to catch my breath. "Ty, baby, make me come for you," I demand, knowing he loves a sexual challenge.

He sucks on my shoulder, marking me as he fucks harder.

"I can take it—give me more!" I cry out as he keeps thrusting.

"You little slut, I feel you coming," he moans as I quiver all up and down his dick. He keeps at it. "Ahh, that's it, baby girl, fuck me back," he says.

I tighten my abs and shove my ass back toward him, pushing him deeper into me as I release once more. I am greedy. He wants to fuck me? Well, I am taking everything he is giving me.

"That pussy is begging for me," he says as he lengthens. He slides his playful fingers around my hips to my hood and begins to flick my pussy as he fucks me from behind.

I instantly start coming for a third time. My whole body tenses as I cream hard on him. "Oh baby, oh my God..." He begins to release inside of me. "Oh, you feel incredible."

I feel him grip my hips as he pulses, finishing himself off, then collapses on me. We are both breathless as I release my hold on the pillowcase.

"Three, Tyler," I say, and he laughs as he kisses my shoulder. He then pulls out and rolls over. "Three," I repeat as I bat my lashes at him in gratitude. I push myself up, crawl over toward him, and thrust my tongue into his mouth.

"Mmm," he says as he kisses me more heavily.

I lick his pouty lips, then lean back and stare into his dark brown eyes, just watching his beautiful face light up as I brush his feathered bangs out of the way. "Three." I kiss his lips again. "Thank you," I say, and he smiles back at me. "You know, when Tristin is here, you have to hold out on all the loud, crazy sex 'til we're alone in the cabin," I tease.

He laughs, searching for a cigarette in the bedside drawer. "That's what visits with Auntie Mick and Uncle Austin are reserved for—so you and I can have a little alone time," he says, and I laugh while I watch him light up a clove. I swipe it from his fingers and inhale.

"Three," I note once again as I blow out smoke and smile proudly.

Tyler stands in front of the mirror in a black button-down dress shirt and black slim-fit jeans, adjusting his chain.

I tighten the back of my earring as I glance down at my pink button-down sleeveless satin shirt and black pencil skirt. "Are we ready for this?" I ask Tyler as I stare at him in the mirror.

He turns toward me, kisses the top of my head, and taps my butt. "Yes, I think so," he says nervously, and I smile.

"We can do this." I try to boost our confidence as he flashes me an innocent grin.

I love him so much.

"I want to do this for you," I say as he pulls me into his chest and holds me.

"It baffles me what you and I have been through, baby girl," he says. "I'm all in, wife," he reminds me.

"I'm all in, husband," I whisper back.

"We better get going," Tyler says, taking my hand.

We walk out of the bedroom and pass the Batcave, giving it one last look. I quickly grab the stuffed Batman toy to bring to Tristin. Tyler smiles. We walk out to the kitchen to collect our keys, and I sniff my fresh bouquet of flowers, squeezing Tyler's hand in gratitude.

"Ready?" he asks. "Ready," I say.

We walk out and lock up the nest behind us.

Arriving at the law office downtown, Tyler turns off the Jeep. He walks around to the passenger side and holds out his hand. I grip it tightly as I jump out and he smiles at me.

"Are you okay?" I look up and our eyes meet. His suddenly begins to gloss over. "You've always been there for me. You've always been a part of me. I know..." He pauses. "I know you'll never leave me."

I smile as I feel his insecurity *finally* take a hike.

"You're everything to me," Tyler says as he leans in and kisses me softly. I nod my head as our hands lock.

We slowly walk up to the set of glass doors leading into the attorney's office. The receptionist recognizes us right away, flashing us a warm smile.

"Hello there, Mr. and Mrs. Black," she greets us. "Big

day today? Let me tell them you are here." She stands up and walks away.

Tyler says nothing, just kisses my hand and gazes out the window toward downtown Dallas as I nervously shift my weight in my black high heels.

"Good morning!" our attorney greets us as he walks over and shakes our hands one by one. "Everything is in place. Tristin is here. Just follow me and you can collect him and head on home," he instructs, and Tyler and I glance at one another before nodding our heads.

We follow our attorney into his private office and look around. The social worker is seated in a leather chair in front of the large mahogany desk; she points toward the window. Next to the bookshelf with all the law books on display is Tristin. He is standing there with his little hands on the window, staring out at the big downtown buildings just as Tyler did a minute ago in the lobby. His back is to us.

"Tristin, someone is here to see you," the social worker sings happily, and he turns around.

Wearing a white cotton T-shirt, blue denim shorts, and white tennis shoes, he looks around, panning his little eyes around the room. His green eyes instantly light up as he smiles at us.

Tyler kneels to greet him. "Hey there, Bruce Wayne."

Tristin bows his head shyly and begins to sway back and forth.

"Do you remember me?" Tyler asks, and Tristin nods his head while staring at the floor. "Your daddy sent me here to pick you up and he asked me to look after you," he says calmly. "Is that okay?"

I inhale deeply and keep quiet.

"Do you want to come home with me so I can take care

of you?" Tyler asks as Tristin looks up from the floor and their eyes meet. "Yeah, buddy, I have everything set up just for you. I promise you'll like it."

Tyler flashes an endearing smile.

"You want to give it a try?" Tyler asks patiently, and finally Tristin nods his head. Tyler opens his arms. "It's okay," he encourages.

Tristin smiles and walks slowly over into Tyler's arms, hugging him tightly. I just stand there with a tear trailing down my cheek and watch the two of them embrace.

"That's better, buddy. I've missed you," Tyler says as he runs his hand through Tristin's chestnut-colored hair. "Are you ready to come live with me and Alex?" he asks.

Tristin twirls Tyler's long black hair with his little finger as he stares at him. "Aww," the attorney and social worker say in unison.

I step up and show Tristin the stuffed Batman toy. He blushes as he timidly reaches for it. "It's okay, it's for you," I say as he pulls the toy closer.

"Should we go to the Batcave now?" Tyler asks. Tristin giggles as he squeezes the Batman toy.

I release a breath, turn, and shake the attorney's hand. I hug the social worker and mouth "*Thank you*" to both of them. They nod their heads as I turn back and smile at Tyler holding Tristin.

"Ready, you two?" I ask nervously.

Tristin smiles as he grips Tyler tighter. Tyler kisses Tristin on the head, takes ahold of my hand, and we walk out of the law office on the warm summer day as a family.

END

ABOUT ATMOSPHERE PRESS

Founded in 2015, Atmosphere Press was built on the principles of Honesty, Transparency, Professionalism, Kindness, and Making Your Book Awesome. As an ethical and author-friendly hybrid press, we stay true to that founding mission today.

If you're a reader, enter our giveaway for a free book here:

SCAN TO ENTER
BOOK GIVEAWAY

If you're a writer, submit your manuscript for consideration here:

SCAN TO SUBMIT
MANUSCRIPT

And always feel free to visit Atmosphere Press and our authors online at atmospherepress.com. See you there soon!

Be sure to pick up
Jacqueline Grandey's other books

BROKEN RECORD

BEHIND THE CIGARETTE

&

BETWEEN US BIRDS

ABOUT THE AUTHOR

JACQUELINE GRANDEY always had a love for creativity, whether it was writing poetry or lyrics or painting mixed media art. She earned a degree in Music Sound Engineering through ARTI, worked live music venues, and even sold her own line of punk rock swag.

After touring for a decade, she started to long for life at home. With her love of cats, she pursued her Animal Science degree through the University of Texas and became CVA certified through the Texas Veterinary Medical Association.

Today, Jacqueline is proud to hold the lead surgical technician position at a "feline-only" hospital as she continues to write, participate in art shows, and root for her Dallas Cowboys.

She resides in Texas with her husband and four cats—Gloria, Genesis, Gabriel, and Iggy—and is very grateful for this balance in her life.

Please follow Jacqueline at www.jacquelinegrandey.com.

* 9 7 9 8 8 9 1 3 2 4 2 1 3 *